Hannah Dennison was b t
spent more than two deca s
been an obituary reporter, ght
attendant and Hollywood story analyst. For many years,
Hannah taught mystery writing workshops at the UCLA
Extension Writers' Program in Los Angeles, California.

Hannah writes the Honeychurch Hall Mystery Series
and Vicky Hill Mystery Series, both of which are set in the
wilds of the Devonshire countryside where she now lives
with her two crazy Hungarian Vizslas.

www.hannahdennison.com
www.twitter.com/HannahLDennison

Tidings of Death at Honeychurch Hall

Hannah Dennison

CONSTABLE

CONSTABLE

First published in Great Britain in 2019 by Constable

A CIP catalogue record for this book
is available from the British Library.

ISBN: 978-1-47212-850-8

Typeset in Janson MT Std by SX Composing DTP, Rayleigh, Essex
Printed and bound in Great Britain by Clays Ltd, Elcograf S.p.A.

Papers used by Constable are from well-managed forests
and other responsible sources.

Constable
An imprint of
Little, Brown Book Group
Carmelite House
50 Victoria Embankment
London EC4Y 0DZ

An Hachette UK Company
www.hachette.co.uk

www.littlebrown.co.uk

For Claire Carmichael.
Writing instructor extraordinaire,
Australian mentor and cherished friend.
With all my gratitude and love.

Earl of Grenville
Created by Henry V in 1414, the title of Earl of Grenville has been passed down the male Honeychurch line and still exists today.

8TH EARL OF GRENVILLE
Rupert James
Honeychurch
B: 1800 D: 1880

EARL *of* GRENVILLE

9TH EARL OF GRENVILLE
Edward Rupert
B: 1835 D: 1899
Fought in Crimean War (1853–56). Decorated soldier, brought back mummified hawk.

Gerald James
B: 1840 D: 1912
Married American heiress – moved to New York. *Died in 1912 in the Arctic. He was a Polar explorer.

Elizabeth Edith
B: 1864 D: 1895
Never married. No children. *Fell from horse and broke her neck out hunting.

10TH EARL OF GRENVILLE
Harold Rupert
B: 1865 D: 1912
Fought in the Boer War (1899–1902).
*Died on *Titanic*.

James Rupert
B: 1873 D: 1950
Married showgirl. Ran a Turkish harem in London, fond of Burlesque & ran with Edward VII set.

Cassandra Mary
B: 1872 D: 1965
Never married. Lived in desert with a sheik, drove ambulances in WWI, war office WW2.

11TH EARL OF GRENVILLE
Max James
B: 1887 D: 1916
No children.
*Fighter pilot shot down over France in WWI.

12TH EARL OF GRENVILLE
Harold Edward
Edith's father.
B: 1900 D: 1940
*Died in London Blitz with wife.

Gerald Rupert
B: 1908 D: 1932
Lived in New York. Lost everything in the Wall Street Crash and committed suicide.

Rose Anne
B: 1907 D: 1988
Married German POW at end of war, moved to Germany. Huge scandal! Had 3 children.

13TH EARL OF GRENVILLE
Rupert James
B: 1921 D: 1959
Spitfire pilot WW2.
*Died in duel with Edith's lover Walter Stark.

Dowager Countess Edith Rose
B: 1927
Married Cousin Edward in 1959 to keep hold of title.

14TH EARL OF GRENVILLE
Cousin Edward
B: 1931 D: 1990
Returned from New York to inherit the title and marry Edith.

15TH EARL OF GRENVILLE
Rupert Max
B: 1963
1st wife: Kelly Jones
2nd wife: Lavinia Carew

Harold Rupert Max
B: 2005

Ad perseverate est ad triumphum

EARL *of* GRENVILLE

Chapter One

'I declare the museum room open day a resounding success.' Mum beamed happily and gestured to the local villagers who had flocked to Honeychurch Hall for a chance to see the legendary collection of artefacts on display. 'You should be proud of yourself, Kat! What a terrific turnout.'

Proud wasn't the word. Relieved was more like it. After a great deal of persuasion, Lord Rupert Honeychurch had agreed to my suggestion of opening the museum room to visitors in order to raise funds to make critical repairs to the east wing.

Honeychurch Hall had never been open to the public before, and even he seemed surprised by the number of people who had streamed through the imposing granite gateposts of the six-hundred-year-old house. The entrance fee was ten pounds and included unlimited mulled wine, my mother's home-made gin and Peggy Cropper's famous mince pies.

'Although I do think this had something to do with it.' Mum gave a nod to the silver tray she was carrying that held a half-litre bottle labelled *Honeychurch Gin* and six cut-glass tumblers frosted with fake snowflakes and adorned with stirrers in the shape of fir trees. 'We've sold twenty-five bottles just this past week – do have a glass, darling. You can relax now. You've done your bit.'

'All right,' I said, and took one.

I'd been on edge all day because Rupert had insisted that no security was necessary. He maintained that Seth Cropper, the ageing butler who stood sentinel next to the 3rd Earl of Grenville's heavy jousting suit by the entrance, could keep watch. He had even refused to put *Do Not Touch* signs in the dozen or so open display cabinets, claiming that his 'people' would never have done such a thing.

As the day drew to a close, it looked as if my fears had been groundless. No priceless artefacts had been damaged, no one had spilled mulled wine over the stuffed white polar bear, and more importantly, the star attraction in the form of a ghoulish mummified hawk had not disintegrated into a pile of dust.

Officially known as the Bleeding Hawk of Honeychurch Hall, the bone-dry creature was thought to be over two thousand years old and was exhibited on a pedestal in the centre of the room. The wooden sarcophagus containing the bird had allegedly been stolen from an Egyptian tomb by the 9th Earl of Grenville and sneaked illegally into England in the 1850s. The hawk supposedly oozed a blood-like substance to warn of an impending death, and it was believed that anyone who touched it would suffer a terrible misfortune.

Since the bird had been sealed in its coffin for over a

hundred and fifty years, it was hard to know if this had ever happened, but today, the lid was off for all to see.

As well as the hawk and a variety of stuffed wild animals festooned in tinsel, there were African relics, rare ostrich and osprey eggs, maritime ship models, scrimshaw, and exotic butterflies set out in specimen boxes. There was also a collection of antique pocket watches, and unusual curios including a nineteenth-century Polyphon music box, an armadillo handbag and a stuffed giraffe head.

'That giraffe looks traumatised,' Mum said, glancing at the red clown nose and red-and-white-striped scarf that the animal was sporting.

'Blame Harry,' I said.

The eight-year-old heir to the Honeychurch estate – otherwise known as Squadron Leader James Bigglesworth – had been put in charge of decorating the room along with his friend Special Agent Fleur Moreau, who seemed to spend more and more time at Honeychurch Hall since her parents had started working out in China.

'Rather over the top if you ask me,' said Mum.

I laughed. If anything was over the top it was my mother's attire. She was wearing a sequinned jumper emblazoned with a reindeer's head, and a pair of red and green tartan trousers that were far too tight. Silver baubles dangled from her ear lobes.

'I love this time of year,' Mum enthused, giving my black tunic, leggings and ankle boots a critical glance. 'You could have tried harder to get into the spirit of things, Katherine.'

I lifted my hair to point to my miniature snowman earrings.

'You can't see them under all that,' Mum grumbled.

'That was the idea,' I said. 'Nick Bond from the *Dipperton Deal* should be here any minute to take photographs of the hawk, and if I'm going to end up in the newspaper, I don't want to look silly.' Our local weekly newspaper would always feature the winner of the largest marrow competition over a sensational 'if it bleeds, it leads' story. Although in this case, Nick had told me that he was hoping the hawk would do just that.

'Oh, I shouldn't worry about looking silly,' said Mum airily. 'Your days of *Fakes & Treasures* fame are old news now.'

'Said with your usual tact. Thanks, Mum.'

But my mother was right. As the former host of *Fakes & Treasures*, a popular reality TV show, I had been followed for years by the paparazzi, who were always determined to catch me in embarrassing situations. But ever since I had resigned and moved two hundred miles away from my old life in London, the media had left me well alone. I was now happily following my dream of running my own antique business – Kat's Collectibles & Mobile Valuation Services.

'And let's not forget Major Leonard Evans,' Mum said with a tinge of malice. 'He'll want his photo taken next to the hawk. He won't miss an opportunity to look brave.'

'You should be happy for your best friend's husband,' I said. When Lenny's name had been put forward to receive the Queen's Gallantry Medal in the New Year's Honours list, Mum had admitted she was just a tiny bit jealous. As a diehard monarchist, my mother's dream was to meet the Queen, and now Delia was going to beat her to it. But I was sure their friendship would survive. The two shared a great passion for Marks & Spencer and drinking gin. In fact it was during one of their boozy lunches that they decided to make their own, and so the Honeychurch Gin label was born.

'Pity the dowager countess isn't here,' Mum said, changing the subject. 'I think she would have enjoyed it after all.'

'I doubt it.' Lady Edith Honeychurch had been so horrified at the idea of opening the Hall to the 'great unwashed', as she called anyone not of her class, that the formidable octogenarian had taken the train and gone to visit friends in London for a few days.

'His lordship looks happy, though.' Mum pointed to where Rupert was holding court with a group of estate workers in the far corner by the polar bear. Balding, and with a trim military moustache, the 15th Earl of Grenville was an attractive man. Dressed as always in beige cords and a green tweed jacket with leather elbow patches, he stood tall and carried himself with an air of entitlement. Occasionally some brave soul would approach their master, reverentially doff a cap or drop a curtsey and then beat a hasty retreat.

'Oh, here comes Nick now,' I said as an earnest young man in his early twenties, dressed in a black leather jacket and jeans, came rushing through the door. His attempt at designer stubble barely covered an unfortunate case of acne.

'Sorry I'm late, Kat,' he said as he joined us by the window. 'I had two weddings to photograph this afternoon and the last bride insisted on a retake. God, I hate doing weddings.'

'We all have to start somewhere,' said Mum. 'Kat's first job was working in a toy shop on a Saturday.'

'Yeah, well I've been in that somewhere now for four years and I'm sick of it,' said Nick, scanning the room. 'Has the hawk started to bleed yet? I grew up on that legend. We all did around here. Do you think it's the real thing?'

'Yes, it's genuine, but I wouldn't hold your breath about it bleeding,' I said.

Nick got out his iPhone. 'I'll do a few spot interviews first, maybe get a quote from his lordship. Where's Major Evans? I need a photo of him – he's quite the hero.'

'Polishing his medals, I expect.' Mum proffered her tray of drinks. 'Can I interest you in some Honeychurch Gin? You'll never taste anything like it.'

That was something I couldn't contest. The proof had to be in the high sixties. I'd only had a sip and it felt like my throat had been ripped out.

'Don't mind if I do.' Nick took a glass and a large gulp. 'Blimey! This stuff is . . .'

'Potent,' Mum said smoothly.

'I was going to say raw.' Nick gave a boyish grin.

'It was made on the estate by myself and Delia Evans, Major Evans's wife . . . well . . . she is still his wife at the moment.'

'What do you mean?' Nick cocked his head. 'At the *moment*?'

I shot Mum a warning look. Just because my mother didn't agree with Delia giving Lenny a second chance after his short-lived extramarital affair did not mean that she should broadcast it to the press.

Nick knocked back the gin and gave a shudder of appreciation.

'I hope you're not driving,' Mum put in. 'The police are out in force.'

'Don't worry,' Nick said. 'I know all the shortcuts. I'm a green-laner.'

'A what?' Mum asked.

'Off-road biking,' he said. 'It's one of my passions. There are hundreds of miles of green lanes around here, good for avoiding the police after a few drinks at the pub . . . Blimey, is that kid still obsessed with Biggles? How old is he now, eight?'

Harry, dressed in his trademark World War I flying goggles and white scarf, along with Fleur in her sunglasses, French beret and oversized trench coat, was heading our way.

'What about you?' I said. 'Didn't you have a hero?'

'Barry Sheene,' said Nick. 'At least when I wanted to be a professional motorcyclist.'

'Has it started bleeding yet?' Harry called out.

'You mean since you last looked twenty minutes ago?' I teased. 'No.'

'Oh good. Phew. We would hate to miss the show.' Having stood guard by the hawk for most of the day, the children had gone to the kitchen for hot chocolate and marshmallows.

Nick offered his hand for Harry to shake. 'Nick Bond, *Dipperton Deal*, and you must be . . .'

'Squadron Leader James Bigglesworth,' said Harry, reverting to his alter ego. 'And this is Special Agent Fleur Moreau.'

'*Bonjour*,' said Fleur coyly.

'It's an honour to meet you, sir,' said Nick. 'I've come to photograph the bird.'

Harry's eyes shone with excitement. 'Would you like to see it? You can't touch it, though. It's cursed.'

'Lead the way,' said Nick.

Chapter Two

'Are we too late? Are you closing?' came a woman's breathless voice from the entrance. 'We've been driving for hours and got hopelessly lost.'

I turned to greet the newcomer and smiled. 'We're not closing for an hour.'

'You're Kat Stanford, aren't you?' the woman said. 'My husband and I used to watch *Fakes & Treasures*.' She was in her mid twenties and strikingly pretty. With her flawless complexion, long blonde hair, huge china-blue eyes and impossibly long eyelashes, she reminded me of one of the bisque dolls that I bought and sold.

She was bundled up in a full-length Moncler parka and carried a Moncler velvet backpack from which dangled an adorable white unicorn bearing the signature Steiff button in one ear.

'Ah! Someone after my own heart,' I enthused. 'I love the Steiff miniatures, in fact I have quite a collection myself.'

'He is cute, isn't he?' she said. 'As a matter of fact, it was you who got me interested in collecting Steiff miniature animals.'

'Oh, lovely,' I said. 'And you are?'

'Just call me Lala.'

I heard Mum mutter something derogatory under her breath that sounded like 'a stripper', and hoped the woman didn't hear.

'What was that?' Lala said sharply.

'I said try some gin, it will make you chipper,' said Mum, all innocence.

'I'm sorry, I'm not drinking.' Lala pointed to her stomach. 'I'm pregnant. Four and a half months left to go.'

'Congratulations,' I said.

'Yes. We're very excited. It's our first – well, my first but not Angus's.' She opened her velvet rucksack and brought out a matching purse. I noticed a perfect French manicure. In fact, everything about Lala was neat. 'Ten pounds each, isn't it?'

'Don't worry about paying,' I said.

'Thanks.' She put her purse away. 'Ah, here's hubby now.' She waved to a stocky man who had to be at least a decade her senior. He looked Mediterranean, with olive skin and jet-black hair, and was wearing the same brand of jacket as his wife, but in black, with black trousers and black boots. The pair couldn't have stuck out more in this room full of country folk if they'd tried.

'This is Kat Stanford,' said Lala to her husband.

'Angus Fenwick.' He gave a big smile. 'We couldn't find the place.'

'Angus refused to ask for directions,' Lala teased.

'Men never do,' Mum put in. 'Do I detect a northern accent?'

'That's right,' said Angus. 'We've come from Richmond, North Yorkshire.'

'Good heavens! That's a long way to drive,' Mum exclaimed. 'Especially in this weather.'

'Angus is interested in taxidermy,' Lala said. 'He'd drive a thousand miles to see a stuffed mouse.'

We all laughed.

'I'm surprised you heard about the open day,' I said, and I was. Although we'd done a small amount of publicity – an announcement in the *Dipperton Deal* and flyers distributed around the neighbouring villages – it had been very much touted as a local affair.

'I can't remember how we found out,' Lala went on. 'But here we are. We're staying at a B and B in the village.'

'Not Rose Cottage, I hope,' Mum said darkly.

'Yeah. Why?' Lala asked.

'Just make sure to ask for a fresh tea bag when Violet Green makes you a cuppa,' Mum replied. Seventy-plus Violet, who ran the only tea room in the area, was frugal to a fault and notorious for re-using her bags until they resembled blobs of grey mush.

'Who's that?' Lala pointed to Lady Lavinia, Rupert's long-suffering wife, who had entered the room with a tray of mince pies and glasses of mulled wine.

'That's the lady of the house,' said Mum. 'Married to the 15th Earl of Grenville.'

Lavinia usually wore grubby jodhpurs and shoved her long blonde hair under a thick slumber net, but today she had made an effort. She sported a white angora sweater – circa 1980 – with large shoulder pads, and a flared red skirt. Her hair surrounded her head in a fuzz of static electricity.

Mr Chips, Edith's Jack Russell, tore into the room after her, racing around in circles and barking before cocking his leg on a Victorian mahogany torchère.

Lala stiffened. 'That dog looks vicious.'

'He's just high-spirited,' I said, although Mr Chips was known for giving the odd friendly nip.

Lavinia sailed over, smiling at everyone she passed. 'Good afternoon. Good afternoon! Goodness.' She noticed Lala. 'You haven't got a glass, dear.'

'She's not drinking,' said Angus. 'She's pregnant.'

'Oh, how lovely,' Lavinia trilled. 'All you do is give a quick *push* and out they *pop*! Children can be *such* fun!' She spoke with the strangled vowels of the upper classes, which often made her difficult to understand.

Lala looked bewildered. 'Pop where?'

'How much loot have we made, Iris?' Lavinia enthused. 'Hopefully *thousands* of pounds!'

'We'll know more at the end of the afternoon, m'lady,' said Mum.

'Good. Carry on, carry on.' As Lavinia fluttered away, I could hear her chirping, 'Mulled wine! Mulled wine! Let's all get squiffy!'

'She must be so rich to live in this big house,' said Lala wistfully. 'They must be billionaires!'

I wanted to tell her that the landed gentry were often land rich but cash poor. I'd seen first-hand what a struggle it was to keep up with the maintenance of these vast country estates. The dowager countess had told me that following her husband's death and subsequent crippling inheritance tax, she'd had to seal off two entire wings at the Hall, one being the east wing and the reason for today's event, because they couldn't afford the repairs.

'But where are the servants?' Lala went on.

'They call them staff these days,' I said.

'Here's a servant.' Mum pointed at Delia as she entered with yet another tray of mulled wine and mince pies. She was wearing a bright red dress and a necklace of silver tinsel, and had topped her outfit off with a reindeer antler Alice band. Her face was flushed. 'She's the housekeeper,' Mum went on.

'Oh so *that's* Delia, is it?' I heard Lala say to Angus. 'She's not what I expected at all – a frump and plump. Is that a wig?'

Poor Delia suffered from alopecia, and frankly, I thought Lala's comments unkind.

And then it all made sense. 'You know Delia?' I asked. 'Is that how you heard about the open house?'

'Yeah, well, no. Not really,' said Angus quickly. 'We know her daughter, Laurie. She lives in Scotland.'

'You mean Linda,' corrected Mum.

'That's right, Linda.' Lala rolled her eyes and nudged her husband. 'Angus is hopeless with names and hopeless with directions.' She paused for a moment before snapping her fingers. 'Isn't Delia married to a famous war hero? Saved some kids in a cave or something?'

'Major Evans,' I said. 'That's right. He's been awarded the Queen's Gallantry Medal.'

Lala scanned the room. 'Shouldn't he be here?'

'Don't worry,' said Mum. 'He'll make a grand entrance, just you see.'

'I would have thought Delia would wear a uniform,' Lala said suddenly. 'You know, like Mrs Hughes in *Downton Abbey*.'

'*He's* wearing a uniform.' Mum pointed out Seth Cropper, who was indeed garbed in traditional attire of starched collar, grey-striped trousers and tails. With his oiled thinning grey hair, he looked the epitome of an Edwardian butler. His eyes were closed.

'Looks like he's asleep,' said Lala with a nasty laugh.

'He pretends to be, but I can assure you he doesn't miss a trick,' said Mum.

On cue, his eyes snapped open. He scanned the room, then retrieved a glass of water from the windowsill behind him and drained it in one go, before putting the glass back and resuming his position.

'What should we look at first?' said Lala.

I gestured to where Harry and Fleur stood with Nick, who was taking photographs of the hawk. 'Well ... that, of course.'

'What is it?' said Angus.

'The hawk.'

He looked blank. 'Hawk?'

There was an awkward pause until Lala gave him yet another nudge. 'Blimey, you need caffeine. The *hawk*! That's the whole reason why we drove all this way.'

'Yeah, yeah! That's it. The hawk.' Angus gave a foolish grin. 'Forget the caffeine. Maybe one of these will sharpen me up.' He reached for Mum's tray and took two glasses, handing one to Lala.

'I'm pregnant, remember?' She replaced the glass, rolled her eyes and mouthed the word 'hopeless' before steering Angus away.

'What a strange couple.' Mum echoed my thoughts. 'Fancy coming all this way, and in this awful weather too.'

It was hard to believe that anyone would have driven what had to be a distance of three hundred miles from North Yorkshire to Little Dipperton. Even though most of the snow had thawed, motorists had been advised not to travel unless strictly necessary because of the possibility of black ice on the roads.

Here in deepest Devon, ninety per cent of the country lanes never saw a speck of grit in the winter months, and the steep, narrow roads were notoriously treacherous and inaccessible to snowploughs. Luckily Little Dipperton had the services of Eric Pugsley, Mum's neighbour, who ran the 'end-of-life' scrapyard next to her home. Eric owned a tractor and made the most of helping out stranded motorists for five pounds a tow.

'Odd that Angus didn't know about the mummified hawk,' Mum said.

We regarded the couple with curiosity.

'They seem to know Delia's daughter,' I said.

'Or they pretend they do. There's something about that Lala,' Mum went on. 'I can't put my finger on it. Just one of my gypsy feelings.'

My mother liked to think she had inherited a touch of the Romany, having spent her childhood living with a travelling fair and boxing emporium.

'I should watch those two like a hawk – no pun intended,' she went on. 'Delia tells me she's missing some of her jewellery: her grandmother's crystal necklace and matching earrings . . . Oh, speak of the devil. Here she comes.'

Delia breezed over with her tray. She took a glass of water off it and handed it to my mother. 'Can you give this to Seth?' she said. 'He looks fit to drop.'

We glanced over, and this time it appeared Seth really was asleep.

'Drop is the word,' said Mum. 'Why can't *you* give it to him?'

'Because I have to go and find my husband.' Delia indicated to Nick, who was holding his iPhone up and sweeping the room. 'We don't want to keep the press waiting. You'll die when you see my Lenny in uniform.'

'It must be wonderful to be married to a hero,' said Mum, barely able to disguise her sarcasm. 'Is there anything at all that he's afraid of?'

'Snakes,' Delia exclaimed. 'But don't tell him I said so.'

Mum did as she was told, nudging Seth and giving him the glass of water. As she did so, she discreetly pointed out Angus and Lala, who were studying the hawk and chattering away to Harry and Fleur.

The room seemed to have thinned out. Dr Smeaton – a man in his fifties with a grey beard and dressed in a navy-blue Christmas jumper with a snowman motif – had cornered

Rupert by a contraption known as the electrical rejuvenator. Invented by Otto Overbeck, it was said to have been extremely popular in the roaring twenties. Patients were wired up to it and experienced an electrical current said to instantly restore youthful vigour.

Rupert had rashly allowed anyone interested to have a go, with Dr Smeaton standing by in case something went wrong. I couldn't help wondering if Lavinia's bizarre hairstyle had been the result of doing just that.

Nick waved me over and switched his iPhone to record. 'Tell me what you know about the mummified hawk, Kat.'

We looked at the creature in the open sarcophagus. It lay, wings folded, in its geometrically wrapped linen shroud. The shape of its beak could be seen through the cloth, with a tiny hole for one eye.

'The hawk was considered sacred by the ancient Egyptians and regarded as the god of the sky,' I told Nick. 'Or as the *ba*, or physical manifestation, of Horus the hawk-headed god, who was the embodiment of divine kingship.'

I went on to explain how the Horus falcon was the guardian deity and protector of the reigning pharaoh, and was frequently depicted with its wings outstretched behind the head of the king.

'And if it starts to ooze blood, that means someone is going to vanish, die or be cursed forever!' Harry said gleefully.

'Maybe it's bleeding under all that cloth,' Lala declared. 'Why don't we give it a little poke and see?'

'You can't touch it!' Harry exclaimed in horror. 'It's bad luck.'

'I'm not superstitious.' She laughed and moved in with her index finger outstretched.

'No! Don't!' Harry shrieked, and suddenly pandemonium broke out.

Mr Chips, fearing that Harry was under attack, lunged for Lala. She screamed and grabbed Angus, who bumped into the pedestal, which began to teeter on its base. Harry just managed to stop it from toppling over, but Angus and Lala, caught off balance, fell to the floor with a tremendous thud and Mr Chips went in for the attack, sinking his teeth into Angus's ankle. Angus cried out in pain.

Rupert hurried over with the doctor, only to collide with Nick, who was capturing everything on his iPhone.

'How *dare* you come here!' Rupert's eyes flashed with fury. 'Leave immediately or I shall call the police.'

'Looks like you might have to anyway,' Nick retorted, standing his ground and continuing to film the ensuing chaos.

'Mr Chips! Leave it! Drop it!' shouted Harry. But Mr Chips seemed to be having far too much fun. There was the sound of tearing fabric.

'Help!' Lala screamed again. 'That dog is killing my husband!'

Mum dashed forward and grabbed the feisty animal's collar just as the door flew open with a bang.

Standing there was Lenny in full military uniform, wielding an umbrella.

'I'm here!' he boomed. 'Stay where you are! Everything is under control!'

'Please save us!' Lala cried.

But then the most extraordinary thing happened.

Lenny stopped dead in his tracks. It was as if he had hit an invisible wall. His face turned deathly white. Dropping the umbrella, he began to back away as if he'd seen a ghost . . . right into the 3rd Earl of Grenville's heavy jousting suit.

Time seemed to slow down.

We all watched in horror as the armour began to sway.

'Seth! Move! Move!' screamed my mother, but the old butler just gave a goofy smile before the metal suit landed on top of him with a resounding crash.

Chapter Three

For a moment, no one moved, and then I heard Rupert shout, 'Get the children out!'

I bounded forward to help, but Lala seemed to have rallied. Grabbing Harry and Fleur's hands she said, 'Tell me where I should take them.'

'The kitchen,' I said quickly. 'Harry will show you the way.'

'She touched the hawk!' Harry said. 'I told you it's unlucky! Is Cropper dead?'

'Of course not,' Rupert said quickly. 'Everyone out! Now!'

'Dead! Dead! Dead!' Fleur sang cheerfully as Lala propelled them out of the room, closely followed by the last of the visitors, leaving just Mum, Angus – with his torn right trouser leg – Rupert and me.

I feared that Fleur could be right about Seth's prospects.

Blood was already creeping across the flagstone floor where his feet poked out from under the plate armour. He wasn't moving.

'I know first aid,' said Angus. 'At the very least, we should lift the breastplate off.'

'No. Yes. Should we?' Rupert was distraught. 'Oh God! The kitchen! I don't want Harry alarming Mrs Cropper!'

'Mum and I will go,' I said.

It was then that I noticed Nick Bond hovering in the corner with his iPhone. He had continued to film everything.

Rupert saw him too, and the expression that came over his face was nothing short of murderous. 'Give me that phone!' he shouted. 'Give it to me now!'

Nick turned and fled. Mum and I followed, and bumped straight into Dr Smeaton holding his black doctor's bag.

'The ambulance is on its way,' he said. 'Let's hope it's not too late.'

Out in the Great Hall, Nick had taken refuge behind one of the heavy brocade curtains. We could see his scuffed boots peeping out. If the whole thing hadn't been so awful, it would have been funny.

'Nick,' I said. 'We can see your feet.'

The young reporter stepped into view and gave a sheepish grin. 'Can't blame a man for trying. Did someone touch the bird? I didn't see.'

'I didn't either,' said Mum.

'I grew up on the legend of the Bleeding Hawk of Honeychurch Hall,' Nick said. 'Other kids were threatened with the boogie man, but us locals got the hawk. This is going to be my big break. No more weddings for me!'

'What do you mean by that?' I said.

'You do realise,' Nick went on, 'that if that had happened

to a visitor, his high-and-mighty lordship would be facing an expensive lawsuit.'

'Exactly!' Mum agreed. 'Thank God it was only Seth Cropper.'

Only? I was appalled. 'Mum!'

'Nick's right,' my mother went on. 'Health and Safety are going to be down on his lordship like a ton of bricks. It's not Kat's fault, though. She recommended that he take out insurance but his lordship just wouldn't have it. Said it was too expensive.'

'And then we have the bloke who was bitten by the dog,' said Nick. *'And* his pregnant wife. What if she has a miscarriage?'

'Exactly!' Mum said again. 'His lordship had better watch out.'

'Where is Major Evans?' Nick said. 'One moment he was there, the next he'd vanished.'

'Good question. I didn't notice Delia either,' said Mum. 'So much for bravery!'

'Yes, so much for bravery,' said Nick slowly. 'I'll definitely want to have a little chat with him about that. Why did he leave?'

All of a sudden I realised that Nick had been recording this conversation too. I was furious. 'OK, I think that's enough, Nick.'

'Were you recording us?' Mum said with horror.

'Thanks, ladies,' he said with a smirk. 'I'll be seeing you.' And with that he left us.

'Oh dear,' Mum said. 'I think I said something I shouldn't have done. His lordship's going to be upset if he finds out.'

'I'll see if I can talk to Nick,' I said, but somehow I doubted he would listen.

Peggy Cropper raced towards us pulling on a dark brown wool coat. She had her mob cap in one hand and a hand-knitted dark green bobble hat in the other.

'Where is he?' she said anxiously. 'It's not true, is it? Seth can't be dead.'

'Let's wait for the ambulance,' Mum said, blocking her path. 'The doctor is with him now.'

Peggy allowed my mother to lead her to a chair that had been randomly tucked away in an alcove. She brought out a packet of Fisherman's Friend lozenges and popped one in her mouth.

'I'll stay with her,' Mum said to me in a low whisper. 'You go and sort those children out.'

'That's nice of you, Mum.' And it was. My mother's feud with Peggy had been raging for months over some old boy-friend from the past that the two of them had shared during their teens. It seemed she had put that behind her. I was glad.

'And try to find a way to stop his lordship being sued,' she called out.

I found Lala chatting to Delia and drinking tea at the vast kitchen table. It looked like Peggy had been baking biscuits. Red and green icing still sat in basins on the countertop. In fact the entire kitchen was in disarray. Unwashed plates were stacked on the draining board and the floor looked filthy.

'So don't get talked into going all natural for the birth,' I heard Delia say. 'Take every drug you can get. That's my advice.'

Lala picked up a packet of Fisherman's Friend from a fruit bowl on the table. 'These are disgusting. They blow your head off. Are they yours?'

'Not likely,' Delia said. 'They're Peggy's. She's always sucking them.'

'Where are Harry and Fleur?' I asked.

'They went through there.' Lala pointed to a door that led to a long flagstone corridor. 'They should be back in a minute.'

'I doubt it.' I explained that the door led to the former larders and storage rooms and eventually out to the rear courtyard. 'Knowing Harry, he'll circle back to the museum room,' I said. 'Rupert specifically wanted the children out of there.'

'Why?' Delia demanded.

'Because . . . because it's very serious.'

'Serious?' Delia said sharply. 'What do you mean? As in . . . Seth isn't going to make it?'

'He'll be fine,' Lala said. 'Angus knows first aid.'

'The doctor is with him and an ambulance is on its way,' I said. 'And I think it would be a good idea if you let Dr Smeaton take a quick look at you, Lala. You had quite a bad fall.'

'Oh, I'm fine,' said Lala. 'But perhaps he should inspect Angus's ankle.'

'Mr Chips is such a naughty dog,' said Delia. 'He's always biting someone.'

Lala's eyes widened. 'You're kidding! What if Angus gets an infection and can't work?'

Which was exactly what I was worried about. These days everyone seemed to be more aware of the Dangerous Dogs

Act than ever before. Mr Chips could easily end up in court, and I would not want to be the one explaining why to the dowager countess, who idolised the animal.

'What does your husband do?' Delia asked.

'He's self-employed, so if he can't work, that would be a problem,' said Lala. 'I'm sure he can come to some arrangement with Earl Wotsit.' She helped herself to another cup of tea, added two lumps of sugar and gave it a vigorous stir. 'I mean. Look at this place. He must be loaded.'

I looked around and saw what Lala saw – a vast room with a high-gabled roof and clerestory windows. Old-fashioned paper chains were strung along various hooks screwed into the rafters, and Delia had put up a miniature Christmas tree on the oak dresser – purchased from Marks & Spencer, of course. There was an old-fashioned range flanked by warming cabinets. A lively fire burnt in the grate under an elaborate arrangement of roasting spits – long since abandoned – but it was never enough to heat the room. Instead, horribly expensive portable electric radiators had been purchased to take off the chill, blasting out pockets of heat. Lala was sitting next to one, and her face was going red.

'Are you sure you don't want to take off your coat?' Delia said.

'I'm fine,' said Lala. 'So what happened to Major Evans? I thought he was coming to our rescue. One minute he was standing in the doorway like Superman, and the next he was gone.'

'I don't know,' said Delia. 'I wasn't there when it happened.'

'He's such a brave man,' Lala said. 'I read about him in all the newspapers.'

'The kids were caving and got caught in a storm,' Delia said. 'They would have drowned had Lenny not saved them.'

'You wouldn't get me anywhere near a cave,' said Lala.

'Nor me.' I suffered from claustrophobia and couldn't think of anything worse.

'They were down there for three days,' Delia went on.

'Must be nice to be married to such a hero,' said Lala.

'It is,' Delia agreed. 'I'm so lucky.'

Lala pointed to the door again. 'Looks like the kids aren't coming back after all. Where did you say that goes to?'

'To the servants' entrance in the rear courtyard,' I said. 'And the original storerooms and larders.'

'Storerooms and larders?' said Lala. 'Angus loves that kind of stuff.'

'They're not used now,' I said, 'but back in the day, before refrigerators, each small room served a specific purpose – cold larders for meat, dairy and fish; flower rooms, lamp rooms, that kind of thing. And a still room where the mistress of the house would make up herbal remedies.'

'So the servants would have had their own toilet out there?'

It was a strange question to ask, but I nodded in agreement. 'It would have been outside originally, but in the 1950s, the family installed a modern one – if you can call it that. The inside toilets – or water closets, as they were known – were for family use only. There's a particularly lovely one off the entrance hall where the toilet bowl is beautifully painted with blue flowers.'

'Yes.' Delia nodded. 'It's like having a tinkle on the best china. The first time I used it, I felt a little naughty.'

We all laughed.

'There are some loyalty portraits in that loo that are worth seeing,' I said. 'Photographs of the staff who lived and worked here from the 1800s until just after World War Two. My mother is doing the Honeychurch family trees for both above and below stairs. It's fascinating.'

'And incestuous,' said Delia. 'A lot of intermarrying. Everyone seems to be related to someone around here.'

'That's because Honeychurch Hall owned – and still does own – most of the village,' I said. 'The main source of employment in those days was on the estate. But it wasn't a bad thing, because livelihoods were secure . . .'

'And you'd get accommodation either in the attics, in the grounds or in the village,' Delia put in. 'Lenny and I have the most adorable cottage here – although it is a little small.'

'I'm a *Downton Abbey* fan,' said Lala. 'You and your husband sound just like the housemaid Anna and Mr Bates. He was a bit of a dark horse, though, wasn't he? Seemed trustworthy on the outside but turned out to have murdered his wife.'

Lala took a sip of tea, but I could tell that her comment had struck a nerve. Delia took out her knitting and started to knit at breakneck speed.

'Maybe I should apply for a job,' said Lala with a grin. 'Angus and I are thinking about moving to the country. I quite like it around here.'

'Did I hear my name?' Angus entered the kitchen.

'They've taken the old boy off in an ambulance, but it doesn't look good.'

'It was very kind of you to help,' I said.

'And the doctor took a look at my ankle,' he continued. 'Just a bad bruise, although the little bugger did break the skin. Rupert was a bit worried, but I said dogs will be dogs.'

Good, I thought. So no court case after all.

'So . . . Dr Smeaton wants to make sure you're OK, babe,' Angus said carefully.

'What? Why! I'm fine,' Lala exclaimed.

'Yeah, I know, but he's insisting.' He gave a brief smile. 'He'll be here in a minute.'

'You should let him have a look,' Delia said. 'My Linda almost had a miscarriage when she fell over.'

'They're friends of Linda's, actually,' I said. 'Isn't that right, Lala?'

'Not A-list friends,' said Lala. 'More D-list.'

Delia frowned. 'Funny. I would have remembered a name like Lala.'

Lala got to her feet. 'I need to use the toilet.'

'Let me show you the one with the loyalty portraits,' I said, and got up too.

'No. I can't wait. I need to go right now.' She gestured to the door. 'Through there, yeah?'

'It's a bit basic,' Delia called out as Angus took Lala's arm and they walked quickly to the door. 'And watch the flush, because if you pull the chain too hard, the cistern falls off the wall, and we don't want another accident.'

'We will. Thanks!' Angus replied.

Moments after they had left, Mum appeared with Dr Smeaton in tow.

'Where is the damsel in distress?' he said cheerfully.

'Using the loo,' said Delia. 'I remember being pregnant. I always wanted to go.'

'How is Seth?' I asked.

A shadow crossed the doctor's kind features. 'Not so good, I'm afraid. It'll be touch and go whether he makes it. Peggy went in the ambulance and Shawn is on his way here.'

Delia suddenly brightened. 'Well, Peggy doesn't need to worry about supper. I can handle the household. I'll get working on a menu straight away. To be honest, the pair of them should have retired years ago. They're just too old.' A comment I thought very tactless given the circumstances.

'Tea or more gin, Doctor?' said Mum.

'Just a nip, and call me Reynard – you know, like the fox,' said Dr Smeaton with a leer. 'I think you're trying to lead me astray, Iris. At least I hope you are.'

I stifled a groan as my mother giggled and gave him a coquettish look.

Mum looked really well. True, her face was a little flushed and her eyes were just a bit too bright, but she was an attractive woman and Dr Smeaton was single too. Nothing would make me happier than for her to meet someone special.

'And speaking of gin,' Dr Smeaton went on, 'I'm afraid that Seth Cropper's reflexes were slow because he was drunk.'

'But . . . that's not possible,' Mum said. 'He's teetotal. Hasn't had a drink for years. Everyone knows that.'

'He was drunk,' Dr Smeaton said again. 'And frankly, if he doesn't die from his injuries, his liver will finish him off.'

'I'm sorry, I just don't understand,' Mum said. 'He was drinking water, wasn't he, Delia?'

Delia didn't answer. She just speeded up her knitting.

Mum gave a cry of alarm. 'Delia? Oh my God! It was gin, wasn't it? You told me it was water, but it was neat gin!'

'Oh for heaven's sakes,' said Delia. 'That poor man wanted some Christmas cheer, and God knows he doesn't get any from Peggy. One or two drinks can't hurt.'

'But . . .' Mum was visibly distressed. 'I personally gave him *four* glasses of so-called water. Tumblers! Filled to the brim!'

'And at navy strength,' Dr Smeaton added. 'It's a miracle he was able to stand upright at all.'

'Didn't you smell it on his breath?' I said, shocked.

My mother shook her head. 'I never liked to get that close.' She turned on Delia, jabbing an accusing finger at her friend. 'You told me to do it!'

Delia didn't answer. She just knitted all the faster.

Mum pulled out a chair and sat down at the table. 'If something happens to him, I've killed him! I've killed him and Peggy will never forgive me.'

'They need to retire,' Delia said again.

'His injuries are pretty severe,' said Dr Smeaton. 'The breastplate broke a few ribs, and he has a collapsed lung and crushed diaphragm.'

'Perhaps because he was drunk he didn't feel any pain?' Mum said in a hopeful voice.

'I believe that is possible,' said Dr Smeaton.

We fell into an uneasy silence, although I was aware that Mum and Dr Smeaton were engaged in some kind of teenage eye-contact game. I thought I heard her say 'mistletoe', but I couldn't be sure.

We waited for Lala and Angus to return, but as the minutes ticked by, I decided to go and look for them.

As I strolled down the rear corridor, I felt a blast of cold air.

The door to the outside cobbled courtyard stood wide open. Lala and Angus had vanished.

Chapter Four

'They've gone!' I said, returning to the kitchen just as Rupert stormed in. He looked furious.

'We've been robbed!' he exclaimed.

My heart sank.

'I knew this would happen,' he fumed. 'I should *never* have listened to you, Katherine. This is your fault. Mother is going to be livid.'

'What exactly has been taken?' I finally managed to say.

'Well, probably not the polar bear,' Mum whispered to Dr Smeaton. They giggled.

'What was that, Iris?' Rupert demanded.

'Nothing, your lordship.' But I caught the doctor giving her a mischievous nudge. She nudged him back.

'I haven't had a thorough look yet,' Rupert went on, 'but the pocket watches that my ancestor brought back from the Crimea have definitely gone.'

'Are you sure?' I had taken photographs of each display

cabinet and listed their contents the day before. I couldn't remember seeing any pocket watches from the Crimea.

Delia took a deep breath. 'Without meaning to speak ill of the dead—'

'Cropper is not dead yet, Mrs Evans,' Rupert said coldly.

'Oh, I know, milord,' said Delia. 'I'm just saying that he wasn't exactly on the ball and he was supposed to be on guard.'

'And that's where I completely disagree with you,' Rupert declared. 'Cropper was very much on the ball. He was able to give us a vital clue shortly before he was taken away in the ambulance.'

I was surprised. 'What did he tell you?'

'The police have been informed and that's all I'm prepared to say for the time being,' said Rupert.

'I think that couple from up north had something to do with it,' Mum suggested. 'They couldn't get out of here quick enough.'

'And she didn't want to take off her coat,' Delia added.

'She could have stuffed the watches in her pocket,' Mum agreed. 'And what with the dog biting her husband and then Seth's fall, it provided the perfect diversion.'

'You mean you allowed people to come into the museum room who weren't *local*?' Rupert sounded horrified.

This was an argument I knew I couldn't win. I wanted to say that I could hardly ask for postcodes, and besides, Rupert had hoped for a big turnout. He couldn't have it both ways.

'No,' Delia declared. 'I've changed my mind. Lala wouldn't have done it. She's pregnant.'

'As if being pregnant makes you a saint,' Mum said. 'I know I wasn't.'

Dr Smeaton perked up. 'Tell me, Iris. I'm intrigued.'

'Mind you,' Delia continued slowly, 'someone has stolen my crystal necklace and matching earrings. They belonged to my grandmother.'

'Well it can't be the northerners,' said Mum. 'They only got here an hour ago. You just forgot where you put them.'

'Sorry, I only just managed to get away, milord,' came a familiar voice, and Santa Claus entered the room. Or rather, Detective Inspector Shawn Cropper, dressed in a red Santa suit and wearing a fake white beard with thick, bushy eyebrows. 'I was manning the grotto at the holiday bazaar at the school,' he added.

'Oh good heavens!' my mother exclaimed. 'Last time we saw you, you were dressed as Paddington at the BearFest.'

In fact it was one of the last times I'd seen the handsome police officer too. Ever since he and Lady Lavinia's eccentric brother had fought like schoolboys for my attention, Shawn had been avoiding me.

Now he shot me a shy smile.

'I'm sorry about your grandfather,' I said. 'We're all hoping he will pull through.'

'Tell Peggy not to worry about things here,' said Delia again. 'Lenny and I are quite capable of holding the fort.'

'We won't know how bad his internal injuries are until after he's had some tests,' said Shawn. 'But he's as strong as an ox. Gran is optimistic.'

'I hope so,' Rupert said doubtfully, and I tended to agree, especially when Dr Smeaton didn't comment.

Shawn retrieved a small notebook from his Santa suit pocket. 'You say some watches were stolen, milord?'

'That's correct,' said Rupert.

'Please tell me everything,' Shawn said.

So we did.

'I must admit, Angus and Lala Fenwick certainly sound suspicious,' said Shawn. 'Don't worry. We'll put a roadblock up at the main gate, if they even get that far. Cars are having some trouble getting out of the park. The snow has turned to slush and now it's deep mud everywhere. Eric is doing a roaring trade pulling vehicles out with his tractor.'

'Well I find it hard to believe that Angus had anything to do with it,' said Rupert. 'He went out of his way to help me with Cropper. Knew first aid too. Nice chap.'

'His wife is having a baby,' Delia put in.

'And they weren't in the museum room for very long,' I pointed out. 'In full view of everyone.'

'Then it must be someone from the estate or the village,' Mum declared. 'Or – and I hate to say this, because I know she's Harry's friend—'

'I agree with Iris,' said Delia. 'That little minx is not a good influence on Master Harry.'

'I'll talk to the children,' said Rupert grimly.

'Does the major drive a black BMW convertible?' Shawn suddenly asked Delia.

'Yes,' said Delia. 'Why?'

'If I hadn't been in such a rush to get here, I would have

pulled him over for speeding. He should be very careful driving like that in these conditions.'

Delia frowned. 'Are you certain it was Lenny?'

'He nearly took the wing mirror off my patrol car,' said Shawn. 'So yes, I'm sure.'

'Where on earth could he be going?' Delia frowned.

'In the wrong direction, if you ask me,' Mum said.

I was convinced that Lenny had knocked over the suit of armour accidentally, but why wouldn't he have stayed to help?

'Will you show me which display cabinet the watches were stolen from?' I asked Rupert.

'I'll come too,' said Shawn.

The three of us left Mum and Delia in the kitchen and trooped back towards the museum room.

'I didn't want to say too much in there,' said Rupert, 'but I'm afraid the culprit is a woman.'

'Sir?' said Shawn, pencil poised. 'Why would you say that?'

'As Cropper was being lifted onto the stretcher, he gestured for me to come closer and said, "Watch her."'

'Watch *her*?' Shawn repeated. 'You're quite certain?'

'Absolutely certain,' said Rupert.

We'd reached the museum room, where Harry and Fleur were standing next to the hawk again. It was just as I had feared when they left the kitchen by the servants' entrance.

Harry had the grace to look nervous when his father strode in. He didn't even make a comment about Shawn being dressed as Santa Claus.

The jousting suit had been reassembled and was back up in its place next to the door, but some old newspapers had been spread over the area where Seth had fallen. I noted that one had a particularly distressing brown stain.

Shawn noticed it too, and immediately blanched.

'The hawk has blood on it!' Harry called out. 'Come and see!'

'Go to your room,' Rupert commanded. 'You shouldn't be in here.'

Harry's face crumpled. 'But Father, we—'

'Why?' Fleur demanded. 'We're not doing anything wrong.' She folded her arms and sat down at the base of the pedestal. Harry hesitated for a moment, then did the same.

'Do as you're told, children,' said Shawn. 'Or you'll be put on my naughty list, and you don't want that.'

'I don't believe in Santa Claus anyway,' said Fleur. 'You're just a policeman.'

'I'm afraid I will have to tell your grandmother about this, Harry,' said Rupert sternly. 'And I'm sure you know what that will mean.'

Harry scrambled to his feet. 'Come on, Fleur. Let's go.'

Fleur didn't budge. She just pouted.

'Please,' Harry urged. He grabbed her hand and pulled her up, and the pair of them walked out. Fleur slammed the door behind her, hard.

'I'm sorry about that,' said Rupert. 'Fleur's parents live abroad and they are also going through a divorce. They don't want to see her until it's all sorted out, so she's having a particularly hard time of it.'

'Poor kid,' said Shawn. 'Is she an only child?'

'Yes, but so is Harry,' Rupert reminded him.

'And so am I!' I said. 'Mum says that what you haven't had, you don't miss.' Although I had often wondered what it would have been like to have siblings.

'At least when Helen died, my boys had each other,' said Shawn.

Ah, Shawn's dead wife and the main reason why things had never seemed to work out between us. His loyalty to Helen was admirable and touching, but her shoes would be hard ones to fill. I waited for him to go on about her virtues, but to my surprise he just said, 'Although that was a long time ago now.'

'Is Fleur going to stay here for Christmas?' I asked.

'It looks like it,' said Rupert.

I felt a pang of compassion for the little girl. It had to be hard knowing that you wouldn't be with your family over the holidays.

'Let's look at these watches,' I said.

Rupert marched to the open display cabinet that held the pocket watch collection. I had counted and photographed seven watches, and seven still remained.

'Nothing is missing,' I said as Shawn scribbled in his notebook.

'There should be two watches that the 9th Earl brought back from the Crimea,' said Rupert. 'One was very unusual in that the watchmaker had engraved his name and a cryptic message about Lord Cardigan inside the case.'

'Lord Cardigan as in the Charge of the Light Brigade?' I said.

'That's right,' said Rupert. 'That one was a gift. The other was picked up on the battlefield at Balaclava.' He turned to me, his moustache bristling with annoyance.

I didn't know what to say other than the truth. 'I would have remembered seeing them, and they were definitely not here.'

Rupert indicated the display case, jabbing his finger at the top right-hand corner. 'That's where they have always been.'

Shawn and I leant together and took a closer look. To my dismay, I could make out two faint circular imprints on the silk padding. But then I remembered something.

When we had first decided to open up the museum room, the display cabinets and stuffed animals and artefacts had all been covered with dust sheets.

'When was the last time you actually viewed the contents of this room?' I asked Rupert.

'Are you implying that I do not know my own property?' He paused. 'Not for quite a few years, actually.'

I had thought as much.

'And what year would that be, milord?' Shawn said.

'Oh for heaven's sake, remove that ridiculous beard,' Rupert said. 'I can't have a serious conversation with a man in a Santa suit.'

Shawn did as he was told, ripping off the beard. It sounded painful, and I noticed him wince.

'Wait . . . what's this?' Producing a pair of tweezers from a hidden pocket, he leant over and withdrew two scraps of paper each no bigger than a postage stamp. It looked like they had been pushed down the side of the seam in the padding.

'What have you got there?' Rupert demanded.

'I think these could be the labels that described the pocket watches,' said Shawn. 'Presumably they would have been held in place by a pin like these others here.'

He straightened out the scraps of paper. The handwriting was faded and hard to decipher, but I could make out the word *Cardigan* on one label and *Sevastopol* on the other.

'Evidence that they were here, milord,' said Shawn gravely.

'Well they weren't here yesterday nor were they here this morning,' I insisted, and pulled out my iPhone. 'Look.' I scrolled through dozens of images until I reached the display cabinet, happy to see that I was right. There were only seven watches.

'Is it possible that someone broke into the house before last night?' Shawn asked. 'Since this room has only just been opened, it could have happened some time ago and no one would be any the wiser.'

Rupert dismissed the suggestion with a grunt of annoyance. 'No. Cropper specifically said "watch her",' he said. 'I told you. I believe he was referring to that young woman . . .'

'Lala Fenwick,' I supplied.

'Or perhaps he said "watches", rather than "watch her",' Shawn mused.

'But why take just those particular items?' Rupert said.

'A history buff, perhaps?' said Shawn. 'Someone who collects rarities just to keep and not sell?'

'Possibly,' I said. 'They're far too distinctive to sell in the usual manner. But they could be sold on the black market to a collector.'

'I'll offer a reward,' Rupert said suddenly. 'A no-questions-asked reward for the safe return of the watches.'

'I'm afraid I cannot endorse that idea,' said Shawn.

'I don't care if you can or you can't,' Rupert exclaimed.

'This is a criminal act and the perpetrator should face the consequences.'

'No. My mind is made up,' said Rupert. 'Put the word out. We'll take an advertisement in the local newspaper, and we can also twiddle it.'

'Twiddle?' said Shawn.

Rupert snapped his fingers with impatience. 'Whatever the term is. I do not subscribe to social media.'

'You mean tweet,' I suggested. 'As in Twitter?'

'Twiddle. Tweet. Whatever you call it,' Rupert said. 'The watches need to be back before my mother returns on Tuesday.'

'Very well,' said Shawn. 'We'll start with a list of everyone who came to the event and go from there.'

'I overheard quite a few people saying they planned on meeting up at the Hare and Hounds this evening,' I said. 'You could ask there as well.'

Shawn nodded. 'Perhaps we should look at disgruntled estate employees?'

Rupert's eyes widened. 'Disgruntled? How can they possibly be disgruntled? I give them work and a roof over their heads. The families who have served the Honeychurch estate have been with us for decades. Have you not seen the loyalty portraits in the water closet? I would trust them with my life. No,' he fumed, 'I am convinced that the guilt will lie with . . . with blow-ins. You know, outsiders. Someone who was not born in Devon.'

Shawn nodded. 'As you wish.'

'I suppose that includes myself and my mother,' I said drily. 'And Major and Mrs Evans.'

Rupert hesitated. 'Well, if we're being thorough, yes.' He snapped his fingers again. 'And question that Jones boy.'

Shawn frowned. 'Which Jones boy would that be, milord? There are quite a few.'

'You know . . . what's his name . . . great-uncle used to be the gatekeeper in my grandfather's day. Yes. Question him.'

'You mean the newspaper reporter, Nick Bond?' said Shawn. 'His mum married—'

'I don't care who she married,' said Rupert. 'She was born a Jones, and anyone connected to that family is banned from setting foot on the estate. Obviously he was up to no good here.'

My heart sank for the second time that afternoon. 'Actually, I invited Nick to cover the event for the newspaper,' I said. 'He didn't say anything about being banned.'

'Of course he wouldn't!' Rupert exclaimed. 'But make sure you question him. He was filming everything, you know. Damn cheek.'

'Sir? May I approach?' Detective Constable Clive Banks stood at the door looking very pleased with himself. With his heavy black beard and pot belly, he always reminded me of Captain Pugwash.

'You'll never believe it,' he said. 'We're in luck!'

Chapter Five

'You've made an arrest!' Rupert exclaimed.

'Not exactly,' said Clive. 'But . . . all the vehicles have left the park except an Enterprise rental car.' He grinned. 'I think it belongs to our suspects. Unfortunately, it's locked so I can't get inside, but I've put young Richard – that's my nephew, newly joined the force – on sentry duty. They'll have to come back at some point and then we can nab them quick.'

'Excellent work, Constable,' said Rupert. 'Good.'

Shawn frowned. 'But that means they're roaming the estate unescorted.'

'Exactly!' Clive exclaimed. 'They're opportunists, make no bones about it.'

'And no one locks their doors here,' Shawn said in a voice heavy with disapproval.

'I expect the safe return of the pocket watches within the hour,' Rupert declared. He headed for the door, then paused. 'And please keep me informed of Cropper's progress, naturally.'

'Of course, milord,' said Shawn.

The moment Rupert was out of earshot, Clive pointed to the pedestal, his eyes alight with boyish excitement. 'Is that *it*?'

'The hawk, yes,' I said.

'Can I look?'

'Yes, but don't touch,' said Shawn. 'We can't risk losing any more officers. We're short-staffed as it is.'

Clive stared at the mummified creature in awe. 'Blimey. I've wanted to see this since I was a kid. We all knew about the curse, didn't we, Shawn? Looks like there's no sign of blood, though. I'd say that's a good omen for Seth Cropper. I reckon he'll pull through.'

'Gosh, is there no one around here who doesn't believe in the curse?' I said.

'*Everyone* does,' Shawn and Clive chorused.

Leaving Shawn to go to the hospital and Clive to deal with the rental car, I stopped by the kitchen to see if my mother had gone home yet.

I found Delia chopping carrots with the same speed she used for her knitting. She was wearing an apron emblazoned with sprigs of holly and fir trees. There was the most delicious smell of cooking.

The kitchen was now spotlessly tidy. Prepared vegetables sat in neat piles on the table, along with a sheet of paper with the heading *MENU* and the days of the week written in Delia's neat handwriting.

'What are you making?' I asked.

'Boeuf bourguignon,' said Delia. 'Peggy always served up

coddled eggs on Sunday nights. The family must have been starving.'

'Where did you find the ingredients?' I said.

'I have a well-stocked pantry at home. I took a course in London once with Gordon Blue—'

'Cordon Bleu?'

'However you pronounce it,' said Delia. 'I told Lady Lavinia not to worry. Between you and me, I think she's excited about tasting something a bit more adventurous. Peggy never altered the menu. It was the same every week – and she calls herself a cook!'

'Well they'd better not get too used to your cooking. Peggy will soon be back,' I reminded her.

'And her eyesight is going,' Delia went on as if I hadn't spoken. 'I had to scrub this table so hard to get all the dirt out that I broke the brush! She really needs to retire.'

'So you keep saying.' In fact, when I thought of the number of times Delia had voiced this opinion, I wondered if she was planning a below-stairs coup.

She set the carrots next to the runner beans, then picked up a cloth and started wiping down the cupboard doors as if to prove her point.

'I assume Mum's already gone home,' I said.

Delia gave a snort of disdain. 'We've had a tiff. She's blaming me for making Seth drunk. I told her he's a grown man. It's up to him if he wants to fall off the wagon at Christmas.'

I saw that she was drinking a pot of black coffee for a change. She noticed me looking at it. 'Yes, it's coffee,' she said. 'I've got to stay sharp for the kitchen tonight. Have you seen Lenny? I can't wait to see him dressed in a butler's get-up.'

At that moment the rear door flew open and Lenny stood there – still in his military uniform – looking bewildered.

'Where is everyone? I run a quick errand, and when I get back, the place is like a morgue. Is that kettle hot?'

'Where have you been?' Delia demanded. 'You've missed all the excitement. Seth Cropper is in hospital, hanging on to life by a thread.'

'Really? What happened?' said Lenny. 'Was it a heart attack?'

I looked at him in disbelief. 'You don't remember?'

'Remember what?' he said.

'You were *there*.' I was incredulous. 'You came into the museum room and knocked into the suit of armour, which then fell on top of Seth Cropper.'

'No.' Lenny shook his head. 'That wasn't me. You need your eyes tested, luv. I was nowhere near the museum room. I've been up at Guy's.' He pulled out a chair and sat down at the kitchen table.

I was stunned. 'But I saw you. Other people saw you.'

'Nope. Not guilty.' He gave an indulgent chuckle. 'I think you've been drinking too much Honeychurch Gin!'

'Well . . . Seth was definitely on the sauce,' Delia said as she set down a mug of tea for her husband. 'Dr Smeaton said he was drunk. The Croppers really should retire.'

'I know what I saw, Lenny,' I said firmly.

'Are you accusing me . . . a man who is about to be

awarded the Queen's Gallantry Medal?' Lenny leant back in his chair and played with the array of military medals across his breast pocket. 'Maybe you should take it up with Her Majesty?'

'Don't be silly,' scolded Delia. 'Take no notice of him, Kat. I doubt if the Queen would take your call anyway.'

They both burst into laughter.

I regarded the pair with growing dislike. The major had lied to my face, and Delia seemed to care more about ousting the Croppers from their posts than about whether Seth would pull through.

'Where did the reporter bloke go?' Lenny asked. 'I thought he wanted my photograph.'

'He left,' I said, and then remembered that Nick had been filming and recording everything. With any luck, he might have captured Lenny falling into the armour so I could prove that I hadn't imagined it.

'Come on, luv,' teased the major. 'Lighten up. If you're going to become family, you'll have to get used to me taking the mickey out of you.'

Family? I knew that Delia and my mother had been thoroughly enjoying playing matchmaker between the Evanses' son and me, but it was still very early days.

So far I liked Lieutenant Commander Guy Evans of the Royal Naval Air Service. He was handsome, charming, witty, talented – and, surprisingly, available. He had recently bought a barn conversion close by that he was in the process of doing up. I had only seen him twice in the last three months, but we had spoken almost daily on the phone.

But I was cautious, and Guy was too. He'd been married and divorced and told me he'd been badly hurt, so we were happy to take things slowly.

'Now you've really scared her, Lenny,' Delia said. 'Don't worry. I promised Guy we wouldn't interfere in your relationship.'

'I'm glad to hear it,' I said.

'So that's why we're going to the pub tonight. Just to keep an eye on you both.' Lenny winked at Delia and they roared with laughter again. 'It's all right. We'll keep out of your way.'

'Lovely.' I forced a smile. 'I'll look forward to seeing you both later. I'm going to go home and change.'

Outside was eerily quiet save for the hoot of a barn owl and the distant strangled cry of a mating fox.

When I'd first moved from the bright lights of London, the strange noises of the countryside had frightened me. I'd been used to the sound of Underground trains outside my flat at Putney Bridge station, the yellow glow of the street lamps and the never-ending buzz of the city. It took me a while to adjust to the silence, but now I couldn't imagine living anywhere else.

I walked briskly to my car, which I'd left in the courtyard by the servants' entrance. Within seconds my face felt numb and my throat raw from the cold night air.

I cautiously set off for Jane's Cottage, thinking how crazy it was that as the crow flies, my home was about five minutes from the rear of the Hall, but because one of Rupert's ancestors didn't want the staff to accidentally wander onto the main drive, he'd created an elaborate network of service lanes. It usually took me fifteen minutes to travel down the drive, turn left at the entrance next to the gatehouses where I ran my antique business, skirt the estate boundary wall along Cavalier Lane and then enter the tradesmen's entrance that would eventually dead-end at Jane's Cottage.

As I rounded the corner, I saw a panda car parked across the five-bar gate next to a wooden sign that made me smile.

Parking £1

Stuck? Towing £5 (ask for Eric)

Clive and Richard were in the front seat of the police car with the engine running to keep the inside warm. In the field beyond was one solitary car that I assumed was the Enterprise rental belonging to Angus and Lala.

The fact that they had not returned to their car only seemed to exacerbate their guilt.

I opened my window and Clive did the same. 'I'll let you know if I see them,' I said.

'Sooner rather than later,' replied Clive. 'It's bloody freezing.'

I exited the main drive and entered the tradesmen's entrance that took me along a narrow potholed lane past Eric's scrapyard, the entrance to the Carriage House, the Victorian walled garden and stumpery, Honeychurch Cottages and the rear access to the stable block.

My home – Jane's Cottage – was a quarter of a mile further on at the top of the hill.

It was when I was approaching Honeychurch Cottages that my headlamps picked out two figures on foot. One was limping.

To my astonishment, it was Angus and Lala. I slowed down, not sure exactly what to do.

Angus wrenched the passenger door open and stuck his head inside.

'Are we glad to see you,' he exclaimed. 'Can we get in?'

Chapter Six

'We got lost,' said Angus as he jumped into the front seat and Lala piled into the back.

I was surprised. 'Surely you haven't been wandering around all this time?'

'I told him we shouldn't have gone out the back door,' Lala grumbled. 'There are no signposts anywhere.'

'That's because we're still on the Honeychurch estate,' I said.

'Most country houses have signs like "Exit" or "Way Out",' Angus went on.

'Honeychurch Hall isn't open to the general public,' I said. 'Today was a special occasion.'

'That explains it,' said Angus. 'We're members of the National Trust. To be honest, we like to go where we're not supposed to.'

'Angus!' Lala wailed. 'Don't tell her that. She'll get us arrested!'

'Is that why you didn't come back?' I wasn't sure if I believed them. 'Because you wanted to go exploring?'

'We just thought we'd have a look down the servants' corridor – you'd mentioned all the little rooms and stuff,' said Lala. 'Then we saw the back door and went outside to look in the courtyard.'

'We lost track of time.' Angus took up the story. 'And then we thought, no point going back the way we'd come, and the next thing we know, we're in this place full of tree stumps.'

'It was like a horror film,' said Lala.

'That's the Victorian stumpery,' I said. 'Think of it like a rock garden but using stumps and logs instead.'

'Where are we going?' Lala demanded. 'Isn't our car back in the other direction?'

'Yes, but it's too narrow to turn around here,' I said. 'Your car is the Enterprise rental, isn't it?'

'Yeah,' said Angus. 'I expect it's the only one left in the park.'

'I thought we'd have to send out a search party,' I told him.

'You should have done,' he said. 'I'm not listening to Lala's directions again. She got us lost on the way down, and then out here too.'

'That's only because the map on my phone doesn't work,' Lala protested. 'I don't understand it.'

'There's no phone signal or Wi-Fi on the estate unless you can get to high ground,' I said.

She looked at me as if I had just told her the world had come to an end. 'That's stupid. How can anyone post on Instagram without Wi-Fi or a phone signal?'

'Walk to the top of a hill or go into the town.' I was going to add that I had a BT hotspot at the gatehouse, but decided against it.

'So you mean you can't get emails anywhere around here?' Lala was still in shock. 'Not even in the village?'

'I think the earl will eventually get broadband installed,' I said. 'But for now, the nearest Internet café is in Dartmouth. My phone works on 4G but I don't always get a signal.'

'Well that certainly explains a few things,' Angus said.

'I thought the old bag at the B and B was just being difficult,' Lala grumbled. 'She kept saying it wasn't working.'

I had a sudden thought. 'I didn't realise you'd already checked in at the B and B.' When the couple had arrived earlier, they'd given the impression that they had driven straight to the Hall.

'Yeah,' said Lala. 'We checked in on Saturday.'

'What are you talking about?' Angus said with scorn. 'We drove down today. Blimey, luv. The cold must have frozen your brain.' He turned to me. 'It's her hormones. Makes her forgetful.'

But I knew he was lying. My suspicions as to why they had come all this way deepened. It would be easy enough to find out when they had arrived, but it made no sense. If they had broken into the museum room days before, why hang around for the open house and risk being caught with the goods?

'How long are you planning on staying in the area?' I asked.

'Angus has got some business in Plymouth,' said Lala. 'And there's an auction in Newton Abbot that we want to go to on Wednesday.'

'That would be Luxtons,' I said, surprised. 'I'll be going there as well.' There was a rare white Steiff Dicky Bear that I was hoping to acquire.

'In case you hadn't guessed,' said Angus, 'we collect stuffed animals.'

'Yeah, we do,' said Lala. 'But the difference is that Angus's used to be alive.'

As the couple continued to banter, I found it hard to imagine that they had stolen the pocket watches, and yet their presence in Little Dipperton still baffled me.

'If you visit Dartmouth, make sure to stop by the Antique Emporium,' I said. 'I have a space there and a zoo of Steiff miniature animals for sale.'

'Trade discount?' Angus said.

'Of course,' I replied. 'Seriously. You should come. There's a Christmas market and the Dartington Morris Men will be performing there. It will be fun.'

Suddenly a pair of headlamps approached at speed. Pulling tightly into one of several turn-ins dotted along the service road, I waited for the car to pass. As it slowed down, I saw Lenny at the wheel of his black BMW convertible. We both opened our windows.

'Just spoke to Guy,' said Lenny. 'He's going to be a bit late getting to the Hare and Hounds tonight and— Oh.' His expression changed to one of confusion. 'Who . . . What the hell . . .' And without another word, he roared away.

'Blimey,' said Angus. 'Where's the fire, mate?'

Lenny's behaviour was nothing short of bizarre.

'Did either of you see what happened this afternoon?' I asked. 'When the armour fell on top of Seth Cropper?'

'I was a bit preoccupied with getting my leg bitten off,' said Angus with good humour, 'and poor Lala here was floundering around on the floor like a beached whale. Why?'

Was I the only person who had seen Lenny walk into the armour? Maybe I had been imagining it after all.

Finally we pulled up alongside Clive's police car. I started to feel nervous, as if I was betraying the couple in some way. I stole a look at Angus, who seemed oblivious to the possibility that they were about to be accused of theft and almost definitely searched.

Clive and Richard leapt out to help them alight from my car, turning on their torches.

'Now that's service for you,' said Angus. 'I think we can take it from here. Thanks, Kat. We'll see you at the auction – if not before.'

'Not so fast, sir,' said Richard, looking stern. 'Will you wait here for a moment, please?'

Clive came around to my side and gestured for me to open the window. In a low voice he said, 'I'm afraid I'm going to need your assistance, for obvious reasons.' He gestured to where Richard was standing guard as if he were stopping sheep from making a run for freedom.

'No sign of Shawn?' I said.

'He's still at the hospital,' replied Clive. 'We need a witness to prove that we're not planting evidence, and we need a woman to search Lala Fenwick.'

'I am definitely not doing that,' I said.

'In that case, we'll have to arrest her and wait for a female police officer to come to the station. As you can imagine, that won't be happening tonight, and it would look bad in the newspapers if it turned out they were innocent.'

I had to agree with him there. With great reluctance, I joined the trio in the gateway.

'What's going on?' Angus demanded.

'We can do this here or go down to the station,' Clive declared.

'It's just standard procedure,' I said quickly. 'We need you to empty your pockets – and if you don't mind, I'd like to look in your handbag, Lala.'

'Yes I do mind,' Lala fumed. 'Bloody cheek! First that ruddy dog bites my husband – who tried to save someone's life, I may add – and now—'

'It's fine, babe.' Angus put out a restraining arm. 'No problem, Officer. Search away.'

He raised his arms and Clive went through his pockets and patted down each of his trouser legs, setting Angus's mobile phone, car keys and wallet on the bonnet of the police car.

Richard picked up the wallet and retrieved a driver's licence. He read out, 'Angus Fenwick, Richmond address.'

'What?' Angus demanded. 'You thought I'd have a fake ID or something? There's a business card in there as well. Take it if you want.'

'We will. Thank you, sir. Everything seems to be in order.' Clive turned to me. 'Over to you.'

Lala gave me a filthy look. 'You can search my pockets and my bag, but don't you dare touch me.'

'I'm really sorry,' I said, and I was. It was mortifying.

'Well go on then,' she sneered. 'What are you waiting for?'

Her coat was so thick and padded she could hardly raise her arms. 'Want to see the lining?' She unzipped it and opened the coat so I could feel the lining and put my hands in her pockets. Other than a crumpled tissue and a raspberry-flavoured lip salve, there was nothing – certainly no pocket watches, though I hadn't expected there to be any.

Lala's baby bump was a fair size, but I suspected it was because she had such a small frame. I resisted the temptation to touch it, and felt a twinge of longing for a child of my own.

'Can you hurry up?' she grumbled. 'My feet are getting cold.'

'Just a quick peep in your handbag,' I said apologetically. Clive shone his torch into the interior of her rucksack.

Lala was remarkably neat, using all the little compart-ments for her mobile, a notebook and pencil, a small make-up bag and her purse. I unzipped the make-up bag to find a lip-stick and mirror.

Naturally, there was no sign of the pocket watches there either.

I gave the rucksack back. 'I'm so sorry,' I said again, then felt compelled to tell them why they had been searched. 'Lord Honeychurch believes that something has been taken from the museum room.'

'What about those two kids?' Angus said. 'Biggles and the French girl.'

'Yeah.' Lala nodded. 'I heard them egging each other on for a dare.'

'What kind of dare?' I demanded.

'Let me see . . . caving at Larcombe Quarry, skating at Larcombe Quarry, stealing the electrical rejuvenator – whatever that is – and touching that old dead bird.'

'Oh dear,' I said.

'If anyone has taken anything, I reckon it's that Fleur,' Lala continued. '*Is* she French?'

'No,' I said. 'But she likes to think she is.'

Leaving the pair to find their way back to Little Dipperton, I called in to see my mother.

As I drove into the entrance, light from Mum's newly installed sensor system flooded the cobbled courtyard, illuminating it like a football stadium.

The Carriage House formed part of a quadrangle and was surrounded by a range of outbuildings, including the old piggery – still with the iron bars on the windows – and the henhouse. The former had been newly renovated to become my mother's writing house and the latter had been turned into a gin still.

I left my car next to the wishing well. The little pitched roof was adorned with fairy lights, and Mum had hung wreaths on every available door.

I'd never forget the first time I saw her new home. I was appalled. The place was semi-derelict, and I thought she'd made a terrible mistake, but now, after spending oodles of money from her royalties as the international best-selling romance writer Krystalle Storm, the two-storey red-brick building with its arched double carriageway door was stunning.

Krystalle Storm's true identity was a closely guarded secret, which was just as well given the biography that featured on my mother's website: an Italian villa on the Amalfi coast, a stately home in Devon, a Pekinese called Truly Scrumptious and, most shocking of all, an international diplomat husband – my *father* – who'd tragically perished in a plane crash. When questioned about these lies – I can't even call them exaggerations – my mother claimed that Dad's real job as a tax inspector hadn't sounded glamorous enough.

Even her publisher had no idea, because Mum claimed to be a recluse who rarely made public appearances. It was such a pity. I was so proud of her accomplishments and I was quite sure that everyone in the village would be thrilled to have a famous author living in their midst, but the lies had gone on for far too long now.

A sliver of light was visible under the door of the piggery, so I knew she was in there, writing. She used to have an office in the Carriage House itself, but with Delia's constant unannounced 'I just dropped by!' visits, she couldn't risk being found out. A dedicated building had seemed the answer.

The piggery had a one-way window, meaning that Mum could look out but no one could look in. When questioned as to what was behind the door, she said it was the priceless

Honeychurch archives. It sounded believable, since Mum had been working on the Honeychurch family tree for Rupert for months, and had been appointed the official family historian.

I rapped out our code on the door. 'It's Kat,' I whispered.

After a moment, I heard a mumbled 'Are you alone?'

'Yes. Of course.'

After a great deal of fumbling, Mum threw the door open and pulled me quickly inside, shutting it behind me. She looked as if she'd been crying.

'Whatever is the matter?' I said.

'It's Seth. He's dead.'

'Oh no!' I exclaimed. 'I am so sorry. That's awful.'

'And it's all my fault.'

'Of course it's not your fault!' I took her hand and gave it a squeeze. She seemed really upset. I was too, but I had to admit to being a little surprised at my mother's grief. I knew she had no time for Peggy, and whenever she had mentioned Seth Cropper, it had rarely been complimentary.

'Reynard called and told me,' said Mum. 'I'd asked him to let me know the moment he heard news. Apparently the alcohol level in Seth's bloodstream was through the roof.'

'Mum, it was Delia who gave you the neat gin to give to Seth,' I said. 'If there is any blame – which there isn't – it should all be hers.'

I sat her down on the sofa in front of the wood-burning stove. The room was cosy and comforting. Mum sniffled quietly into a tissue while I headed over to a corner unit where she had set up a mini kitchen area.

As the kettle boiled, I scanned the room, impressed with everything my mother had accomplished completely by herself and with no encouragement from anyone, simply because we just hadn't known.

Floor-to-ceiling custom-made bookshelves covered one wall, displaying all her writing awards. Her first-edition books ran for entire shelves, and I knew that she had boxes of copies up in the attic in the Carriage House too.

A grey metal filing cabinet five drawers high stood in one corner. In another was a standard lamp and Dad's battered leather wingback chair that she used for reading. Next to that was a hexagonal table piled with editions of *The Lady* magazine and the weekly *Dipperton Deal*.

Another wall held a corkboard showing the official Honeychurch family tree.

Half of it was covered in black-and-white photographs of Honeychurch Hall and the formal gardens in what must have been its heyday at the beginning of the twentieth century – the golden age of the English country house. Colour photographs dating from the 1950s and early 1960s showed the interior of a shell-lined grotto and the exterior of the Carriage House before it was abandoned for the new stable block. I noted a recent addition: an old black-and-white photo of the stumpery before nature took its course and covered it with a variety of ferns.

Dad's Olivetti typewriter sat on a walnut partner's desk beneath a window that looked out to the pine forest beyond. Mum told me that she often watched the deer. Tonight the fabric blind was pulled down.

I handed her a mug of hot tea. 'I can't stay long.'

'And I can't concentrate,' Mum said. 'I know you might not believe this, but I had a soft spot for Seth. He wasn't *always* a boring old fart. He was quite the Casanova in his youth. It's rotten getting old.'

In the past year or so, I had learnt more about my mother's childhood and wild teenage years than I had in the entire time I had lived at home. To say her past was colourful was putting it mildly.

'Please don't tell me you had a fling with Seth Cropper as well as . . . as well as all the other names that seem to keep surfacing,' I said.

'I was sixteen and he was twenty-four,' Mum began wistfully.

'That's disgusting.' I pulled a face. 'He'd be arrested these days.'

'As you know, Bushman's Travelling Fair and Boxing Emporium used to camp in the park every summer—'

'Yes, I know,' I said. 'Yet another reason why Peggy has never liked you.'

'It wasn't only me,' Mum protested. 'We used to say Seth had desert disease . . . wandering palms.'

'Ugh.'

Thinking of Seth reminded me of Lenny and his past indiscretion. My mother listened in amazement as I told her how Lenny had denied having anything to do with Seth's accident. Unfortunately, although Mum had seen him arrive, she hadn't seen him actually fall into the armour, because she was grabbing the dog at the time.

'All Delia is saying is that she thinks the Croppers should retire,' I added. 'And now Seth is dead.'

My mother took a deep breath. 'I think Delia deliberately set me up.'

'Mum—'

'She wanted Seth to fall off the wagon so that he'd be unfit to work. That would mean that she and Captain Bravado could move into the Croppers' cottage and take their jobs.'

'That sounds too far-fetched if you ask me,' I said.

'Wait there,' said Mum. 'I want to show you something.'

She retrieved several copies of the *Dipperton Deal* from the hexagonal table. Local news represented the whole world of those who lived in this small community. Friends fell out over what seemed to be the most trivial of things – a hedge pruned too low, someone's prized marmalade being placed second instead of first, and even, in my mother's case, a kiss that had happened decades ago.

'I knew you read that newspaper, but I didn't think you kept copies,' I said.

'Of course I keep copies,' Mum declared. 'It's full of ideas for stories – especially on page five.'

She opened it to the page in question and handed it to me. 'See?'

It was the problem page hosted by an anonymous agony aunt called Amanda. At one point we were convinced that Amanda had to be the local postmistress, but when she died, the problems continued to pour in and Amanda remained.

The weekly column had always been a point of derision for Mum and me. When I first moved to Devon and lived in her spare bedroom, we'd do the crossword together and then have fun guessing which tortured soul in the village was seeking Amanda's no-nonsense advice.

Now Mum pointed to a problem that she'd circled in red. 'Read that one.'

> Dear Amanda,
> I'm troubled by two old people I work with who really should have retired ten years ago since they are no longer capable of working the long hours required on the job or the physical demands, e.g. sweeping the floor and polishing shoes. I find I am constantly covering for their mistakes. What should I do?
>   Signed: Desperate
>   Amanda advises: Get them sacked!

I couldn't help but laugh. 'And you think that's from Delia?'

'That was last week,' Mum said. 'And here is this week.'

> Dear Amanda,
> I only used to see my husband forty days a year, but now that he's retired he's under my feet all the time. I think he needs to get a part-time job but he wants to write his memoir. I'm waiting for the couple next door to retire and then he could have a job. Their cottage has a cellar. What should I do?
>   Signed: Desperate
>   Amanda advises: Get them sacked!

'But does Lenny even want to be a butler?' Somehow I couldn't imagine him taking orders when he was used to giving them. 'And only seeing him for forty days a year? Is that true?'

'Sarah Ferguson said she only saw Prince Andrew for forty days a year, so I assume it is. "Desperate" has been writing in every week,' Mum went on. 'The first few were all about whether she should give her husband another chance, to which Amanda said, "On your head be it. A leopard doesn't change his spots", which is my belief too.'

'Everyone deserves a second chance, Mum.'

'Delia is only giving him one because she's going to meet the Queen,' Mum declared. 'If the scandal of his affair came out, she'd drop him, I'm sure of it.'

'Well hopefully it won't,' I said.

'To be honest, their reconciliation has been quite helpful in writing *Betrayed*.' Mum passed me two sheets of type-written pages. 'Do you think this scene works?'

It would seem that my mother's grief over Seth had ended as quickly as it had begun.

I read: *Colonel de Lacy Evans cornered the housekeeper in the meat larder. His sword dragged along the flagstone floor. Startled, Delilah spun around. Her face burnt with desire as he closed the door behind him. It was just the two of them alone. 'Take off your—'*

'No, Mum. Absolutely no!' I threw the pages down. 'You cannot possibly—'

'That's what happened,' Mum protested. 'Delia told me. Lenny caught her by surprise and—'

'OK. I'm leaving now,' I said quickly. 'You're playing with fire. Colonel de Lacy Evans? Delilah?'

'No one ever recognises themselves in a book.'

'Delia's a huge fan of Krystalle Storm, as you well know.'

'De Lacy Evans existed, actually,' said Mum. 'He fought in the Crimea.'

At the mention of the Crimea, I was glad to change the subject and fill my mother in on the missing pocket watches and how I'd had to frisk a pregnant woman.

'They could easily have taken the watches and hidden them somewhere in the grounds to pick up later,' Mum mused. 'Don't be fooled by the fact that she's pregnant and that he tried to save Seth's life. It could be a cover.'

'Since when have you become so cynical?' I exclaimed.

'Ever since I started reading the *Daily Mail*.'

But it was a good point. The couple had been wandering the estate for a long time. They had even mentioned finding the stumpery, which would definitely be an excellent hiding place, with its many nooks and crannies. But I thought it unlikely.

'Seth must have seen something, because his last words to Rupert were "watch her",' I said.

'What?' Mum said sharply. 'What did you say?'

'"Watch her".'

'Oh. Wait a moment.' Mum fell quiet. 'Let me think.'

'Are you all right?' I said.

'No . . . Oh dear,' she said slowly. 'Oh my God, Katherine! The pocket watches! Has his lordship already reported the theft to the police?'

'Yes,' I said.

She looked at me, her eyes wide. 'How can you possibly have forgotten? This is not good. Not good at all.'

Chapter Seven

'The insurance scam,' Mum said.

My heart sank. 'The million-pound payout?'

'Remember?' Mum exclaimed. 'The dowager countess's husband – that would be the 14th Earl, Rupert's father – staged a fake break-in to get the insurance money in order to cover the crippling inheritance tax when he died. It was a very good idea.'

'Only it was illegal,' I said.

'No one else in the family knew – not even the dowager countess,' Mum went on. 'I only remembered because I'm constantly reminded every day staring at that!' She pointed to the family tree on the wall.

I hadn't been at the Hall for very long, but I recalled that the only people who had known about the earl's plan back in 1990 were Seth and Peggy Cropper, and Shawn's father Detective Chief Superintendent Robert Cropper, who was long retired and now lived out in Spain.

This wasn't the first time the deed had come back to haunt the family.

As the years passed, various 'stolen' items started to reappear in the household. The Steiff *Titanic* mourning bear sat on Harry's bed; paintings were hanging in the dining room and Great Hall again, and all the silverware seemed to have been put back where it belonged. And these were just the items I knew about.

And the reason I had known about the insurance scam was because David Wynne, international art investigator and my ex-boyfriend, had found out and told me when I first moved to the estate.

I realised what this could mean. The fact that the pocket watches might have been stolen from the display cabinet in 1990 didn't matter. The items would pop up on David's Art Loss Register hot sheet and he would be down here in a flash.

'Dylan,' Mum whispered, as if reading my mind.

'His name is David,' I said. 'And yes, I know.'

'He'll be here before you can blink. Just you see.'

'Let's hope not.' I had wasted so much of my life waiting for David to divorce his estranged wife Trudy, and now I had moved on and did not want to revisit the past. 'I need to double-check the list.' David had given me a copy. 'It's at the gatehouse.'

'Let's not panic quite yet,' said Mum. 'As long as the watches *don't* resurface, it should be OK. But if they *do* resurface and the culprits, as in Angus and the lovely Lala, admit they stole them after all, David will have a field day.'

'Rupert reported that they'd only just been stolen, Mum.'

'I know. But didn't you say that he hadn't been in the museum room for years?'

I nodded.

'Perhaps he can be persuaded that he made a mistake,' she said hopefully.

I was dubious. 'Maybe.'

I could feel her watching me. 'Is there something else bothering you?'

'Like what?'

'David?' she said. 'You *are* over him, aren't you, darling?'

'Yes, of course,' I said. 'Why?'

'No reason,' Mum said. 'No reason at all. And anyway, what does he matter? You've got the gorgeous Guy now.'

'Which reminds me. I'm going to be late. Can't I tempt you to come to the pub?'

'What? And be the third wheel?'

'Fifth actually,' I said. 'Delia and Lenny are going to be there.'

Mum must have caught the expression on my face, because she laughed. 'Your future in-laws, you mean.'

'Don't you start!' I felt irritated. Of course I knew that Mum had my best interests at heart. Apart from the fact that she was desperate to become a grandmother, she and Delia had got it into their heads that Guy and I were perfect for each other. On paper, how could he not be?

Being a navy helicopter pilot, he'd travelled extensively and lived overseas. He was fluent in French and German, played the guitar and was a keen amateur painter – I was surprised by how much he knew about the Impressionists.

During one of our long phone conversations, he'd confided that he'd wanted to study art but his father had insisted he follow the family tradition and join the armed forces.'

'And a word of advice,' said Mum. 'Don't encourage Shawn. We don't want a repetition of what happened with Lady Lavinia's brother, do we? I would think that in this instance, Guy would win hands down.'

'Give me some credit. Please,' I said.

'I saw how Shawn looked at you behind that Santa beard,' Mum went on. 'Delia told me that Peggy told *her* that Shawn has been in grief counselling.'

'Delia should mind her own business,' I said.

'Forewarned is forearmed,' Mum said cheerfully. 'Now, off you go. I'm behind with my word count today.'

After changing into fresh clothes, I stopped by the gate-houses on my way to the pub. I just had to know for sure whether the pocket watches were on the list of 'stolen' items.

I disabled the alarm to the West Gatehouse, the building I used as a showroom and office, and stepped into the warmth.

I had spent a fair bit of my own money doing the renovation – replacing cracked windows, repairing damaged cornices and installing new guttering and central heating. I'd also put in a new alarm system that could be activated from my iPhone.

There was a single large living area, one-and-a-half storeys high, with a gabled ceiling and two tiny dormer windows. At one point there had been a mezzanine level with a ladder that led up to a sleeping area, but the floorboards had been rotten and I had taken them out. A galley kitchen, bathroom and large cupboard that held a wall safe were at the rear.

The place was light and airy, with three bay windows that looked out onto the driveway.

I loved my showroom. Lined with lighted shelves that displayed dozens of my most expensive antique bears and dolls, I regarded it as my sanctuary. Mum thought it was creepy and claimed it reminded her of a scene from a horror film.

I kept some stock in the East Gatehouse, though ever since I'd taken a space at Dartmouth Antique Emporium, I had moved a lot of it there. But it was in the West Gatehouse that I met serious collectors who were willing to spend thousands of pounds on high-end porcelain character dolls and vintage bears. It wasn't that long ago that I had sold a one-of-a-kind Gund bear for ten thousand pounds. It was exquisite, with Tahitian pearls for eyes. I was hoping to buy the white Dicky Bear for the same collector. It would be a great way to start my Christmas.

I headed straight for the wall safe and keyed in the code.

David had given me a copy of the original police report from the night of the supposed break-in, along with a list of the items stolen. Sure enough, the Crimean pocket watches were on there.

I wondered if he knew I still had a copy. He'd never asked me and I had forgotten about it up until now.

According to the report, the intruder had come in through the French doors in the middle of the night. No alarm. No broken windows. No witnesses. All the family were away, except for one or two staff – i.e., the Croppers.

David had noted the names of those who had lived on the estate at the time – familiar names that my mother had put on her below-stairs family tree. Only Peggy Cropper and Eric Pugsley still lived here.

I ramped up my computer and logged on to the Art Loss Register. The Crimean pocket watches were still there, with the date they'd been reported stolen: 21 June 1990.

For a moment, I wondered if I should tell Shawn, but then I reminded myself that this was nothing to do with me. My mother had a point. As long as the watches didn't resurface, everything should be fine.

Eventually I set off for the Hare and Hounds, and soon forgot about the watches as the butterflies in my stomach took over at the thought of seeing Guy again.

Cresting the narrow stone bridge that had stood there since the twelfth century, I drove into the village of Little Dipperton.

There was just one narrow road, which snaked around the village green past the Norman church of St Mary's. A series of whitewashed cottages, some in dire need of re-thatching, others with slate roofs, and all desperate for a coat of paint, formed a crescent around the churchyard, which was encompassed by a low stone wall. Ancient yew trees and hedges flourished among the dozens of gravestones, many of which bore the names of families who still lived here. The village itself had been mentioned in the Domesday Book.

Most of the cottages belonged to the Honeychurch estate and were painted in a distinctive blue. They had no front gardens and there was no pavement. The low front doors opened directly onto the road.

Tonight, under a bright moon and star-covered sky, the whole place sparkled with frost. Christmas trees stood in windows and outdoor festive lights hung from rafters. Someone had even decorated the red telephone box, which, no longer housing a phone, now had a life-saving role as a defibrillator station.

As I drove through the village, I spied the Enterprise rental car parked in the alley between the post office and Rose Cottage – Violet Green's tea room and B and B.

Parking was always difficult here, and since many of the people who had been at the museum room had been planning on heading to the pub afterwards, I knew it would be busier than usual. In fact, the car park was full.

Rupert's black Range Rover was in its reserved spot, and Lenny's black BMW convertible took up two spaces outside the front parking bay. *How typical!* There was also a Suzuki DR-Z400 with a distinctive lime-green fender and mudguard.

I circled back to the church car park, but that was full too. In the end, I left my car partially mounted on a grass verge next to the entrance to a rutted track signposted *Unmetalled Road* – another term for a green lane – and cut through the churchyard. The cold was raw and almost took my breath away. The brick path was slick with ice. It was then that I heard voices.

Glancing over, I saw two figures huddled together under the boughs of a yew tree. They must have heard me coming, because they fell silent and drew back further into the shadows.

As I reached the lychgate, though, I was startled by another figure crouched behind a headstone close to the boundary wall. To my dismay, I slipped and went crashing down onto the hard ground, landing on my elbow. It really hurt!

The figure sprang out. 'Oh my God, Kat, are you OK?'

I looked up to see a man dressed all in black and wearing a balaclava.

'Nick?' I said, astonished. 'Is that you? What on earth are you doing skulking around here?'

Chapter Eight

Nick helped me to my feet.

'Thanks,' I said. 'It's just as well I recognised your voice. You scared me.'

'Sorry,' he said. 'I just popped out for a bit of air. The pub was getting stuffy.'

'In a balaclava?' I said.

'It's cold!' He took the balaclava off, making his hair stand up in spikes. 'Force of habit. I came here on my bike.'

'Ah, is the lime-green motorbike outside the pub yours?'

'I happen to like lime green,' he said.

'Come on, Nick,' I teased. 'What are you really doing out here?'

He grinned. 'Following a hunch.'

I wondered if it had something to do with the figures I'd seen in the churchyard, but looking over his shoulder, all seemed quiet now.

'Well I'm sorry if I blew your cover,' I said. 'Is this about the pocket watches?'

For a split second, he hesitated. 'Maybe.'

My stomach turned over. 'You *know* something?'

'Maybe,' he said again. 'Why . . . do you?'

'No,' I lied. 'But Rupert is offering a reward.'

'He sure is,' said Nick. 'He's in the pub asking questions.'

'Has anyone come forward?'

'Maybe,' he said for the third time.

'And of course you won't tell me.'

'I can't.'

'Can't – or won't?'

'Both,' he admitted. 'Sorry to hear about Seth Cropper.'

I smiled. 'Nice change of subject. But yes, it's very sad. News travels fast. Are you going back to the pub?'

'Not yet,' he said.

I left Nick in the churchyard and headed for the Hare and Hounds.

I loved this old pub. It was my favourite. Mum and I came here often. It was a typical Devon longhouse, with a low, heavy-beamed ceiling and a massive inglenook fireplace. It was so enormous that seats had been cut into the bricks of the enclosed hearth that flanked the grate. A roaring log fire burnt in front of a decorative cast-iron fireback bearing the inscription *1635*. Christmas decorations were everywhere.

Two threadbare tapestries depicting battle scenes from the Civil War jostled with a plethora of pikes, maces and swords. Dozens of heavy antique keys dangled from wires along the beams overhead, and copper of all descriptions filled what little wall space remained.

Tables grouped in clusters were set with oak chairs or embraced by high-backed curved oak benches to provide intimate settings. Through a low arch – where a sprig of mistletoe was getting a lot of attention from a handful of young couples – was a small room known as the snug. It led to a latch door and a back staircase that went up to a handful of bedrooms for B and B, where until recently Lenny had been living until Delia allowed him to come home.

In the corner stood a wainscot chair with a tattered tapestry cushion that was reserved for the dashing Cavalier Sir Maurice. Centuries ago, Sir Maurice had courted Lady Frances Honeychurch, and his ghost was said to roam Hopton's Crest on his black steed. No one was allowed to sit in this chair, otherwise a terrible misfortune would befall them. Bottles had been known to explode, dogs refused to lie by the fire. I was amused that even though the pub was packed, everyone gave that chair a wide berth.

As I fought my way through the crowd, I told myself again that the Honeychurch robbery was not my problem, and yet Nick's comments worried me. What exactly did he know?

Let it go, Kat. Tonight I was meeting a man I found attractive and who was just as interested in me as I was in him.

'Let her through!' came a shout. 'Let our lovely Kat through, lads!' I looked up to see Doreen Mutters waving.

It had taken me a while to feel part of the village, but now I really felt I'd come home.

Doreen and her husband Stan had run the pub for over forty years. Mum called them Tweedledum and Tweedledee. Voluptuous and rosy-cheeked, Doreen was the epitome of an old-fashioned barmaid. The pair were well known for their unusual pets, the current one being an Indian Runner duck called Fred.

I reached the bar, where Fred was nestled on his small pad wearing a red bow tie made of tinsel.

'Here you go.' Doreen handed me a glass of Sharpham Sparkling Blanc without me even asking. 'I haven't seen your man yet,' she said.

And that was the one thing I didn't like about living in a small community. Everyone knew everybody else's business.

'But Delia is guarding that table as if her life depended on it.' Doreen pointed to where Delia sat. She had staked her claim by hanging a knitted woollen bobble hat, her canvas tote bag and her coat over the backs of three empty chairs. Someone came over to try to take one of them, but with lightning speed Delia held onto it.

I assumed that meant Guy and I would be sitting with his parents. *Great.*

Word of Seth Cropper's death had flown around the village like wildfire. A tin collection bucket sat on the bar with a sign saying: *Seth's Final Shindig. Give Generously.* Two photographs were propped against the bucket. One showed Seth and Peggy on their wedding day, emerging from the village church through a tunnel of kitchen utensils – presumably held by the servants who worked below stairs at the time. Another showed them celebrating their fiftieth wedding anniversary on a wooden bench in front of a ruined brick building with a tall chimney. There was a small lake framed by trees in the background.

I took out five pounds from my purse and dropped it into the bucket.

Doreen smiled. 'Thanks, luv.'

'That's a nice thing to do,' I said.

'He used to be a permanent fixture here until Peggy gave him an ultimatum.'

'Oh,' I said carefully. 'I didn't know.'

'Oh yes,' she continued. 'Seth was very popular. Could spin a good yarn when he'd had a few, and of course he always had a bit of an eye for the ladies. We used to say he had desert disease – wandering—'

'Palms, yes, I've heard that expression.'

'Poor Seth. We were all so proud of his sobriety.'

Clearly news of Seth's fall from grace hadn't reached the pub quite yet.

'When did he stop coming here?'

'Let me see.' Doreen thought for a moment. 'He got breathalysed one time too many and Peggy threatened to divorce him unless he gave up the drink. So he did. That was about fifteen years ago, and he never took another drop.'

Apart from the four glasses he imbibed today, I thought, but I kept that to myself. Gesturing to the photographs, I asked, 'Where was that photo by the lake taken?'

'That's Larcombe Quarry,' said Doreen. 'It's just a mile from here. The old earl – Lord Rupert's father – closed it down in the forties and flooded the pit. But it was a well-known spot for lovers back in the day. It's all in ruins now.'

'Is that near Larcombe Woods?' I knew that bridleway well.

Doreen nodded. 'That's right. The bridleway comes out at the back of the churchyard. A footpath runs all the way to Honeychurch Hall.'

Recalling Lala's comment about Fleur daring Harry to go caving, I said, 'Are the underground workings accessible at the quarry?'

'No. They've all been fenced off, but that doesn't stop kids trying to get in. There was a rumour once that one of the operational bases was down there – you know, when England feared a Nazi invasion. Something to do with the Home Guard building underground bunkers.'

Doreen suddenly grabbed my wrist and leant across the bar. She was so close that I could smell the alcohol on her breath, mixed with the pungent aroma of a musky perfume.

'Peggy doesn't have a pension, Kat,' she said urgently. 'Just a small amount from the government, which hardly counts. You have the ear of his lordship – make sure she isn't thrown out.'

'Thrown out? Why would she be thrown out?'

'You don't understand,' said Doreen darkly. 'There's them and there's us. Upstairs. Downstairs. They'll want a new couple taking on the roles of butler and cook, and those folks will move into the Croppers' cottage. Peggy will be out on her ear with nowhere to go.'

'That's terrible,' I said. 'But I don't see how I can help.'

'What do I have to do to get a drink around here?' shouted a florid-faced man in a flat cap and tattered tweed jacket. I'd seen him in the museum room earlier in the afternoon, wearing the same sour expression as he was wearing now. Rudely he elbowed me aside to get to the bar.

I saw my chance to escape, but Doreen kept hold of my wrist, yelling over her shoulder, 'Stan! Serve Mr Jones, won't you? I'm busy.' She leant in closer, turning away from the man, who was clearly unhappy at being passed along.

'And what's more,' she went on, 'his lordship thinks one of us stole those pocket watches! As if anyone would have the nerve other than a blow-in— Oh look. Here comes one now, and it looks like he knows you.'

It was Angus Fenwick.

'Can I buy you a drink, Kat?'

Chapter Nine

I was surprised to see him. 'Where's Lala?'

'Tucked up in bed,' he said. 'She caught a chill and thinks she's coming down with a cold.'

He looked around the bar and gave a nod of approval.

'I think we could happily settle in Little Dipperton – once they get broadband, of course. Nice place to bring up a kid.'

'Yes. I like it here,' I said.

Gesturing to the collection bucket, Angus added, 'I'm sorry about the old boy. Nasty way to go.'

Mr Jones tapped him on the shoulder. 'It was your wife who touched the bird, wasn't it?' he said in an accusing voice.

'Excuse me?' said Angus.

'The hawk. She touched it.'

'She didn't touch it,' Angus said mildly. 'Only pretended to.'

'It was enough, though, wasn't it?' Mr Jones exclaimed. 'We all know the bird is cursed.'

'Oh let him be, Douglas,' Doreen scolded. 'Not everyone believes in all that nonsense.'

I remembered Douglas Jones now. He'd spent at least half an hour studying the hawk with his magnifying glass, until Rupert had inexplicably told him to leave.

Now he stood his ground. 'Those of you who weren't born here, maybe.'

'Rubbish!' Doreen exclaimed. 'I came here when I was five.'

'Not a local, then,' someone called out, and everyone laughed.

Douglas was not amused. 'Those of us whose folks grew up knowing all about the hawk think differently. Same as someone touching Sir Maurice's chair.'

There was a murmur of agreement. Sometimes I forgot what a superstitious lot these villagers could be.

'Seth's death was a freak accident,' Doreen declared. 'Now, let's not have any trouble. It's Christmas.'

'If anyone needs sympathy, it's me,' joked Angus. 'I almost got my leg bitten off by that damn Jack Russell!'

There was another explosion of laughter.

'Don't say you weren't warned!' And with that, Douglas spun on his heel and, shoving people out of his way, headed for the snug and the sign marked *Toilets*.

A sudden cheer went up as he collided with Lenny under the archway where the mistletoe was hanging. Someone yelled out, 'Kiss him! Kiss him!' and the whole bar erupted in thunderous applause.

Lenny roared, 'I'm game if you are!'

Douglas thrust him violently aside and vanished from sight.

I had no idea that Lenny had become so popular. I caught snatches of conversation – 'going to London to see the Queen', and 'saved some kids caving up north'. A couple of people brought out their iPhones to take his photograph.

I felt Angus stiffen beside me, and when I turned to talk to him, I noticed he was watching Lenny with a look I couldn't quite fathom. Dislike? Disgust?

Lenny spotted me and waved, and was about to come over when he noticed Angus. He turned away abruptly and plunged back into the crowd.

And then I saw Guy and forgot everything else.

He joined me and kissed my cheek. 'Sorry I'm late. You look beautiful.'

I stared into his piercing grey eyes, surprised at how happy I was to see him. Dressed in a leather jacket over a black crew-neck sweater and jeans, he seemed far more handsome than I remembered.

'I haven't been here long myself,' I said.

He glanced around. 'This place is packed. We'll go somewhere quiet once I've spent some duty time with Mum and Dad.'

'I'd like that,' I said.

Rupert headed towards us. His face looked flushed. 'Good evening, Katherine.'

I made the introductions, but he didn't seem to realise that Guy was Delia's son until I told him.

'Good to meet you, sir,' said Guy deferentially.

'Ah, good, good . . .' Rupert replied vaguely, already moving on. 'Katherine, I've put the word out about the pocket watches and made it clear that all information will be gratefully received, with no questions asked.'

'What's happened?' Guy asked. 'Something stolen?'

'I'll tell you later,' I said.

'Your lordship!' called out Delia breathlessly as she joined us. 'Can I have a quick word?'

'Oh no,' Guy whispered. 'I never know what she's going to say.'

'Lenny wants you to know that now Seth Cropper is dead – God rest his soul – he's more than happy to take over Seth's duties as butler. That way the smooth running of the household won't be interrupted.'

Rupert looked embarrassed.

'And of course we're very happy to switch cottages with Mrs Cropper,' Delia blundered on, 'since ours is a little cramped and number two is so much more spacious and has a cellar.'

'Mum!' Guy sounded horrified. He took his mother's elbow. 'Let's go and find somewhere to sit, shall we? Where's Dad?'

But Delia, fortified by gin, dug her toes in. 'Although frankly, Peggy should retire. I think there's an empty cottage next to the post office. Maybe she would prefer to live in the village.'

'Mum!' Guy exclaimed again.

'I'm afraid that is something you should take up with the dowager countess,' Rupert said frostily. And with that he walked away.

'Oh yes. We shall,' she called out after him. 'Thank you!' Turning to Guy, she added, 'Good. I think we're in!'

I caught Guy's eye, and he pulled a face and mouthed, 'Awkward.'

'You'd better do what he says, Mum.'

'Not likely,' Delia laughed. 'I'll take it up with Lady Lavinia. She's easier to manage.'

Guy scanned the room. 'Where's Dad gone?'

'He was here a moment ago,' I said.

'Oh no! Would you look at that!' Delia pointed to the seats she had been saving. Her tote bag, coat and hat had been unceremoniously dumped on the windowsill. 'Someone has stolen our table!'

'We're not staying anyway,' Guy said firmly.

'But why not?' wailed Delia.

'Because I feel like we're being watched like two Chinese pandas.' And as if to prove a point, he picked up my hand and kissed it, prompting a flurry of comments.

I felt a rush of affection, and then I heard someone say, 'Shawn's not going to be happy.'

'Here's your father now,' Delia exclaimed. 'At least wait and say hello.'

Lenny joined us, but he seemed agitated.

'Where have you been?' Delia demanded. 'They're not staying. They're going now.'

'Can't a man use the gents?' Lenny said crossly.

'*Again?* You were there an hour ago,' Delia grumbled. 'What's the matter? Have you got the trots?'

Guy groaned. 'Oh God. I apologise for my parents.' But he regarded his father with concern. 'Is everything all right, Dad?'

Lenny didn't seem to hear.

'Seth Cropper's dead,' Delia said. 'Have you heard?'

But Lenny was watching Angus talking to Nick over by Sir Maurice's chair. Delia must have noticed him too, because she said, 'That's Angus Fenwick. He has a lovely wife called Lala and they're thinking of moving into the area. She's pregnant.'

'And why should that be of interest to me?' Lenny snapped.

'Because they know our Linda,' said Delia. 'I thought I'd knit them some baby socks.'

'Why would you do that?' Lenny said. 'You don't even know her!'

Delia recoiled, stung.

'Steady on, Dad,' Guy said anxiously. 'Whatever's the matter?'

'Nothing! Excuse me.' And with that, Lenny turned away and headed off to the toilets again.

'I shouldn't have said that about him having the trots,' Delia mumbled weakly. 'He gets stroppy when he's not feeling well. Thinks it's not manly. But we all—'

'I'll go and see if he's OK. Just be a minute,' Guy went after him.

'I'll come too!' said Delia.

As I stood there on my own, thinking about the odd scene I'd just witnessed, Shawn walked into the bar. I was surprised to see him, given that his grandfather had just passed away. To my dismay, he scanned the room, and when he saw me, his face lit up.

I felt a surge of panic. It wasn't as if there was anything

between Shawn and me, but for some reason, I felt guilty being in the pub with someone else.

As Shawn fought his way through the crowd, Guy reappeared, and the two men reached me at the exact same time.

Shawn moved in to give me a hug, but Guy was faster. He threw his arm around my shoulders and thrust out his other hand in greeting.

'Guy Evans,' he said. 'And you must be Detective Inspector Cropper. My mother has told me all about you.'

Chapter Ten

For a moment, Shawn seemed frozen, and then he managed to pull himself together. Mum and Delia had been speculating on my non-existent romance with him for weeks, and it was obvious that Guy knew this. I felt horrible for Shawn, especially as I could sense a gazillion eyes enjoying this uncomfortable meeting between the three of us.

What made it even more awkward was the fact that Shawn and Guy were dressed the same. For the first time ever, Shawn had left his trademark trench coat behind. Guy wore his outfit with flair, while Shawn looked a little uncomfortable – as if he was wearing someone else's trousers.

'I'm really sorry about your grandfather,' I said.

Guy rested his hand on my shoulder in a move that was clearly territorial. 'Yes. Sorry for your loss, Officer – or should I call you Shawn, since it looks like you're off duty.'

'Thank you,' said Shawn. 'And yes, Shawn is fine for now.'

'How is Peggy?' I asked.

'She'll be staying with us for a few days,' he said. 'She's

very upset, as you can imagine. Kat . . .' He cleared his throat. 'I need to talk to you.'

'Of course,' I said.

'In private.'

'Oh,' I said. 'Right.'

'Take whatever time you need,' said Guy, making it clear that I was his property. I was flattered but at the same time not sure if I liked it.

Shawn and I found a quiet corner away from prying eyes, but we did not sit down. Nor did he ask me if I wanted a drink.

'I thought I would find you here tonight,' he said.

'I'm surprised to see you,' I admitted. 'Given the circumstances.'

'Surprised or pleased? No, I didn't mean that – I've got a thief to catch,' he said briskly, and pulled out his notebook and a pencil. 'Clive told me that you searched Angus and Lala and came up with nothing. He also told me that you found them wandering around the estate in the dark. Can you give me some more details?'

'I thought you were off duty,' I said.

'I just wanted an excuse to wear my new leather jacket.'

I recounted how I had come across Angus and Lala in the service road, what we had talked about, that they were staying in the area for a few days, and then pointed Angus out, now talking to Rupert. 'His wife isn't here tonight.'

Shawn nodded. 'They check out,' he said. 'The rental car is registered to an Angus Fenwick for two weeks. No criminal record. Not so much as a parking ticket.'

'And Lala?'

'Ah. Lala.' Shawn tried to look serious, but failed. 'She used to be an exotic dancer at a club called the Peppermint Panda in Leeds.'

'Oh!' I exclaimed. 'Wow.'

'And yes, Lala is her real name. She was known as . . .' he cleared his throat again, 'Limbo Lala. Apparently she could limbo-dance under a ten-inch bar. If my sources are to be believed, she was a close rival of Shemika Campbell from Buffalo, New York, who holds the limbo record.'

'And what is the limbo record?' I said.

'Eight and a half inches,' said Shawn. 'Not many people know that.'

I burst out laughing. This was a side of him I hadn't seen before. Maybe the grief counselling was working.

Shawn grinned. 'No one can ever accuse me of not doing my homework.'

This is when I should tell him about the insurance scam. But I hesitated. It was not my secret to tell. And then I remembered that it was Shawn's father who had been the investigating officer at the time. 'Have you told your father about the stolen items?'

Shawn seemed taken aback. 'Dad? Why would I talk to him?'

'Perhaps there is . . . some parallel with the robbery that happened thirty years ago,' I said wildly. 'Maybe some things were taken from the museum room back then as well.'

'I don't see the connection.' Shawn looked puzzled. 'Besides, my dad had a stroke and is in a nursing home in

Spain. He's in a very bad way and wouldn't remember anything about that time now.' He frowned. 'Why would you think there was a connection?'

I shrugged. 'I don't know why I said that.'

'You think it might have been someone in the village back then and that it might be the same person now?'

'Really, I don't think anything,' I said hastily.

'Fortunately his lordship was able to supply me with photographs of the missing pocket watches,' Shawn said. 'Time is of the essence – no pun intended.' He grinned again. 'I believe he would prefer the dowager countess not to hear about it . . . Ah, here comes your . . . boyfriend.'

I turned to see Guy and Delia heading our way.

'Did you get everything you need, Shawn?' asked Guy.

'There is just one more thing,' said Shawn. 'I understand that you and Iris have been making your own gin, Mrs Evans?'

'That's right,' Delia declared. 'We've made a killing this Christmas. It's a very good price and makes an excellent gift, but if you want some, you had better order it now. We're about to start on a new batch.'

'That sounds very nice, but are you aware that it's illegal to distil alcohol in your own home without a licence from HMRC – that's Her Majesty's Revenue and Customs?'

Delia's jaw dropped.

'Oh come on, Shawn,' said Guy lightly. 'Don't be such a killjoy.'

'Right this minute, it's Detective Inspector,' said Shawn. 'And I'm afraid your mother is breaking the law.'

'Lighten up, mate,' said Guy. 'She couldn't have sold more than a dozen bottles.'

'Are you talking about today or over the last two months?' Delia mused.

'How many in total?' Shawn said.

Delia thought for a moment. 'Over a hundred.'

'*A hundred!*' Shawn was shocked. So was I.

'We sold a lot at the WI Christmas party,' she continued proudly. 'They make excellent stocking fillers – though not for children, obviously.'

Shawn's jaw hardened. 'We can talk about this tomorrow at the police station.'

'You are joking, aren't you?' said Guy, but I knew he wasn't. I'd seen the pompous side of Detective Inspector Shawn Cropper before.

'You'll have to ask her ladyship if she can spare me,' said Delia. 'With Peggy gone, I'm in charge.'

'Wait – didn't you tell me that it was Iris's idea, Mum?' Guy put in.

'Yes, that's right.' Delia nodded. 'It was. She pushed me into it.'

I was indignant. 'It was a decision you made together, Delia. I was there when you discussed it.'

Guy must have sensed my dismay, because he added, 'I'm sure they're both as bad as each other.'

I remembered it distinctly. They'd been sitting at the kitchen table in the Carriage House, having polished off the last bottle of gin and complaining about the price. Delia had said it would be cheaper to make their own, so Mum had found a gin-making workshop at Dartington and the pair had spent a raucous afternoon cackling like the witches in *Macbeth* over a cauldron.

Guy thought for a moment. 'Doesn't Iris have the gin still in one of her outbuildings?'

I couldn't believe it. He seemed determined to throw my mother under the proverbial bus.

'Yes.' Delia nodded again. 'She does. It's in her old henhouse.'

Shawn seemed horrified. 'Iris has an illegal gin still on the Honeychurch estate?'

'It's hardly a gin still,' I protested. 'It's a kit. She bought it on Amazon.'

'Exactly,' said Delia. '*Her* idea.'

Shawn gave a heavy sigh. 'Then I'll expect both you and Iris down at the station tomorrow morning at nine. You're not under arrest—'

'I should think not!' Delia exclaimed.

'I'm not being a killjoy,' said Shawn. 'But HMRC are clamping down on this sort of thing. With the current gin-making craze hitting the country, there are a lot of illegal stills being set up, and people are selling without a licence.' He shrugged. 'I'm sorry, but there it is.'

My stomach dropped. Even the remotest possibility of an investigation by HMRC into my mother's business affairs would be devastating. For decades she had been squirrelling her book royalties away into an offshore account in the Channel Islands and not declaring it. I'd told her gazillions of times that she had to come clean, but she refused to talk about it. This was all the more ironic given that Dad had been a tax inspector! No, it was too big a risk.

'Not a problem, Officer,' I said smoothly. 'Mum and I will be there first thing.'

'We will too,' Guy agreed. 'I'm sure we can sort this out. And I'm sorry about your grandfather again.'

'Thank you,' said Shawn. 'Unfortunately, it appears that someone plied him with alcohol – filling his water glass with neat gin. I fear that this affected his reflexes, so that when the armour fell, he was unable to move out of the way fast enough.'

'Oh that's a shame,' Delia mumbled.

'My grandmother is very upset and wants to press charges.'

Delia gasped. 'Press *charges*?'

I was speechless.

'It was common knowledge that my grandfather had given up drinking fifteen years ago. Ask anyone in the village – and since you worked with my grandmother, Mrs Evans,' Shawn went on sternly, 'you would have known that too, wouldn't you?'

'Of course I knew,' Delia declared. 'But I didn't give him anything. You should be talking to Iris.'

Yet again I was appalled. Why should my mother be made a scapegoat for everything? She wasn't even here to defend herself!

'It could be viewed as a malicious act,' Shawn continued. 'A deliberate intention to inflict harm on another person without provocation.'

'Steady on,' said Guy. 'Don't you think that's a bit extreme?'

'My grandmother told me that she knows Mrs Evans wanted them to retire—'

'I didn't say that,' Delia muttered, which was a flat-out lie.

'Anyway – please bring a bottle of your gin with you,' Shawn said. 'It will be sent away for testing and we'll take it from there.'

'*Testing?*' Guy laughed. 'Good God, man. You think the gin was poisoned?'

'There are much more important things to worry about than the gin,' Delia said suddenly. 'The stolen pocket watches for one, and my crystal necklace with matching earrings that belonged to *my* grandmother.'

'You think they were stolen, Mum?' Guy asked. 'I didn't realise.'

'I know it!' Delia declared.

'We can talk about that tomorrow too,' said Shawn. 'For now, I bid you all goodnight.' And with that, he actually clicked his heels and left.

Finally Guy spoke. 'Well, that was interesting.'

'I want to go home now,' whispered Delia. 'Will you take me?'

Guy shot me an apologetic look. 'I'm going to walk Kat back to her car, and then we'll go.'

'Where is Lenny?' I asked.

'He's not feeling well,' said Guy. 'He already left.'

I felt a stab of disappointment, and hoped that Guy would not turn out to be a mummy's boy.

As we left the pub, he said, 'Sorry. She's upset. I promise I'll make it up to you.'

'It's fine. Really. Looks like we have an early start tomorrow anyway, since we have to go to the police station.'

He took my arm and linked it through his.

'I'm parked on the other side of the churchyard,' I said.

We entered the lychgate. 'I think that copper has a giant crush on you,' Guy teased. 'But I beat him to it.'

'Of course he hasn't,' I said. 'He's widowed and still madly in love with his wife.'

'And looking for a mother for his children, according to Mum,' said Guy. 'Do you want kids?'

The question took me by surprise. 'Yes. Eventually. And you?'

'Yep. Definitely. And I don't want to wait too long either.'

I felt light-headed with nervous excitement. Guy was sounding me out, I knew it.

'This way,' he whispered, and led me off the path onto the crisp grass covered in frost.

'Where are we going?'

'Away from prying eyes.'

We weaved our way through the headstones until we stopped in the shadow of the imposing Honeychurch mausoleum. The family motto – *Ad perseverate est ad triumphum* – was carved above heavy bronze doors that were framed by a pair of hawks in flight. The style was similar to the architecture of the Hall, albeit in miniature.

Guy whispered in my ear, 'To endure is to triumph.'

'You know Latin?' I said.

And then I found myself pressed against the cold stone wall of the mausoleum as Guy kissed me deeply. I had to pull away and catch my breath.

'Sorry, I couldn't help it.' He drew me into his arms and held me fast. 'I told myself that we were going to take things slowly, but I'm afraid I'm losing my resolve.'

'Me too,' I said. And I was. The last man who had found me attractive was Lady Lavinia's brother Piers, but I had never quite trusted him. He had a reputation as an international playboy and I'd always wondered if he had regarded me as a challenge. Nothing physical had ever happened between us, and of that I was glad.

And then there was Shawn. Why he popped into my head at that moment, I couldn't say. But it was confusing.

'Perhaps it's just as well I have to take my mother home this evening,' Guy said in a low voice. 'I don't think I could restrain myself. But tomorrow . . . can I cook you dinner?'

Dinner. Dinner meant being alone together. *Come on, Kat. You can't hide away forever.* 'Yes. I'd like that.'

'I want to show you the barn. It's not finished. Dad is helping me with the painting. I don't have any furniture either, but there is an Aga, and I have a saucepan.'

'I'd love to see the barn,' I said.

'What are your plans tomorrow?'

'Well . . . after taking my mother to the police station,' I said wryly, 'I'm stopping by the Dartmouth Antique Emporium. There's also a sale in Newton Abbot I want to view. And you?'

'Probably worrying over what to cook for you with my one saucepan,' he joked.

That was when we saw him.

Tucked behind a headstone was a black-clad figure lying face down on the ground.

It wasn't moving.

'Oh my God,' I whispered. 'It's Nick.'

Chapter Eleven

Guy dropped to Nick's side and immediately felt for a pulse.

'He's not . . . he's not dead, is he?' I said.

'No, thank God,' said Guy. 'You know him?'

'Yes. He's our local newspaper reporter, Nick Bond.'

Guy repeated Nick's name half a dozen times before shaking his head. 'He's unconscious. Do you have a torch?'

I got out my iPhone and tapped the flashlight feature. My hands were trembling.

'Shine it here.' He gently touched Nick's head and sniffed his fingers. 'Blood. Yes. He's been hit on the back of the head.'

'Oh God. He's been *attacked*? You don't think he just fell?' I was stunned and felt sick. 'Shouldn't we call an ambulance? Or I can run back to the pub. Shawn may still be there.'

'We don't need him yet,' said Guy briskly. 'Nick's pulse is weak but he's alive. It's just as well that we were here. If he'd been outside all night, he would almost certainly have died of hypothermia.'

'I think we should—'

'Kat, I'm trained in this, OK? Give me a minute.' Guy expertly checked all Nick's vital signs before turning him onto his side and into the recovery position. 'I'm leaving the balaclava on, because if this was an attack it could provide—'

'Evidence. Oh Guy, who would do such a thing?' I thought of all the happy revellers in the pub. 'I'm going to call for an ambulance.'

'Yes, you're right. You should.' Guy glanced at my phone screen. 'Although you'll be lucky. There's no signal. It's like the Dark Ages in this village.'

I looked over to the cottages beyond the boundary wall. I could see a light on in Rose Cottage. 'Violet's always home. I'll use her landline.'

I took off across the grass and hurried along the path, slipping and almost losing my balance twice. My heart was racing. Whatever Nick was up to seemed to have gone horribly wrong.

With just two windows flanking the front door of the tea room, Violet's cottage looked small from the road but was actually deceptively spacious. I knew she wouldn't be able to hear me knock at the front, so I went to the back, taking the alley where she always left her Morris Minor.

I expected to see Angus's Enterprise rental car there too, but it had gone.

I rapped sharply on the back door, glad that since Angus was out, Violet would still be up.

It took some moments until I heard her turning the locks. 'That was quick,' she said as she opened the door wide, only to look at me in confusion, peering blindly through her bottleneck glasses. 'Why, Kat? Is that you?'

I told her I needed to use her phone but didn't say why. She was a nervous old lady and easily scared. I didn't want to frighten her.

As she led me into the kitchen – which had more teapots on the shelves than I could count – Violet said, 'I thought it was Angus and Lala. I thought to myself . . . goodness, you're back early.'

'Lala isn't here?' Angus had said she wasn't well.

'No, they went out,' said Violet.

I called 999 to request an ambulance, and then tried Shawn's mobile on the off chance. Happily, he answered, having only got as far as the top road to Dartmouth, and said he would come straight back.

'What happened?' Violet asked in a querulous voice. 'Why are you calling for an ambulance?'

'Someone fell over in the churchyard,' I said. 'The path is very slippery.'

'Was it Lala?' Violet said. 'Is something wrong with the baby? She's pregnant, you know.'

'No, it wasn't her. I'm glad she's feeling better.'

Violet cocked her head. 'Better?'

'I saw her husband at the Hare and Hounds,' I said. 'He told me she wasn't feeling very well.'

Violet looked blank. 'Oh no. We sat and had a lovely cup of tea. We were choosing baby names. She wants to settle in the village, you know. And then she went out to meet Angus.'

My heart gave a peculiar jolt. 'Do you remember what time she left?'

Violet frowned. 'Now let me think. I wanted to watch *Vera* on ITV – they're running a marathon – and she left before that started, which would have been about seven thirty.'

That was the same time I had left the gatehouse to drive to the pub. I'd seen Angus after that and he'd told me that Lala was in bed. Violet must have her timings wrong.

'That's right,' Violet went on. 'They were hungry – I only do a light breakfast here.'

'They could have eaten at the pub,' I pointed out.

'Lala was craving ice cream,' said Violet. 'My mother ate coal when she was carrying me. So they went to Morrisons in Totnes. It's open until eleven at night, you know.'

And that was when we both heard a knock at the door. Violet beamed. 'That'll be them now.'

Sure enough, it was. And not only that, Lala was holding a giant tub of vanilla ice cream.

'I hope you don't mind if we take it to our room, Mrs G,' she said cheerfully 'We'll be very careful not to spill anything. Oh, hello, Kat. What are you doing here?'

'Using the phone,' I said.

'Don't you want to take your coat off?' Violet asked as Lala headed for the narrow flight of stairs that led to the bedrooms above.

'No, she feels the cold,' said Angus. 'And you've only got storage heaters upstairs.'

'You only have to ask for an extra blanket, Mr Fenwick,' Violet said. 'I don't want to get a negative review on Trippy.'

Angus grinned. 'What's going on in the churchyard? I saw a police car with a flashing light.'

'Someone fell,' Violet declared. 'It's the icy paths. Probably hit a headstone going down, I shouldn't wonder. That's why I don't like to go out in this kind of weather.'

'Seems like everyone is falling over today,' he said.

'How is your bite?' I asked.

'I'll survive.'

When I got back to the churchyard, I was relieved to see that Nick was sitting up. A foil blanket had been wrapped around his shoulders and he was resting his head in his arms. Shawn was prowling the cemetery with a torch, clearly looking for something.

Guy came over and pulled me to one side, saying in a low voice, 'He'll be all right. Stubborn bloke. Refused to go to the hospital.'

'What if he has concussion?'

'He says he's fine. Apparently he fell backwards and hit his head on a gravestone.'

I stared at Guy in disbelief. 'Surely you don't believe that. He was lying face down when we found him.'

'If he says that's what happened, then that's what happened.'

'First of all,' I said, 'he was nowhere near the path. He was on the grass. So I'm not sure how he could have slipped. And secondly, he would have had to have fallen backwards quite a long way to hit his head.'

Guy shrugged. 'That's his story and I don't see why we should be bothered about it.'

I was surprised by his attitude. It seemed a little callous. 'Are you OK?'

'Yes. Of course,' said Guy, but I could tell that something was bothering him. 'Sorry, Mum will think I've forgotten her. I have to go.' He gestured to Shawn, who had now moved into the undergrowth along the far boundary wall. It was where I had seen the figures retreat into the shadows earlier that evening. 'I'm sure he'll be only too happy to look after you. I'll see you tomorrow at the police station.' He leant over to kiss my forehead, but as I moved in to give him a hug, he pulled back, saying, 'Let's not torment Shawn too much,' and hurried away. It was most odd.

I went to talk to Nick. 'How are you feeling?'

'Crashing headache.' He winced.

'Apparently you tripped,' I said drily. 'Which I find hard to believe.'

'Has he gone?'

'Shawn? No. He's skulking around the cemetery searching for something, by the looks of things.'

'Not him,' said Nick. 'The major's son.'

'Guy? Yes, he's gone. Why?'

'He kept asking me if I'd seen anyone.'

'I think he was just trying to help,' I said.

'Help? I don't think so. He was asking too many questions. Even accused me of stalking his daddy.'

'*Stalking?*' I was stunned. '*Guy* said that? Are you sure?'

'Warned me off him, in fact.'

'I think that blow to your head has made you delusional,' I said.

'No. After you left me in the churchyard and went into the pub, Guy arrived and cornered me in the car park.' Nick pulled the foil blanket closer. He was shivering. 'I just told him I had a job to do and to back off.'

'Guy warned you to stay away from his father?' I repeated. Knowing how much Lenny courted the spotlight, I was sure Nick was way off base. 'But the major knows you want to take his photograph. He even mentioned it to me a few hours ago.'

'Believe what you like,' said Nick. 'I'm just telling you what your boyfriend told me.'

I crouched down beside him. 'And *did* you see anything?'

'No, but I heard someone. Came from behind and hit me twice with a brick. At least that's what it felt like. Then whoever it was stole my iPhone.'

'I couldn't find anything,' Shawn said as he joined us. 'We'll have another look in daylight.'

'What are you searching for?' I asked.

'The culprit could have tossed the weapon into the undergrowth.'

'I don't care about that,' Nick said. 'I need my phone – there are critical interviews on there.'

'I don't doubt it,' said Shawn wryly.

Nick got unsteadily to his feet and had to reach out to grab my arm.

'Leave your motorbike here.' Shawn's voice was firm. 'You're not driving anywhere. I'll take you home via the hospital.'

'I already told you, I'm fine,' Nick said. 'I'll ring my mum. She'll come and get me.'

'Shawn's right,' I told him. 'You should definitely get a doctor to take a look.'

I headed to my car. It really had been the most extraordinary day, but I had just one more thing to do before I could fall into bed.

Chapter Twelve

Mum answered the door dressed in an emerald-green velour kaftan. Without her make-up on, she looked younger than her seventy years.

'Oh no!' she cried. 'What are you doing here? Have you had a lovers' tiff?'

'No, Mum, I have not, and if you're going to start, I won't come in.'

'Promise I won't. Kettle boiled just ten minutes ago.' She ushered me into the warmth. 'Let me make you a cup of tea, darling.'

'I love it when you fuss over me,' I said.

'That's what mothers like to do.'

We went into the kitchen. I took a seat at the pine table, where a half-drunk cup of tea sat with an array of Post-it notes covered in scribble. Scissors and clippings from the *Dipperton Deal* were set in a pile along with the latest copy of *Star Stalkers*, with its predictably tacky headline: *SexTortion! Celebrities Caught With Their Pants Down!*

Mum lunged forward and snatched the magazine off the table.

'I don't know why you're trying to hide it,' I said with disgust. 'I know you read that rubbish.'

'Research,' she declared. 'All of it. Where do you think I get my love scenes from – real life, that's where! And since your father was the only man I ever knew in the biblical sense, I have to rely on other people's experiences.'

'*Star Stalkers* is not real life,' I said. 'Everything is always out of context.'

'Hmm. Which cup for you tonight, I wonder.'

'And don't change the subject,' I said.

Mum regarded the oak dresser, where her collection of royal commemoration plates, reproduction Buckingham Palace china and Queen Elizabeth II Diamond Jubilee mugs ranged along the shelves with framed photographs of Prince William and Kate Middleton.

'I think Princess Margaret for you tonight.' She took down a bone-china mug featuring the heads of HRH Princess Margaret and Lord Snowdon on their wedding day. 'Because she led such a tormented life, just like you.'

'I am not tormented!' I protested. 'If you must know, I am not here to seek your advice or' – I gestured to the *Dipperton Deal* – 'that of Dear Amanda. I'm here to tell you that you are wanted at the police station tomorrow morning for questioning.'

Mum gasped. 'Whatever for?'

I relayed Shawn's conversation from the pub about the illegal gin still.

'It's just a hobby,' she wailed. 'Why on earth do we need a licence?'

'It doesn't matter,' I said. 'You don't want HMRC delving into your finances, do you?'

'Oh God. No.'

'And I'm afraid you'll need to bring a sample with you,' I said.

'Of what? Urine?'

'No need to be vulgar, Mum.'

'Really, I just don't have time for this.'

'If you stop behaving like a child, I'll tell you what a fascinating evening I have had, and why I am here and not indulging in hot sex with my helicopter pilot.'

'Good grief!' Mum's eyebrows shot up under her hairline. 'Now who's being vulgar? And that's a bit fast, darling. You've only known him five minutes.'

'I'm joking,' I said with a groan.

'Well, let me know if you need any tips. I'm grappling with a particularly juicy scene with Colonel de Lacy Evans and Delilah in the meat larder.'

'Are they *still* in the meat larder?'

'He's having a problem with his sword.'

I burst out laughing. 'You are incorrigible.'

Fortunately the kettle boiled, putting a stop to the risqué conversation. Mum set down a cup of Night Time tea in front of me and pulled out a chair. 'So tell me what happened.'

When I'd finished filling her in about finding Nick unconscious in the churchyard, she said, 'And you say you saw figures in the undergrowth earlier in the evening?'

'The first time I came across Nick, he was hiding behind a headstone by the lychgate – although I'm not quite sure how he could have heard anything from so far away. The second time, he was unconscious by the Honeychurch mausoleum.'

'The *mausoleum*?' Mum frowned. 'What on earth was he doing there? Wait, what on earth were *you* doing there?'

I felt my face redden. 'Showing Guy around.'

'Say no more!' Mum winked, but then suddenly went very still. 'It's obvious! Nick knows about the insurance scam. That's what this is all about.'

'But how? He wouldn't even have been born when that happened.'

'Since we know the Croppers were in on the secret, chances are others were too,' she declared.

'I think Nick's great-uncle was the gatekeeper here,' I said.

'I'll check on the below-stairs family tree tomorrow,' said Mum. 'From what I remember, that family bred like rabbits. I'm certain he's related to one of them.'

I went on to tell Mum about the earl's intense dislike for the young man. 'Some scandal from the past, but I have no idea what that could be.'

'Hmm. Interesting.' Mum scribbled something on a Post-it. 'Let me see what I can find out about that too.'

'There is one more thing . . .' I wondered whether to open up this can of worms. 'Nick told me just now that Guy had warned him to stop stalking Lenny.'

'What do you mean by *stalking*? I thought Lenny *wanted*

to be stalked,' said Mum. 'He loves being the centre of attention. Perhaps that blow to the head has affected Nick's senses. I should take no notice.'

'My thoughts exactly,' I agreed and got to my feet. 'Well, fortunately it's not our problem. I'll pick you up tomorrow at eight forty-five.'

As I got ready for bed, my thoughts turned to poor Peggy Cropper and her future. As brutal as it sounded, Delia had a point. Peggy had to be closer to eighty than seventy, and she really shouldn't be working full time. I recalled the kitchen sink piled high with unwashed dishes and the dirty floor in need of sweeping because her eyesight was not what it used to be. Delia must have spent a long time cleaning all that up.

With Seth gone, the dowager countess would want to engage a new couple to live in Peggy's cottage. Doreen Mutters was right about the possibility of Peggy being evicted, but I didn't know how I could help.

My mobile pinged and Guy's name popped up on my caller ID just to wish me goodnight and to apologise again. We arranged to meet for lunch the following day, even though we'd see each other at the police station first thing.

That night I had dreams about a bloodied hawk wearing a pocket watch perched on Shawn's shoulder. Guy appeared in a Santa suit carrying a sword. The two began to fight.

I woke up wondering if I was better off staying single.

'Delia had better turn up,' Mum declared as we drove to the police station the next morning.

'Why wouldn't she?' I said.

'She didn't answer the phone last night. I used to look forward to our evening chats. I think Lenny is too possessive.'

I hadn't realised just how much Lenny's return would alter their friendship. Mum and Delia used to be inseparable, even if they bickered from time to time. My mother had told me that Delia was the first true friend she'd ever had, so I did feel for her.

'I don't particularly like Lenny much either,' I admitted. 'But I think we should give him a chance.'

'All right, I'll try,' said Mum grudgingly. 'I suppose when a man is only home for forty days a year, he's going to be tempted by other women.' She must have seen my face because she quickly added, 'I'm sure Guy won't be like that.'

With her usual gift for finding my weak spots, my mother had echoed my own concern about starting a relationship with a man who was away for so many months at a time. Right now, though, I wasn't involved enough to be heart-broken if it didn't work out.

We pulled up outside the tiny police station, which could easily be mistaken for a shed were it not for the lone police car parked on the forecourt. Guy's Freelander was already there.

'Well, I've brought my sample.' Mum brandished a half-litre bottle. 'Let's get this over with – and let me do the talking, if you don't mind.'

Chapter Thirteen

The police station comprised just one room, sparsely furnished with an uncomfortable looking bench seat and two hard chairs. There had been an attempt to imbue the place with festive cheer, with some home-made paper garlands taped to the four corners of the ceiling.

A bell sat on the counter designed to keep the general public at bay. There was no sign of Shawn, but since the door to a walk-in cupboard behind the counter was ajar, I assumed he must be in there.

Delia sat on one chair, dressed in an identical navy wool coat to that worn by my mother, with Guy next to her.

He jumped up to give me a warm embrace. 'Ready for this?' I was glad to see he seemed more cheerful this morning.

Mum and Delia pointedly ignored each other.

We took the bench. Mum gave me a nudge and gestured to the noticeboard that stretched along one wall.

Stolen!
PRICELESS pocket watches from the Crimea
Property of the 15th Earl of Grenville
HUGE reward for their return or information
pertaining to said items
No questions asked!

The sign was fixed next to a large grainy photocopy of the pocket watches. Unfortunately it had been blown up from an original and was far too blurry to show the details.

Shawn emerged at last holding several sheets of paper. He nodded a greeting and then ducked under the counter and headed over to the noticeboard, where he tacked one more photograph next to the stolen pocket watches. It was of a beautiful art deco crystal necklace with matching drop earrings.

'Thank you, Officer,' said Delia. 'Hopefully whoever took the pocket watches has my jewellery too.'

'I told you not to keep it in that outbuilding,' Guy scolded.

'I don't have any room in the cottage,' Delia retorted. 'What with all your father's boxes from the base, we've had to use the potting shed in the walled garden.'

'Which is not a safe place at all,' Shawn put in.

'They're very pretty crystals,' I said.

'My grandmother's,' Delia replied. 'They're all I've got of her. I'm very upset.'

'But you still don't remember when you last saw them,' Guy reminded her. 'They could have been stolen before you moved here.'

'No,' said Delia firmly. 'I checked them about four weeks ago and thought they would be nice to wear for Christmas. I had them hidden on one of the shelves under a pot in a small velvet pouch.'

'It seems a bit random for someone to steal them from the potting shed,' Mum pointed out. 'Whoever it was would have had to know that they were there in the first place.'

'That's what I told her,' said Guy.

'Can't you claim on your insurance?' Mum asked.

Delia shook her head. 'When I moved to Honeychurch, I didn't notify the insurance company of the change of location.'

'And some insurance companies won't pay out if the goods aren't kept under lock and key,' added Shawn.

'Well they don't need to know that,' said Mum. 'Just say they were in the cottage. Everyone else around here seems to do that.'

'No,' Delia declared. 'Lenny is adamant. He doesn't want to lie about a thing like that.'

'But he lied about his affair,' Mum said under her breath.

'I heard that, Iris,' Delia snapped.

'Shall we proceed?' Shawn returned to his post behind the counter and took out his notepad. 'Thank you for coming here this morning. I won't keep you long. I've printed out the application form DLA1 so we can complete the details today and get the paperwork going.'

'Why do we have to fill out a form?' Mum said.

'To produce and hold any form of alcohol, you need to have a licence that has been approved by HMRC,' said

Shawn. 'Furthermore, to sell to the public you have to have a personal licence, and the premises from which you are conducting the business need to be licensed for off or on trade as appropriate.'

'Oh for heaven's sake!' Mum grumbled. 'Whatever next? A licence for home-made strawberry jam?'

Shawn pretended he hadn't heard. 'Once that's done, someone from HMRC will visit your plant—'

'Plant? It's in the henhouse!' Mum protested.

I gave her a subtle kick and hissed, 'Just listen.'

'I must remind you that your application can be rejected if you do not produce more than three thousand pints a year,' said Shawn.

'*What?*' Mum and Delia chorused in horror. 'It's just a few bottles!'

'And naturally, you will have to pay excise tax,' he went on.

I had a feeling that he was actually enjoying this, and I wondered if he was being particularly hard on them because he blamed them in some way for his grandfather's death.

'Oh come on, Shawn,' said Guy. 'They were just having a bit of fun.'

'I'm sorry, but rules are rules.' Shawn turned to Mum. 'Did you bring a sample, Iris?'

At least he was addressing her by her first name. That was a good sign. Whenever she had been in trouble in the past, he'd always called her Mrs Stanford.

She delved into a tote bag and produced her half-litre of gin. It had a pretty label of a sheep on the front and the words: *Honeychurch Gin. Made by Iris.*

'You see!' Delia said with triumph. '"Made by Iris"!'

'You know very well that we have some saying "Made by Delia",' Mum said coldly. 'Would you like me to go back and get one in case you don't believe me, Officer?'

'That won't be necessary,' said Shawn.

Mum marched to the counter and handed him the bottle. 'Why don't you keep it? Consider it an early Christmas present.'

'I like the label,' said Shawn. 'Nice touch having a sheep – gives it a country feel.'

I had a thought. 'So if Mum and Delia make gin and don't charge for it, is that legal?'

'I'm afraid not. Nor is it legal for personal consumption.'

'It's like Prohibition,' Mum grumbled.

'There may be a small fine,' Shawn added.

'Well Iris will have to pay that,' said Delia.

Mum shot her a filthy look. 'Why should I be the one to pay the fine?'

'I wasn't left money by a rich husband like you were,' Delia whined. 'Lenny is really struggling at the moment on his pension.'

'How is that possible, Mum?' Guy demanded.

'He started dabbling in the stock market and made some bad business investments.'

Guy's expression darkened. 'Since when?'

Delia shrugged. 'I don't know – a few weeks ago. He told me he needed a hobby.'

'But he doesn't know the first thing about the stock market!'

Guy seemed worried. 'I'm going to have to have a word with him.'

'Perhaps he shouldn't have bought that fancy convertible,' Mum suggested.

'It's a lease,' Delia retorted.

'I'll pay Mum's fine,' said Guy wearily. 'Please, let's just get this sorted out.'

Shawn gave a big smile. 'But since it's Christmas, I'm going to let you both off with a caution!'

I was right. He had been enjoying himself.

'Oh, that's so kind!' Mum enthused.

'Thank you, sir,' Delia said meekly.

'I still want to have a look at the gin still,' Shawn said. 'And of course, if you plan on continuing with this enterprise, I'm afraid you will have to go through the proper channels.'

Mum nodded. 'Of course.'

We all stood up.

'Then we're free to go?' I said.

'Actually,' said Shawn. 'There is one more thing.'

We all sat down.

'I knew it!' Mum whispered.

'I just have a couple of questions for Kat and Guy.'

'However we can help,' Guy said.

Shawn picked up his pencil and turned to a fresh page in his notebook. 'Can you tell me exactly what you saw in the churchyard last night when you found Nick unconscious?'

'Nick? The newspaper reporter?' Delia turned to Guy in shock. 'You never mentioned any of this to me.'

'I don't tell you everything, Mum.' Guy appealed to me

for support. 'I'm sure Kat doesn't tell *her* mother everything either.'

'Oh yes she does,' Mum said smugly.

'What were you were doing in the churchyard?' Delia said suddenly.

'I told you, Mum,' said Guy. 'I was walking Kat to her car and then I came back to take you home.'

'Where was Major Evans at this time?' asked Shawn.

'He wasn't feeling very well,' Delia said helpfully. 'He had a touch of the trots and he went home.'

'What time was this?'

'About nine.'

'And Kat, you and Guy left the pub together,' continued Shawn. 'What time was that?'

I shrugged. 'I'm not sure. Nine thirty, perhaps?'

Shawn nodded. 'So, Mr Evans, you very gallantly offered to walk Kat back to her car but got sidetracked by . . . what? Nick was found quite some distance from the path.'

'Katherine wanted to show Guy the Honeychurch mausoleum,' Mum put in smoothly. 'And as you know, it's tucked away in the corner of the churchyard.'

Mum knew very well what Guy and I had been doing, but for some reason she seemed to want to spare Shawn's feelings.

'Why is the timing so important?' Guy said. 'Nick told me that he just fell and hit his head.'

'I'm afraid that is not the case at all,' said Shawn. 'He was attacked and his iPhone was stolen.'

'I asked him.' Guy seemed annoyed. 'Why on earth didn't he say so? Why lie about something like that?'

'Attacked! Here? In Little Dipperton?' Delia's eyes widened. 'Perhaps it was the same person who stole my crystal necklace and matching earrings.'

'Possibly,' said Shawn. 'Kat, I take it that you and Mr Evans arrived separately at the pub?'

'Yes,' I said. 'We agreed to meet there.'

'Can you talk me through your movements before you arrived?'

I gave him a brief account of the early part of the evening.

'And I definitely got the feeling that Nick was watching the couple in the churchyard,' I finished.

'And you have no idea who that couple could have been?'

'Well it wasn't Dad,' said Guy. 'Because he was in the pub.'

'How do you know?' Delia declared. 'You weren't there.'

'You told me that he had an upset tummy and was in the gents for most of the evening.'

'What about that chap Angus?' Delia said suddenly. 'He could have cut through the churchyard on his way to the pub. They're staying at Violet's B and B. And by the way, I called my daughter Linda and she told me that she had never heard of an Angus and Lala Fenwick. Don't you think that strange?'

'Interesting,' said Shawn.

'I think it has something to do with those.' Guy pointed to the photograph of the pocket watches on the noticeboard. 'Rupert was in the pub asking everyone for information. Maybe he agreed to meet someone in the churchyard and Nick saw them.'

Shawn nodded. 'That certainly seems the most logical explanation.'

'But didn't you search that couple last night?' Mum said. 'Kat told me she had to go through Lala's pockets.'

'Well that's not very thorough,' said Delia. 'They could have hidden the stuff anywhere on the estate and gone back to get it later.'

Which was exactly what my mother had thought, too.

'Did you search their room at the B and B?' Delia demanded.

'We would have to have reasonable cause to get a warrant,' said Shawn.

'I bet they've got my jewellery,' Delia muttered.

Shawn scribbled in his notebook. 'Mrs Evans, did Major Evans and Nick have a good relationship?'

'Very good,' said Delia. 'Nick wanted to photograph him yesterday, but with all the hoopla going on with Seth Cropper, he didn't get a chance.'

'That's not what Dad told me,' Guy put in. 'He said that Nick was being annoying.'

'No, dear,' said Delia. 'You've got that wrong. Nick is taking his photograph this morning otherwise it won't make this Saturday's newspaper.'

'Why didn't he tell me?' Guy seemed agitated. 'Where are they meeting?'

'Violet's tea room,' said Delia.

'Why meet there?' Mum wondered. 'Violet's coffee tastes like dirt!'

Delia shrugged. 'Because it's the only tea room in Little Dipperton, and apparently Nick left his motorbike at the Hare and Hounds last night.'

'What time are they meeting?' Guy asked.

Delia checked her watch. 'In about twenty minutes. That's why he couldn't come with me this morning.'

'I'd better go and find him.' Guy got to his feet. 'I don't particularly trust this reporter, and Dad can be so gullible.'

Mum caught my eye and mouthed, 'Gullible?' I must admit, I had never seen Lenny in that light at all.

'Are we finished here?' he continued.

'You may leave, sir,' Shawn said politely.

'I'm sure Kat and Iris will be able to run me back to the Hall,' said Delia. 'Will I see you later?'

'Yes, Mum,' said Guy. 'And Kat, I'll meet you at the Dartmouth Antique Emporium and then we can go for a late lunch.'

Delia was uncharacteristically subdued on the drive back to Honeychurch Hall. She sat quietly in the rear seat looking small and defeated. It was only when we drew close to Honeychurch Cottages that she finally spoke.

'I'm sorry if I've been a bit prickly today, Iris,' she said. 'I'm not . . . Um . . . It's a bit of an adjustment with Lenny at home for good, and much as I love Guy, the two of them just take over my life. They're so controlling!'

'That's all right,' Mum said. 'I'm sorry. I've been snappy too.' She took a deep breath. 'I just don't want to see you get hurt. You know what they say about leopards and spots.'

'What's that supposed to mean?' Delia said sharply.

'Mum!' I hissed. 'Don't go there.'

'What I meant was that we haven't been to Marks and Sparks for weeks now,' said Mum. 'And I miss you.'

'That's a nice thing to say,' said Delia. 'I miss you too, but I've got so much on my mind. With Seth dead, I'm worried that her ladyship might bring in a new couple, and perhaps I'll lose my home.'

'Don't be silly,' said Mum.

'After all, I'm just the housekeeper. Lady Lavinia told me that before I came along, they used to use someone from the village. Perhaps they'll go back to doing that. They could even rent out my cottage for a holiday home. People do that these days on big fancy estates.'

'I can't imagine it ever happening here,' said Mum. 'They'd have to spend a fortune to bring the cottage up to scratch.'

'And what if his lordship wants me out for selling gin illegally?' Delia said miserably. 'You own your house, Iris, but Lenny and I could easily be out on our ear.'

Eric Pugsley emerged from his cottage brandishing a brown paper parcel and waved us down. He wasn't wearing a coat, just a checked flannel shirt, jeans and ... goodness, were those Ugg slippers? I had never seen him without his beanie and was surprised to realise that despite his heavy eyebrows, he was completely bald.

'Look out, here comes Beetle-Brows!' Mum exclaimed.

I pulled up and opened the window. A blast of cold air sent us all shivering.

'Got another package for Lenny,' said Eric. 'It was left on the front doorstep at the Hall again. I already told him he must use the correct address.'

Delia gave a gasp of horror. 'Did his lordship find it?'

'Unfortunately, he did,' said Eric.

'Oh God!' Delia exclaimed. 'Was he angry?'

'Given that it's nearly Christmas, you won't be evicted today.' Eric kept a straight face. I hoped he was joking.

Delia let out a whimper of dismay.

'Just make sure that your friends have the correct address in future,' said Eric.

'Wait,' said Delia. 'Did you say that another parcel had been delivered for Lenny at the Hall?'

'That's right,' said Eric. 'I gave it to him on Saturday.'

Delia frowned. 'Oh. Funny. He never mentioned it.'

'It was probably your Christmas present,' said Mum. 'A surprise.'

Eric handed me the parcel through the open window. I noticed that it sported half a dozen Christmas stamps in an effort to make up the right postage. The address simply read: *Evans, c/o Honeychurch Hall, Little Dipperton.*

'How on earth did it ever get this far?' I exclaimed.

'Oh, the postman knows everyone,' Mum said. 'No, wait, there's no postmark. There are stamps but no postmark! How extraordinary! This must have been hand-delivered.'

'Give me that,' said Delia quickly. 'I wonder what it is. Do you think it's for me?'

'There's only one thing to do,' Mum declared. 'Let's open it and see.'

Chapter Fourteen

Delia hesitated. 'I don't know . . . Oh, all right.'

'And that means I have to come in too,' I grumbled, 'since Mum will need a lift back to the Carriage House and you'll want one to the Hall.'

'It'll only take two minutes,' said Mum.

'I don't know,' Delia said again. 'If it's for me, I don't want to spoil the surprise.'

But my mother had already got out of the car.

We headed for Delia's cottage, Mum holding the parcel as if it were an unexploded grenade, and stepped into the tiny living area. With a sofa, armchair, dining room table and six chairs, TV table, coffee table and an enormous Christmas tree, the place resembled a second-hand furniture store. It was incredibly claustrophobic. Boxes marked *Storage* were stacked in every available space.

I had been in Delia's cottage before Lenny retired, and it had been immaculate.

'Well . . . it's rather cosy in a cramped sort of way,' said Mum tactfully.

'It's all Lenny's stuff,' Delia moaned. 'I'm not used to it. Peggy's cottage has a cellar. I hate being in a mess.'

'It's not really a mess, though,' I pointed out. Everything was neatly labelled. 'You've just got a lot of stuff.'

'Guy suggested we use one of his outbuildings,' Delia said. 'Or we could use one of yours, Iris?'

'They're leaking,' Mum said quickly. 'I wouldn't want your things to get ruined.'

'They're not mine, they're Lenny's,' said Delia. 'But you've just had the courtyard all done up! You've got bags of room. What about the piggery?'

'I told you, I'm using that for the Honeychurch family archives,' Mum lied. 'Come on, let's get this over and done with.'

She set the parcel down on the dining room table and gave the tape a professional once-over, not bothering to hide the fact that she was relishing doing something not totally above board. 'Kat, go and put the kettle on.'

I did as I was told, although it took me a while to locate the kettle. There were so many appliances along the counter-top – two blenders, two toasters, a mixer, an egg cooker, a coffee machine, some with European plugs presumably from when Lenny had been based overseas.

'I don't think I have time for tea,' I heard Delia say. 'I told her ladyship I'd only be an hour and a half.'

'We're not stopping for tea,' said Mum.

I returned to wait for the kettle to boil. Delia looked miserable.

'We use the steam to remove the tape,' Mum declared. 'Have you got any more tape?'

'Maybe we shouldn't do this.' Delia looked nervous. 'I'm not sure—'

'You're right,' Mum said suddenly. 'Peggy's cottage is much larger. You would have more room if you moved in there.'

'That's what I was going to suggest to Lady Lavinia,' Delia said eagerly. 'I'm going to meet her this morning to talk about it.'

'Lavinia? You're wasting your time with her.' Mum's voice was laced with scorn. 'She's as thick as two short planks. The person with the power is the dowager countess.'

'But she's away until tomorrow, and we need to strike whilst the iron is hot.'

'As in . . . when Peggy is prostrate with grief,' Mum said drily. 'Lady Edith has the last say in everything, and you definitely don't want to annoy her.'

'Unlike you, Iris,' said Delia with a sniff, 'I'm not afraid of that old bag.'

Mum was taken aback. She was fiercely loyal to the elderly lady who had been so kind and generous to both of us.

'Oh, I'm not worried,' Delia went on airily. 'Lenny will charm the pants off her.'

'Yes, you can certainly say he's good at doing that,' Mum muttered.

Delia reddened. 'What's that supposed to mean?'

'Do I have to spell it out?'

'You know it was only once, Iris,' said Delia primly. 'Why can't you give him a break?'

There was a loud ping. *Thank God!* 'Kettle's boiled!' I cried.

With surprising speed, my mother deftly steamed off the parcel tape. 'Ta-dah!'

'I think you've done this before,' said Delia.

Swiftly Mum removed the outer brown paper to reveal a slim rectangular box covered in festive wrapping paper and tied with a big red bow.

'Well it's definitely a Christmas present,' she said.

'Isn't there a card?' Delia asked.

Mum checked the discarded brown paper and carefully flipped the box upside down. 'No,' she said. 'I bet he's ordered you some sexy lingerie.'

Delia pretended to look shocked but soon did a U-turn. 'My Lenny *does* like nice underwear. He likes me to dress up as one of those Wild West saloon girls, you know – a lady of the line.'

Mum gawked. 'You mean . . . a *prostitute*?'

'Argh!' I said. 'Please, no! Too much information!'

Delia cackled. 'Our sex life has—'

'You told me about the meat larder.' Mum sniggered. 'I had to go and take a cold shower afterwards. It sounded exhausting.'

'Please!' I begged again. 'No details!'

'He may be retired,' Delia went on, 'but he's certainly not retiring in that department.'

They exchanged dirty laughs. I was disgusted, but relieved that they seemed to be friends again.

'Well let's just see what it is,' Mum said, and ignoring

Delia's protests about quite liking a surprise, she carefully undid the next round of tape.

Beneath the Christmas wrapping paper was a beautiful gift box with the Harrods logo.

Delia's eyes widened. 'Harrods!' she exclaimed. 'He can't afford anything from there. Oh bless him. So sweet.'

'I think Harrods sells Agent Provocateur,' said Mum. 'It's very expensive. Ready to take off the lid?'

'I've changed my mind,' said Delia. 'I don't think I want to know—'

'But I do.'

Mum removed the lid. Inside was a layer of black tissue paper. With painstaking care, she gently opened it up. A whiff of cheap perfume immediately assaulted my senses.

'Oh, good grief,' she said, wrinkling her nose. 'That's pungent.'

And then everything changed. Delia had turned white.

'Don't,' she said sharply. 'Wrap it up. I don't want to see it.'

'Don't be silly.'

'Mum, she doesn't—'

'Wrap it up, Iris!' screamed Delia.

But my mother was on a mission. Carefully she brought out the most exquisite cashmere scarf. It was black and cobalt blue and was without a doubt a gift for a man.

Delia clapped her hands over her mouth in horror.

Mum seemed bewildered. 'Who would send Lenny a man's scarf smelling of perfume?'

Delia gave a cry and made a run for the door that led to

upstairs. She thundered up to her bedroom, and we heard the door slam.

'Oh Mum,' I said. 'Poor Delia.'

'I knew it,' Mum said in an I-told-you-so tone of voice. 'It looks like he's still carrying on with her. Look! There is a note after all.'

Written on a beautiful vellum card in exquisite hand-writing were the words: *With you for always, forever.*

I felt terrible for Delia and annoyed with my mother. 'What should we do now?'

'I know you think I'm unkind, but I don't want her hurt,' said Mum defensively. 'I had a feeling—'

'You shouldn't have done that,' I said. 'What do we do with the scarf?'

'I'll take it,' Mum said. 'I'll wrap it back up and hang onto it until she decides to confront him.'

Once she had finished, the parcel looked as good as new. She went upstairs to see if Delia was all right, but came back down shaking her head. 'She refuses to come out of her bedroom.'

I tried too, but it was futile. 'Delia,' I said. 'We're leaving now. I know you have to go to work, so if you want me to take you, please come out now.'

There was no reply.

'She'll just have to walk,' said Mum.

Leaving Delia to her misery, I drove my mother back to the Carriage House. Mum was not remotely sympathetic to Delia's predicament. She was more concerned at having to change the governess in *Betrayed* to a Wild West lady of the line.

Not only did my heart go out to Delia, I felt disappointed and let down. During the numerous conversations I'd had with Guy over the last few weeks, he had told me that his father was filled with remorse, and that he would lay down his life for things to be back the way they had been before he hit his midlife crisis – Guy's words, not mine. Personally, since Lenny was nearer seventy than fifty, I thought it a poor excuse, but Guy seemed to believe him.

As we pulled into Mum's cobbled courtyard, a Kawasaki quad bike was parked next to the wishing well.

'Good heavens,' said Mum. 'Whose is that?'

The children came running out of the arched carriageway doors waving with excitement. They were dressed in their usual outfits – Harry as Biggles and Fleur as a French special agent.

'It must be Harry's!' I said with surprise. 'He *is* growing up.'

'Surely his lordship doesn't allow him to drive that thing,' said Mum. 'I mean – is it actually legal?'

'On private land, I think so,' I said. 'I don't really know.'

'Stanford! Stanford!' Harry yelled as Mum and I got out of the car. 'You'll never guess! It's true! The legend is true!'

'I'll leave you to it,' said Mum, and clutching Delia's offending parcel, she hurried into the house.

'Slow down and tell me what you're talking about,' I said.

'We've been looking for you everywhere!' Harry lifted his goggles to reveal horn-rimmed glasses that had left deep impressions around his eyes. He was very red in the face. 'You have to come with us right now!'

'I can't,' I said. 'I don't have time.'

'No, it's important.' He took a deep breath. 'The hawk is *bleeding*!'

'Really?' I said drily.

'It's true, Kat,' he said, dropping his alter ego. 'And Cropper died, Father told me, so the curse is *true*!'

'Cropper is dead,' repeated Fleur quietly. 'He is dead. Very scary.'

'All right,' I said reluctantly. 'But five minutes. That's all I have.'

The children jumped onto the quad bike and I followed them to the rear of the Hall – which took a lot longer than five minutes.

Despite the number of times I had used this entrance, I was always fascinated by the different architectural periods that were in evidence. It was here that the old house showed her age, with a series of exposed wooden beams hinting at its Tudor beginnings. It was as if the Hall kept being swallowed up by bigger and more fashionable additions as time went by.

It was also here that you got a sense of how enormous the estate really was. Paved pathways led away from the court-yard in a dozen different directions.

The extensive formal grounds stretched to the south in a confusion of neglected box hedges and topiary. Overgrown flower borders rolled down towards the River Dart. There were avenues of ancient oak trees, a ha-ha, a shell-lined grotto and an equine cemetery. The terrace of cottages, the Victorian walled garden and its adjacent stumpery – accessed by a concealed wooden door – stood to the east.

As the quad pulled into the rear courtyard, Mr Chips darted in front of it and Harry swerved, catapulting Fleur off the vehicle. She hit the ground with a thud and lay there without moving.

I slammed on the brakes and raced over to see if she was OK.

Harry jumped off the bike, shouting, 'Man down! Man down!'

I dropped to my knees. 'Fleur? Fleur!' I whispered. 'Can you hear me?'

She didn't answer.

Harry turned pale. 'She's not dead, is she? I think . . . I think she touched the hawk.'

'She's not dead, Harry,' I said. 'She's just winded.'

'Oh golly!' Harry said anxiously. 'Father is going to be furious. Come on, Agent Moreau! Wake up!'

But Fleur just lay there with her eyes closed.

Then Mr Chips bounded forward to cover her face in kisses, and she exploded into giggles, squealing as she wriggled away from the little dog's frantic licking.

'You scared us,' I scolded, but stopped as a large envelope fell out of her trench coat pocket.

In a panic, she shoved the Jack Russell aside and tried to grab it, but I was faster and snatched it up.

I couldn't believe my eyes. The envelope was stuffed with cash in a variety of denominations. There had to be at least a thousand pounds there, maybe more.

'Where on earth did you get all this money?' I demanded.

Chapter Fifteen

Fleur stood there looking defiant. 'I will never tell,' she declared. 'Torture me if you must.'

'This is not funny,' I said as Mr Chips continued to dance around the three of us, barking madly, before finally giving up and dashing away.

'Special Agent Moreau is instructed to only give you her name,' said Harry, reverting to his alter ego.

'I'm not joking, Harry,' I said firmly. 'Is this your father's money?'

'It's for ammunition,' he protested. 'The Germans have a camp at Larcombe—'

'Harry!' I exclaimed. 'Where did you get that money? How much is in here?'

'There is one thousand pounds,' said Fleur. 'I counted it.'

'Did you take it from Mrs Cropper's housekeeping jar, because if you did, that's stealing and it's a very serious crime.'

'It wasn't from the housekeeping jar,' Harry said. 'I promise.'

'Where did you find it?' I demanded.

There was no response. Fleur shot a sideways glance at Harry and seemed to send a secret signal.

When neither answered, I said, 'Fine. In that case we are going to go and give it to your father and see what he has to say about it.'

'No!' said Harry.

'I'll also tell him that you are far too young to drive a quad bike. Fleur could have been seriously injured.'

'But I wasn't injured,' Fleur said in a sulky voice. 'See.' And she did a quick tap dance.

'Please don't tell him,' Harry said. 'We'll put the money back, won't we, Fleur?'

'Why should we? Finders keepers, losers weepers,' said Fleur.

I heard Harry gasp. He never seemed to have been a disobedient child until he met Fleur.

'Fine. Then you give me no choice.' I strode off in the direction of the rear entrance.

'No!' Harry came tearing after me and grabbed my arm. 'Please don't tell Father,' he said urgently.

'Where did you find all this money?' I said yet again.

Harry glanced over at Fleur, who had stayed by the quad bike. She looked furious. I could see that he was in an agony of indecision.

'Harry,' I said in a low voice, 'I know that you are a good boy. You must do the right thing.'

He looked downcast. 'We found it in the stumpery.'

'The *stumpery*?' I was confused. 'Show me where. Get in my car.'

With one last look at Fleur, who stood watching us, I drove out of the courtyard.

'She's awfully grumpy,' Harry said. 'Girls are such hard work.'

'I'm afraid we are sometimes,' I agreed. 'How about we go riding tomorrow? Just the two of us?'

Ever since Fleur had come to stay for the Christmas holidays, we had forgone our weekly ride.

'Yes please,' he said. 'Can we go to Larcombe Quarry?'

'Whatever do you want to go there for?'

'To see how much ice is on the water. Fleur told me that her brother drove a snowmobile across a lake in Colorado.'

'That's America, and very different from a pond in Little Dipperton,' I said. 'I didn't know that Fleur had a brother.'

'He's going to be her half-brother when her father gets divorced and marries again,' Harry went on. 'He's twenty-five. She hates him.'

I decided to make allowances for Fleur's difficult behaviour. It couldn't be easy for her, especially being so far away from her family at Christmas.

'We'll see what the weather forecast is like first, OK?' I said. 'But I thought the quarry was fenced off?'

'Some of it is,' said Harry.

We pulled up outside the Victorian walled garden just a short distance from Honeychurch Cottages. It was here, if you followed the boundary wall into the woods, that the entrance to the stumpery could be found. It would be hard to locate in the summer months because the wall was so over-grown with ivy. In fact I had only discovered it recently myself. It reminded me of Frances Hodgson Burnett's children's classic, *The Secret Garden*.

In the box of old black-and-white photographs that Rupert had given Mum in her unofficial role as family historian, she had found several pictures of this peculiar Victorian curiosity. Started in the late 1800s, it was an arborist's version of a rockery – and I loved it.

We pushed open the gate and stepped inside. The woodland garden was a confusion of ferns, mosses and lichens that sprouted out of tree stumps, dead trees and root wads to create a plethora of bizarre shapes and hidden nooks and crannies. In the spring there would be a carpet of primroses, celandines and violets.

It was a very weird yet magical place, and I liked to come here just to sit. I always thought that if fairies existed, they would live here.

Today the trees were still covered in snow. There were two paths – one to our left and one to our right. Harry set off down the left-hand one. He stopped at the first dead tree and pointed to a cavity partially covered by ferns. 'The money was in there.'

I was astonished. 'How did you even think to look in there?'

'We wanted a tree to drop secret notes,' he said. 'We looked at other places, but this was the best.' He turned to me, his face creased with worry. 'I'm not in trouble, am I?'

'It's a lot of money to find in a tree,' I said. 'Didn't you think to tell your father?'

It occurred to me that Rupert could have left the money for someone as a reward for information about the watches.

'We can put it back?' he said hopefully.

'No,' I said. 'You are going to give it to your father.' I smiled. 'Don't worry. You haven't done anything wrong.' I gave him a hug. 'Come on. Why don't we go and see that hawk now?'

'OK.' But he said it without his usual enthusiasm.

Fifteen minutes later, I was back in the museum room with Harry and Fleur.

'*Voilà!*' Fleur said, pointing to the pedestal. 'Blood!'

I gave a start. It was true. A tiny cluster of bright red speckles ran along the seam of the bird's wax binding. 'Well, it certainly looks like it.' I regarded Harry with suspicion. 'Did you two do that? Because if you did, your father is going to be very angry.'

'*Non!*' Fleur exclaimed. 'It's blood! It's real blood.'

'What are you doing in here?' Rupert strode into the room. 'Harry! You know you're forbidden to come into this room alone— Oh, Kat. I'm sorry. I didn't see you there.'

Harry looked stricken, and even my stomach lurched. 'They wanted to show me the hawk—'

'Someone else is going to die,' Fleur said quietly. 'The bird has foretold the future. The bird has seen it. The bird knows.'

'What are you talking about?' Rupert said. He joined us, and his face darkened. 'Harry! Did you touch it?'

'No. No, I promise I didn't do anything.' Harry seemed close to tears.

'If either of you has touched this bird . . . you, Fleur, will go straight back to boarding school and spend the rest of the Christmas holidays there. Harry, you will no longer be permitted to ride the quad bike or leave this house. You will be grounded for the entire Christmas holidays.'

I felt terrible for Harry and angry with Fleur, who I was convinced was to blame.

'I swear we did not touch the bird, *monsieur*,' she said. 'I swear on my mother's life.'

Rupert hesitated, and even I wondered if there was some truth in what she said. She was so earnest in her denial, and Harry was unusually quiet. It wouldn't be the first time I had experienced supernatural phenomena at the Hall.

'I have a colleague who is an expert in ancient Egyptian artefacts,' I said. 'I could give him a call.' I thought for a moment. 'It might be a reaction to being exposed to central heating yesterday. Maybe there was some residual moisture that seeped through the bindings.'

'All right,' Rupert said grudgingly. 'Give your chap a call.'

'There's something else,' I said. 'Harry? Do you want to tell your father, or should I?'

'You,' Harry whispered.

I took the envelope of cash out of my jacket pocket. Fleur gave a little gasp, and I saw her shoot Harry a look of disgust.

Rupert frowned. 'What is this?'

'It's one thousand pounds,' said Harry. 'Special Agent Moreau—'

'No!' Rupert exclaimed. 'Enough of these childish games. Where did you get this?'

'In the stumpery, sir,' said Harry.

'The kids were playing there,' I put in. 'They . . . they thought it might be important and that you should have it.'

'Why was it there, Father?' Harry said.

'That's not your concern,' said Rupert. 'Now off you go before you get into any more trouble.'

The children couldn't wait to get away, but as they reached the door, Rupert called out, 'Wait! If you're taking the quad bike, what are the rules?'

'No further than the boundary fence,' said Harry. 'And always make sure we each take a radio handset and leave another one in the dry box on the bike.'

Rupert nodded. 'Off you go.'

'That's a good idea,' I said.

'It's the only way I feel confident that I can find them.' Rupert put the envelope full of cash into his inside jacket pocket. 'Thank you for this.'

'I thought it might have been something to do with the reward you're offering,' I ventured.

'I would ask you to keep this between us and do not mention it to Shawn or your mother.'

'Oh.' I was taken aback. 'Of course.'

I waited for him to say more, but he didn't. Instead he gestured to the hawk. 'Do you think we should put the lid back on?'

'It might be a good idea,' I said.

'Do you want to do it?'

'Me?'

For the first time, Rupert cracked a smile. 'Not that I'm

superstitious, you understand. It's just that it was Cropper who took the lid off, and . . . well . . .'

I had to admit, I didn't want to do it either, but it seemed so silly. 'Let's leave it for now. But we should turn the heating off in this room.'

'Already done,' he said. 'I fear the money we made on the event will all go to pay for heating this room for one day.'

As we left the museum room and crossed the black-and-white-checked marble hall, Lavinia emerged from the drawing room with Delia and – to my surprise – Lenny. His meeting with Nick Bond must have been very fast.

He looked as if he was going to a funeral. He wore a dark suit and his regimental tie. His shoes were so shiny that I could practically see my own reflection in them.

Lavinia was dressed in her usual attire of jodhpurs and a sweatshirt with her hair clamped under a slumber net.

Rupert seemed surprised. 'What's going on?'

'Oh, hello!' Lavinia beamed. 'Allow me to introduce the new butler. This is Evans.'

'Lenny, please,' said Lenny. 'This is the twenty-first century, after all.'

Lavinia turned pink. 'We've always addressed our staff by their last names.' She appealed to Rupert. 'Though I suppose—'

'No,' said Rupert firmly. 'The use of first names encourages familiarity. We don't want to give you any ideas above your station. Besides, I would have thought you would have been used to it, being a military man.'

Lenny visibly bristled. 'As you wish, sir.'

'You have to say "your lordship",' Delia told him coldly. For someone who had got exactly what she wanted, she didn't seem as happy as I would have thought. But then I remembered the incriminating scarf doused in cheap perfume.

'A bit soon, isn't it?' Rupert said. 'Cropper's not even been buried yet.'

'As Mrs Evans pointed out,' said Lavinia nervously, 'we have the annual Honeychurch gift-giving event coming up and we'll need a butler—'

'Wait . . .' Rupert frowned, then snapped his fingers. 'Evans? *Evans?* Are you two related?'

Typical, I thought. Had Rupert really not known that they were man and wife?

'Of course they are.' Lavinia's pink cheeks darkened with embarrassment. 'The major has just retired. He'll be super. And guess what! He's going to be awarded the Queen's Gallantry Medal.'

'I'm sure that will come in very useful when he's polishing my shoes,' said Rupert drily.

Lenny's jaw dropped. 'Polishing *shoes*?'

'Ah, didn't my wife tell you?' said Rupert. 'A modern butler's duties cover a multitude of sins.'

'He'll do it,' Delia snarled.

'Evans rescued some children caving,' Lavinia burbled on. 'It was in all the newspapers! It was frightfully dangerous. *Ab-so-lutely* terrifying. He's such a hero.'

'I'm sorry . . .' Rupert frowned again. 'I thought Mrs Evans was a widow?'

Lenny blinked. 'A widow?'

Now it was Delia's turn to look embarrassed. It had been the story she'd told anyone who would listen when she had first come to Honeychurch Hall as the housekeeper just a few months ago. Rather than admit that her husband had run off with another woman, she had claimed that her husband had died, leaving her penniless.

My mother had managed to smooth over the lie with the dowager countess and Lavinia – who claimed that Delia was the best housekeeper ever. Obviously no one had thought to inform Lord Rupert Honeychurch or Lenny, who looked utterly crushed.

'A widow?' he said again.

'It was a *misunderstanding*,' I said, catching Lavinia's eye.

For a moment she looked blank, and then she gushed, 'Oh! Yes, of *course*! No, you're thinking of someone else, darling. It was another housekeeper at . . . another country estate. Evans is such a common name!'

'A widow?' Lenny said yet again. Delia's expression remained cold.

'Very well.' Rupert just shrugged. 'Below stairs is your department, Lav, but you must remember to run it past Mother first before making any decisions.'

'Yes. Yes, of course.' Lavinia smiled, but she looked uneasy.

Rupert left without uttering another word.

Delia seemed worried. 'Does that mean we can't move into Peggy's cottage yet?' she asked. 'I'd really like to be settled by Christmas.'

Lavinia adjusted her slumber net. 'Um. Well. Perhaps—'

'Our son Guy is home on leave and he can help with the move,' Delia went on. 'As you know, the Croppers have lived at number two since Noah's Ark, and the place is in a terrible state. There is a lot of cleaning to do.'

'A widow,' I heard Lenny say for the umpteenth time.

'And we can move Peggy into our cottage,' Delia went on. 'We'll even pack and unpack her things. She won't have to do anything at all. I'm sure Guy and Lenny can shift the furniture. It's only going next door.'

'Um. Well . . .' Lavinia said again. She looked to me for help, but this was an area I was definitely not getting involved in. For a start, Rupert was right. It was extremely insensitive of Delia to get her husband installed as the new butler so quickly, but to expect Peggy to move out of her home in her absence was just plain wrong.

Lenny cleared his throat. 'Maybe we should wait for your mother-in-law to come back.'

Lavinia blanched.

'Sorry. There's no rush, is there, luv?' Lenny reached for Delia's hand, but she stepped quickly away.

'Don't touch me!' she hissed.

'Lovely!' Lavinia trilled. 'So glad it's all sorted.' And with that she mumbled something about going out riding and hurried away, leaving the three of us in an uncomfortable silence.

'That went well,' Lenny ventured.

'Did it?' Delia snapped. 'Really? You were late!'

'I told you I had to talk to the newspaper reporter. You wanted me to talk to him so I did. You want me to be a butler so I am!'

Delia glared at him and walked off.

Lenny looked at me all hurt. 'I don't understand. I've done everything she asked!'

I guessed he knew nothing about the delivery of the cashmere scarf.

'It happened once,' he went on. 'And she's going to punish me for the rest of my life.' He shook his head in despair. 'Did *you* know that I was supposed to be dead?'

'Sorry,' I said. 'Got to go.'

Leaving Lenny looking bewildered, I hurried to my car and set off for Dartmouth.

Chapter Sixteen

As I crested the brow of the hill above the picturesque town that nestled at the mouth of the River Dart, I resolved to push everything and anything related to the Honeychurch family aside. I was not going to obsess over the cash in the stumpery or the stolen pocket watches or the mummified hawk. Instead, I was determined to enjoy the day with my lovely new boyfriend.

It was a beautiful crisp morning with a cobalt-blue sky and a handful of puffy white clouds. The harbour was full of all manner of sailing vessels and the entire town was decorated with festive lights. Trying to park was always a nightmare, but fortunately, Dartmouth Antique Emporium had its own dedicated car park for customers.

When I first started Kat's Collectibles & Mobile Valuation Services, I felt very isolated. It was lovely having such a beautiful showroom in the gatehouse, but having worked in the public eye for so long, I missed the buzz and human contact.

When I first saw the space at the converted barn complex, I wasn't sure if I would fit in. Even though I had never been an A-list celebrity when I hosted *Fakes & Treasures*, women tended to seek my friendship either because they wanted to be photographed with me or because they hoped I could introduce them to people of influence.

But after the initial few weeks of working shifts at the Emporium, I began to make friends. I also realised that in this part of the country, no one really cared about who you were – or in my case, what I used to be.

The car park next to the Emporium was packed. Next to the front entrance was a Victorian-garbed choir belting out 'O Little Town of Bethlehem' watched by a crowd of Christmas shoppers.

I stepped inside, where Fiona Reynolds, who owned the Emporium, was handing out mince pies and glasses of mulled wine. I had a feeling that by the time Christmas was over, I would never want either again!

My friend Di Wilkins waved to me. She was a beautiful woman just a little younger than me, sporting a pixie cut that suited her elfin face perfectly. Tall and rangy, she reminded me of a colt. She specialised in vintage jewellery, and since her space was opposite mine, we often kept an eye on each other's stock.

'I sold Esther for you this morning for the full price,' she said. 'She went to a lovely couple. I made sure of that.'

I was glad. It probably sounded childish, but I always wanted to know what kind of home my bears went to. I had been particularly fond of Esther, a large German Hermann bear that I had bought from an elderly lady during my *Fakes & Treasures* days. Made in the 1930s, Esther stood two feet tall and had long two-tipped mohair fur and a working growler.

'And a couple stopped by and asked after you,' Di went on. 'Angus and Lala Fenwick? Unusual name.'

'Lala?' I grinned. 'She's a champion limbo dancer apparently. Did they say whether they were coming back?'

'I didn't ask,' said Di. 'Actually, you're really in demand this morning. There was a very handsome man asking for you as well. I assume he's your helicopter pilot.'

'Guy's here already?' I was surprised but pleased, and zipped off a quick text to tell him where I was, but that having only just got here, I couldn't leave for a while.

'Oh, here he is now,' said Di.

'Kat?'

I'd have recognised that smooth voice anywhere. It was David, my former fiancé. I felt the colour rush to my cheeks.

'I'll leave you to it,' Di said with a wink and moved away.

Seeing David again after so long did not lessen the physical impact he always had on me, although I noticed that he looked older and very tired. He had more salt in his salt-and-pepper hair now, and he was wearing a Barbour and jeans. That came as a shock. I'd only ever known him wear smart city clothes – blazers, slacks and Florsheim shoes – never country attire.

'You look like a deer caught in headlights,' he said with a grin, and pulled me into a hug. I could smell his familiar scent and for a moment felt a rush of nostalgia. I had spent over a decade with this man. We had been a powerful couple in the London art and antique world, and even down here, I heard a few murmurs of recognition in the Emporium.

'Hello,' was all I managed to say.

'The extra weight looks good on you,' he said.

I had to laugh at the back-handed compliment. It was *so* David. A year ago I would have been horrified, but now I didn't care.

He suddenly realised what he'd said. 'No! I meant that as a compliment,' he stammered, flustered. 'I've put on a few pounds myself.'

He was *nervous*! I had never known David nervous before.

'And the Barbour?' I said. 'That's a new look for you.'

'Ah. Yes, it is. It certainly saves on dry-cleaning bills.'

'But it still screams city,' I teased. 'You need to lay it down in a muddy farmyard and run over it in a Land Rover a few times.'

'Just like they do with the carpets out in India?' he said.

'Exactly. Make them distressed.'

'Remember that train we took from Delhi?'

'The Palace on Wheels,' I said.

'And the chap who got the black tongue?'

I laughed. 'It was disgusting.'

So many shared memories came flooding back. We stood there looking at each other, then David reached out to touch my hair. Instinctively I took a step back.

'Sorry. I couldn't help it,' he said sheepishly. 'It's longer than I've ever seen you wear it. I had a dream – more of a nightmare – that you cut it all off.'

Moving into a personal conversation made me surprisingly uncomfortable. I had to remind myself that after ten years of promises, David had reconciled with his estranged wife.

He gestured to the space where I sold my antique dolls and bears. 'Nice layout. Good spot here.'

My space was small but light, with a large arched window that overlooked the courtyard. A skylight spanned the gabled roof that stretched the length of the Emporium, where over thirty dealers sold their stuff.

I had decorated my lair – as my mother liked to call it – with sprigs of holly that I'd collected from the estate. Matching walnut bookshelves and glass cabinets lined the partition walls, displaying vintage bears and a selection of porcelain dolls. The floor was covered in an Afghan rug in blues and reds. In the corner next to the window was a pretty Queen Anne oak bureau and a Queen Anne walnut and leather desk chair. In the other corner was a leather wingback chair.

David went and sat down.

'Kat's Collectibles & Mobile Valuation Services. I like it.' He pointed to the bespoke sign that Di had created for me. She was a wonderful calligrapher. 'You always wanted your own business. I'm happy for you.' He scanned the area and gave a nod of approval. 'Nice selection of stock, too, and I like the way you've displayed it. Not too cluttered.'

'Thank you.' I felt off balance. The last time I had seen David had been humiliating for him. I knew him well, and was aware that he didn't forgive easily, especially when it came to damaging his reputation.

He was in Devon for a reason, and I had an awful feeling that I knew what that reason was. The Crimean pocket watches. It had to be. When Shawn had reported the theft, it would automatically have flagged on David's watch list. Mum was right.

A handful of collectors stepped into my space, and for ten minutes I was caught up in showing them three of my favourite Kammer & Reinhardt dolls, aware that David was watching my every move. It made me feel self-conscious.

They left saying they would think about it.

'They'll be back to buy one,' said David. 'Just you see. I can tell. But don't drop the price.'

'I wasn't intending to,' I retorted.

'How is the incorrigible Iris?' he asked, changing the subject. 'Is she still writing bodice-rippers?'

'Mum is very well, thank you,' I said. 'How are Trudy and the kids?'

'Well too, thank you.'

I didn't want them to be well – at least not Trudy. Even though I was happy living here, with a new boyfriend, it still hurt.

'How about the kid who was obsessed with Biggles?' David went on.

'You mean Harry,' I said. 'Still obsessed with Biggles.'

'Do you think he'd like my first editions?'

'Why? Are you giving them away?' I was stunned. Among David's many antiquarian collections were first editions of W. E. Johns's Biggles books. 'Why on earth would you do that?'

'Don't look so surprised,' said David. 'My kids aren't interested.'

'You're not ill, are you?'

'Nice of you to be concerned, but no, I'm in perfectly good health. I just thought he would like them. It can be a Christmas present. From you, if you prefer.'

I shook my head, thoroughly confused. 'No. It should be from you.'

Another couple stopped by to look at the bears, and when they left, David said, 'Don't you miss London? Although I must say, Dartmouth is quite lovely.'

'So what brings you here to the Emporium? Oh, wait, doesn't Trudy's father live around here?'

'Hugh passed away,' he said simply.

'Oh. I'm sorry.' And I was.

'No, I'm here on business,' David continued. 'And of course I had hoped to see you.'

'Well here I am,' I said.

'There's an auction at Luxtons on Wednesday. I wondered if you knew anything about it?'

'You mean you're on the trail of a priceless artefact?' I said lightly.

He grinned. 'You know me far too well. But then we were together for so long.' He thought for a moment. 'I'm staying at the Dart Marina Hotel; will you have dinner with me tonight?'

'I can't,' I said firmly. 'Sorry.'

'You can't or you don't want to?'

I had fantasised about this moment for such a long time. 'I'm seeing someone.'

'Of course you are,' he said quietly. 'I didn't expect for a moment that you would be alone. I knew the snakes would come slithering in the moment you ended our relationship.'

I felt a surge of anger. 'David,' I said. 'I ended our relationship because you refused to divorce your wife!'

'And I told you that you had to give me time, but you wouldn't wait.'

'I waited for ten years!'

'I told you that I would do it when Hugh died,' David retorted.

'Only instead you renewed your vows in Hawaii!' I was painfully aware that my heart was thundering in my chest. Seeing David again was opening up old wounds. I'd thought this was all behind me, but now I realised it wasn't at all.

'You heard about Hawaii?' he said incredulously. 'Even down here?'

'Seriously?' I struggled to keep my temper. 'You thought I wouldn't find out? I do read the tabloids, you know.'

'Clearly you *don't* read the tabloids, because . . .' he took a deep breath, 'I'm divorced now.'

I thought my knees would give way, I was so shocked. But then the shock changed to an unexpected wave of jealousy. 'Who is she?'

'What?' David seemed taken aback. 'You mean you think I would have moved on to someone new just like that?'

I was speechless, the rush of emotions making me feel so light-headed that I had to sit down too.

'As I said,' David went on, 'clearly you don't read the tabloids. Trudy divorced me. She went off with her cameraman.'

My jaw dropped. 'That scrawny guy with the big nose?'

David actually laughed. 'Yes. That's the one. He's ten years her junior.'

'Well, I'm sorry,' I said, and oddly enough, I was. 'How are Chloe and Sam taking it?'

'It's difficult. I got a black Labrador puppy as an incentive for them to come and visit me.'

'I can't believe you actually got a dog!'

David looked sad and even a little lost. It was all I could do not to put my arms around him and hold him tight. When a long relationship ends, it's not like a switch that just goes off. The feelings still remain rooted somewhere deep inside.

There was a moment as we looked at each other, and then I saw Guy making his way through the crowds holding two glasses of mulled wine aloft. He gave a huge smile, and in that smile I saw a new chapter. *Don't look back, Kat.*

'So who is my rival?' said David lightly. 'That funny little policeman who wears the awful ties?'

'You can meet him,' I said. 'He's heading this way right now.'

Chapter Seventeen

David got to his feet as Guy entered the lair. For the first time in all the years I had known him, he seemed unsure of himself. At eight years his junior, Guy brimmed with energy and confidence.

The two wore identical olive Barbour jackets. But while David's identified him as a DFL – down-from-London – a city person wearing country attire as a fashion statement, Guy's looked pretty beaten up and he fitted right in.

He handed me a glass and kissed my cheek before turning to David, whose expression I could only describe as rigid.

Sensing the tension, Guy thrust out a hand. 'Guy Evans, hello. And you are?'

'David Wynne,' said David. 'Drinking so early in the day?'

'Here, take mine,' Guy said gallantly.

David sneered. 'I was being sarcastic.'

'Really? Whatever for?' Guy raised his glass to mine in a toast. 'Cheers! Merry Christmas!'

I took a larger gulp than I'd planned on. My nerves were going through the roof as David just stood there watching.

'Guy's a helicopter pilot at the Royal Naval Air Station in Yeovilton,' I said.

'Rescuing people off clifftops?' David said.

'Small dogs usually,' said Guy. 'We prefer to leave the people behind.'

I laughed. David didn't.

'David is an art investigator,' I said.

At this, Guy frowned. 'I thought the name sounded familiar. You're the male version of Rene Russo in *The Thomas Crown Affair*.'

'I loved that movie,' I gushed.

'I preferred the original version with Steve McQueen and Faye Dunaway,' said David with a sniff.

'I believe that version is playing at the Totnes Cinema,' Guy said. 'They show old movies. Wait . . .' He snapped his fingers. 'I know where I've heard your name before. You impersonated an art dealer and recovered a painting in Venezuela that had been stolen by the Nazis. It was all over the newspapers.'

'Guy is a bit of a painting connoisseur,' I put in.

Instead of preening his feathers at being recognised, David seemed miffed. 'Kat didn't tell you about us?'

I didn't think things could get any more awkward. The truth was, I hadn't told Guy too much about my past. We'd not spent enough time together to go there. And when I'd asked him about the circumstances surrounding his divorce, he had just said, 'I never look back. No one lives there any more.'

'Tell me what?' Guy asked.

David looked at me and smiled. 'She and I were . . . an item for a long, long time.'

'And you let her go?' Guy laughed. 'Bad luck, mate.' He grabbed my shoulders and pulled me close. 'Thank you for that. I'm a lucky man.'

I braced myself for another of David's cutting remarks, but all he said was, 'You're right. I made a mistake. But as the saying goes, nothing is over until the fat lady sings. I'll see you at the auction on Wednesday. Enjoy the mulled wine.'

And with that, he was gone.

I felt a little shaken and was grateful when the couple who had come by earlier returned to buy the doll – just as David had predicted. Even though David and I were most definitely over, I'd not expected to see him again, and I had never imagined he'd actually get divorced.

After I had wrapped the box containing the doll, adding a sprig of holly for a festive touch, I finally turned to Guy, who was sitting in the wingback chair watching me.

'Are you OK?' he said gently.

'Yes, of course,' I said. 'We had a history or whatever you call it. I'm sorry. I was going to tell you.'

'We've all got history, Kat,' he said. 'It's today that matters – and the future.' He regarded me with concern. 'There's something else bothering you, though, isn't there?'

'If you're asking if I still have feelings for him,' I said, 'I don't.'

'Well it's obvious that he still has feelings for you. First the copper and now Mr Big Shot – I'm going to have to fight them all off!'

'Don't be silly. He's here on business. There's an auction on Wednesday in Newton Abbot.'

Guy thought for a moment. 'A man like that, used to travelling the world, hunting down priceless pieces of art, suddenly turns up at a local auction? What's he up to?'

'No idea,' I said, and focused on sorting out my desk. I had never been very good at lying and I certainly wasn't about to tell Guy about the insurance scam.

'If he's not here for you, then I think it's got something to do with those stolen pocket watches,' he said. 'What do you think?'

Fortunately another wave of shoppers stopped by so I didn't have to answer.

'I can see you're busy,' said Guy, and suggested we meet at the Royal Castle Hotel at two. He'd had the foresight to book a table.

The rest of the morning flew by. I sold two more bears and another doll and had three requests for mobile valuations that I set up for the following week. Despite my initial reservations, renting a space at the Dartmouth Antique Emporium had been one of the best decisions I had ever made.

I was in good spirits as I made my way to the hotel. The streets were full of Christmas shoppers browsing the holiday market. Tented stalls lined the pavements selling a variety of items made in the West Country: cheese and wine from the Sharpham estate, hand-made pottery and carved wooden platters and bowls, locally woven linens and textiles and even home-made dog treats.

A round of rapturous applause welcomed the Dartington Morris Men as they took their places and got ready with sticks and bells to perform the peculiar dance sequences that had been in existence since the mid fifteenth century.

I entered the Royal Castle Hotel and looked for Guy.

Built in the 1600s, the hotel had a white castellated facade and gazed out at the harbour and the River Dart. Inside there was ancient panelling and beams of hand-hewn timber reputedly salvaged from the wreck of a Spanish Armada vessel. One of the hotel's best-known features was a great winding staircase that rose from the original courtyard.

Guy had snagged a round table close to the log fire that blazed in the inglenook fireplace. A large bottle of Perrier and two glasses were already there.

When he saw me coming, his face lit up, and I felt a burst of happiness. *Yes, look forward, Kat. Don't look back.*

He stood up and pulled out my chair for me. 'We'll order in a minute, but I hope you like Perrier. I wasn't sure if you preferred flat or fizzy.'

'Fizzy is fine. Flat would be too. Thank you.'

'Fascinating place.' Guy brandished the menu, with its brief history of the hotel. 'Apparently Charles II's mistresses were sent into polite retirement here once he grew bored with them. And it also says that the place is haunted.'

'Yes, I know,' I said. 'The story goes that in 1688, when William and Mary came from the Netherlands to claim the

English throne, they were due to stay at the hotel. A storm in the Channel prevented William from reaching Dartmouth, and he was forced to stay in nearby Torbay instead. Mary, however, reached the hotel in a carriage at two in the morning, and it's this phantom coach that continues to arrive at the same time ever since.'

'Superstitious nonsense.'

'I'm serious,' I said. 'Guests and staff have often been woken up by the sound of horses' hooves clattering over the cobblestones, and then carriage doors closing, the crack of a coachman's whip and the sound of a clock striking two.'

'Then we should stay here and find out.' Guy gave me a look that made his intentions clear. 'Purely for research, of course.' He took my hand and kissed it.

I was pleased but also embarrassed. I was completely out of practice with this kind of thing. David had never been the kind of man who liked public displays of affection, and it had rubbed off on me. I gently extricated my hand and poured us both some Perrier.

'Mum filled me in about the Bleeding Hawk of Honeychurch Hall,' Guy said. 'She says it's cursed, which of course is ridiculous.'

I told him about the blood speckles, and he roared with laughter. 'Those kids had something to do with it,' he scoffed. 'It's obvious.'

'Rupert doesn't think so, and to be honest, I've experienced some supernatural stuff up there.'

Guy just laughed all the harder. 'This makes such a nice change from keeping world peace. There is more subterfuge and conflict going on at Honeychurch Hall than in a war zone!'

'You're right about that,' I said. 'Speaking of war zones, how did your father's interview with Nick go?'

'It didn't.'

'Oh. That's strange,' I said. 'Are you sure?'

'What do you mean?' Guy said sharply.

'Only that I saw him at the Hall and he said that was the reason why he'd been late to meet with Lavinia.'

'What time was this?' he demanded.

'Ten thirty? Eleven?'

Guy went very quiet, then: 'I must have misunderstood. What do you want to eat? Let's order.'

I picked a home-made beef cobbler and he chose grilled Dover sole. We agreed on a Sharpham rosé as the perfect compromise.

As we tucked into our lunch, Guy became serious. 'Look, about this gin-making palaver. If your mother wants to carry on with it, that's fine, but Mum wants out.'

'I'm sure they'll figure it out between them.'

'My mother is easily persuaded,' he went on. 'She's led such a sheltered life. When you're in the army and live on base, everything is done for you. Adjusting to civilian life has been quite difficult for both my parents.'

'I can only imagine,' I said.

'They're very institutionalised. Dad seems lost without his rules and regulations. He's got his memoirs, but he needs a proper interest. Something structured.'

'He's going to be the new butler,' I said.

'I don't think he's too thrilled about that, but he'll do whatever Mum wants. Yes,' he said slowly, 'this is a good fresh start for them. A new beginning.'

Personally I thought Guy should stay out of his parents' marriage, but I kept that thought to myself.

'Your mother doesn't like Dad and that's going to cause a problem for everyone,' he added. 'Can you talk to her?'

'Mum's just being protective, that's all,' I said. 'Delia is her friend.'

'I know you know what happened. It wasn't Dad's fault,' he persisted. 'He told me that it was only the one time, and I believe him. The girl was crazy and stalked him. It was like something out of *Fatal Attraction*!'

I was growing increasingly uncomfortable. It was obvious that Guy thought his father could do no wrong. I thought of the cashmere scarf from Harrods.

'Kat, come on!' He put down his knife and fork and regarded me with concern. 'You aren't saying anything. Out with it. Something is bugging you. What is it?'

So with great misgivings, I told him what had happened earlier that morning.

As Guy listened, he pushed his half-eaten lunch aside. When at last he spoke, his tone was icy. 'Your mother had no right to unwrap that parcel. She has done incalculable damage.'

'It's really none of your business,' I retorted.

'Yes it is, because . . .' he took a deep breath, 'that gift was meant for me.'

Chapter Eighteen

I was mortified, and also confused. Who was this mystery woman who had sent my new boyfriend such an expensive Christmas present? I wished I hadn't said anything at all.

'How were we to know?' I stammered. 'The parcel was addressed to Evans care of Honeychurch Hall. You don't even live there.'

'So *you* wanted to open it as well?' Guy shook his head with disgust. 'Incredible.'

'Actually, I didn't!' I said hotly. 'I just happened to be there. And anyway, your mother wanted to see what was in it.'

Guy's jaw hardened. 'But it was Iris's idea.'

I pushed my plate to the side as well. 'I don't believe this.' I picked up my glass and drank the rest of my wine, thoroughly irritated.

'Don't believe what?' Guy demanded.

'We're actually having an argument over our *mothers*!' I expected him to smile, but his expression remained cold.

I could feel my anger rising. It was ridiculous, and very

childish. I didn't need this aggravation, especially since we hardly knew each other. I noticed that people in the restaurant were watching. I hoped they couldn't hear what we were saying. I suppose I was still a minor celebrity of sorts, and that made it all the more embarrassing.

'Tell me again exactly what happened,' Guy said. 'Where was this parcel?'

'It was left on the front step at the Hall,' I said coldly. 'Rupert found it and he was not happy. Apparently this has happened before.'

'What has happened before?' Guy said.

I was getting exasperated. 'There was another parcel left there for your father. Ask him, don't ask me.'

'OK. No need to raise your voice.'

'Eric was told to deliver it to your mother's cottage,' I said. 'The three of us happened to be there when he was doing just that.'

It was hard to tell what was going on in Guy's mind, but at this point, I didn't care. He had shown a side of himself that I didn't particularly like, and if there was any hint of a girlfriend in the background, I was just not interested. I'd been down that road before.

'So no title or rank on the envelope?' he went on. 'It just said Evans?'

'What does it matter?' I said.

Guy thought for a moment. 'And the box contained a man's cashmere scarf?'

'Yes, an expensive one. From Harrods. Doused in cheap perfume, by the way.'

'I see. And tell me again what the note said?'

'"With you for always, forever".'

When he didn't comment further, I said, 'Look – I'm really not bothered. As you said, we all have a past.'

He turned on me, his eyes flashing with anger. 'Well I *do* care. I need to know who sent it, and when. It's very important.'

'You mean you don't know who it's from?' I didn't believe that for a moment. 'Have you really got that many admirers?'

He refused to look me in the eye. 'I assume my mother still has the scarf?'

'No, mine does,' I said. 'Delia was upset and Mum thought it was better to take it away. I am more than happy to give it to you later. You can even put it around your Christmas tree.'

He muttered some expletives under his breath. Then all of a sudden, he smiled. 'Sorry,' he said. 'I'm just . . . disappointed. I don't want this to come between us.'

But it already had.

'It's so easy to find out anyone's whereabouts these days on the Internet,' he continued. 'You know I've not led a blameless life before I met you—'

'You don't have to explain or justify anything to me.'

'Can we just forget all this and enjoy the rest of the day?' he said hopefully.

I nodded. 'Sure.' But I didn't mean it.

'I want to show you the barn,' he said. 'We could go via your mother's and pick the scarf up first if that's OK.'

'Sure,' I said again.

'All right, I surrender.' Guy raised his hands in defeat.

'I know I overreacted about the scarf. I suppose . . . I suppose I'm a little jealous.'

'Of what?'

'You and Thomas Crown.'

'David?' I was shocked. 'I already told you, I don't have any feelings for him.'

'I suppose I'll have to believe you. Friends?' He offered his hand, and I took it. 'Are you ready to leave?'

'I have to go back to the Emporium first,' I said.

In the end, we agreed to meet each other back at the car park in forty-five minutes and went our separate ways.

It was when I was leaving the Emporium a little later that I saw them by the recycling dumpster at the far end of the car park.

I thought my heart would stop. Lala was standing by Guy's car, engaged in what definitely looked like a heated conversation, judging by her wild hand gestures.

It was clear that the two of them knew each other.

And then, with a sickening jolt, it hit me. The scarf must have been from her. *With you for always, forever.* Lala was pregnant. What if . . . what if the child was Guy's?

I was gutted. She was married to Angus Fenwick – who I couldn't see anywhere in the car park – and they seemed very happy together, but from the moment I'd met them, I had felt that something was off.

I watched as Lala handed Guy a piece of paper through the open window, then turned and stormed off. Even from this distance, I could see that he was fuming.

Thrusting the Freelander into gear, he roared away, fishtailing across the icy road and attracting more than a few angry stares. I heard someone yell, 'Bloody maniac!'

What on earth was going on? He was supposed to be waiting for me! I wasn't sure what to do. Call him? Should I say I'd seen him with Lala? But wouldn't that make me out to be a paranoid girlfriend? I was utterly miserable – so much for a magical day.

And then I remembered the voices in the churchyard. Guy had been late coming to the pub that night. I bet he had been meeting Lala. Good God. What if it had been Guy who had struck Nick over the head? But why would he do that? I could feel myself growing hysterical, and it was so unlike me.

I stepped away from the dumpster and straight onto someone's foot.

There was a cry of pain.

'Oh God! I am so sorry,' I said, and looked up. It was Angus. 'Did I stand on your bad foot?'

'Fortunately it's the other one,' he said. 'What's the matter? You look like you've seen a ghost.'

'No. I'm fine.' I felt flustered and confused. Had Angus been watching me watching Lala talking to my new boyfriend? Did he know about the pair of them? Did he even care?

'We came back to the Emporium hoping to see you,' he said. 'Ah – here she is now.'

Lala walked towards us all smiles, giving no indication whatsoever that she had just been having a heated discussion with Guy.

Angus brought out his iPhone. 'Excuse me. Must take this call.' He walked out of earshot. I knew that if I didn't ask the question, it would eat me alive.

'I didn't know you knew Guy Evans,' I said lightly.

A flicker of surprise crossed Lala's face, and she looked across at Angus, who, judging by his body language, was not going to get off the phone any time soon.

'I'm sorry, who?' she said.

'I saw you talking to the man in the Freelander,' I said. 'Guy Evans?'

She hesitated. 'Oh . . .' She shrugged. 'I have no idea who he is. He was asking for directions.'

'Guy was asking for directions?' I repeated.

'Why?' she said. 'Is he a friend of yours?'

'He's my boyfriend,' I said. 'Where was he planning on driving?'

Lala looked me straight in the eye. 'Did I say he was asking me?' She gave a silly laugh. 'I meant I was asking him. Angus and I want to visit Berry Pomeroy Castle and we thought he might know where it is.'

'Nowhere near here,' I said. 'And anyway, it's closed in the winter. Excuse me.'

And with that, I hurried to my car, just as Guy reappeared in his. He flashed his lights and pulled up, opening the window.

'Did you do everything you needed to do?' he asked, smiling.

'Yes, thanks.'

'Why don't you follow me? It's quite hard to find the barn once we leave the main road.'

I hesitated. And then made a decision. When we got to the barn, I'd demand to know the truth.

As I followed him out of Dartmouth, I wondered what Dear Amanda would make of it all.

Dear Amanda,

I have just started dating a navy helicopter pilot. Since I will only see him forty days a year, trust is everything. Today he received a Christmas present doused in perfume from an old girlfriend, who then turned up out of the blue. She is pregnant. She is married now to someone else, but his behaviour hints at unfinished business. What if the baby is his? What should I do?

I was quite sure that Amanda's reply would be: *A girl in every port. Move on.*

The main roads had been gritted and so were clear, but when Guy turned into a narrow lane signposted to Larcombe Quarry, it all changed. Snow clung to the towering hedgerows and settled along the channel of grass that ran down the middle.

The lane grew even narrower as it twisted and turned down a steep incline. Below us was a flashing blue light, and as we rounded a bend, we came upon a stationary ambulance. It completely blocked our way – not difficult given that the lane was less than seven feet wide. I couldn't see what lay ahead.

Guy stopped and got out. He squeezed past his Freelander and then past the ambulance and disappeared from view.

I pulled up behind him and did the same, but when I stepped out beyond the ambulance, Guy gesticulated wildly. 'Go back!' he said. 'You don't want to see this.'

Over his shoulder, about twenty yards further down the hill, I could see a raised triangle of rough grass covered in snow below a three-way signpost. And beyond that, I saw two paramedics, the Cruickshank twins, crouched over a figure on the ground.

'What's happened?' I said.

And then I saw a flash of lime green and the mangled remains of a motorbike lying on the road.

'It's Nick!' I gasped, and made to hurry forward, but Guy grabbed my arms and stopped me.

'It's Nick,' I said again. 'Is he hurt?'

'Go back,' repeated Guy. His face was ashen.

'Please let me pass,' I said.

For a moment he couldn't speak, and then he said, 'Kat, Nick's dead.'

Chapter Nineteen

'Dead?' I whispered. 'But . . . how?'

'I don't know what he was doing around here,' said Guy. 'Idiot. He must have taken the hill too fast and clipped the mound at the bottom. He hit the boundary wall to the quarry.'

I still couldn't believe it. Another freak accident. First Seth Cropper and now Nick.

'The problem is that we can't get past the ambulance,' said Guy. 'There is no other way in to the barn.'

I scanned the thick banks of laurel trees above but couldn't see any buildings. 'Where is your house exactly?'

Guy pointed vaguely ahead. 'The entrance is about a hundred yards past Larcombe Cross . . . Wait, here comes one of the paramedics now. Good, let's find out how long the road will be blocked.'

Tony Cruickshank waved a greeting and headed in our direction, leaving his brother John with Nick. Usually I could never tell the identical twins apart, but today Tony was conveniently wearing a red beanie hat with his name on it.

As he came over, I was able to get a better look. Nick's body was on the ground close to the stone boundary wall, a good twenty feet from where his bike had come to rest. There was a deep tyre groove in the snow-covered mound.

'What happened?' Guy asked.

'Poor bugger was killed instantly,' said Tony. 'Broke his neck as he hit the wall.'

I felt sick, and so sad.

'Tragic it is,' he added. 'So close to Christmas. We see a lot of these accidents on green lanes. Kids go too fast and the ground's uneven.'

'Where is the green lane?' I asked.

Tony pointed vaguely behind him. 'Just off Larcombe Cross. It leads back to the village but you can't take a car down there. It's too steep and narrow.'

He regarded Guy with suspicion. 'Was it you who called it in?'

Guy frowned. 'I don't follow.'

'Someone dialled 999 but didn't leave a name.'

'Not me,' said Guy. 'Why?'

'Do you live in these parts, sir?'

I could see Guy stiffening. 'Yes. I just bought Larcombe Barn . . .'

'Oh, right. On the ridge.' Tony gestured to the forested hill above us. 'I'm afraid you're going to be stuck here for a while. The police are on their way.'

'I want to get home.' Guy turned to me. 'We can leave our cars and walk.'

But I didn't want to. The events of the day had really taken their toll. I was tired and very emotional.

'Actually, I'm going to go,' I said. 'I'll reverse back to the main road.'

'You're mad!' Guy exclaimed. 'It's got to be a mile.'

'Trust me, I get a lot of practice.'

'Oh. I see.' Guy seemed disappointed. 'Well at least let me walk you back to your car.'

We left Tony at the ambulance.

'I wish you weren't going,' Guy said. 'Can't you just stay for a bit? Come and have a cup of tea?'

'No, really. I just want to get home.'

He took both my hands in his and looked deeply into my eyes. 'Something has changed between us. I can feel it.'

I took a deep breath. 'I don't know what's going on, but you're not being completely straight with me.'

'Everything is going to be fine,' said Guy. 'Just trust me.'

'I'm not looking for complications, Guy. I'm too old for that.'

'Nor am I, believe me,' he said earnestly. 'I really like you, Kat. And yes, you're right. There are some things I have to sort out, but you have to believe me when I say they have nothing to do with you. Nothing at all.'

'OK,' I said. 'So answer me this. That woman today – Lala Fenwick, she's staying in the village with her husband . . .'

Guy didn't flinch.

'I saw you talking to her in the car park outside the Emporium this afternoon.'

'I'm sorry? Who?' He looked blank. 'Oh! The pregnant woman?'

'Yes. Her.'

'She wanted directions,' he said, but as he held my gaze just a little too long, I knew he was lying.

'So you've never met her before,' I persisted.

'Jesus, Kat. Is this what it's going to be like? I'm away for weeks and months at a time, and if you can't trust me—'

'You can't blame me!' I said. 'You get a present from an old girlfriend—'

'OK. I think it's best that you go home and think about things,' said Guy coldly. 'I'll call you tonight.'

I wanted to tell him not to bother, but he'd already turned away and was squeezing past his car. I was gratified to note that he caught his Barbour sleeve on the wing mirror.

I felt upset. How could our relationship have disintegrated so quickly? I just didn't understand.

It took forever to reverse to the main road, because I couldn't manage to hold the Golf steady. I kept clipping the hedge and having to realign the car. Finally I found an open field in which to turn around.

As I nosed back into the lane again, Shawn's panda narrowly missed the front of my car. He slammed on the brakes and opened his window.

'What are you doing here?' he called out.

'Guy lives at Larcombe Barn,' I said. 'We were on our way there and ran into the ambulance. It's awful. Poor Nick.'

'Was it you who called 999?'

'No. We just came upon it. I was following Guy in his car.'

I must have looked awful, because Shawn said, 'You've had a rough time of it. Are you OK to drive home? I can take you. I mean . . . Nick's not going anywhere, is he?'

I forced a smile. 'What with seeing your grandfather yesterday, and then finding Nick in the churchyard last night . . .'

'Did your boyfriend call for the ambulance?' said Shawn suddenly.

'No. It couldn't have been him. We spent the afternoon together in Dartmouth. He wouldn't have known.'

'And Larcombe Barn is the only house in the area.' Shawn frowned. 'Is anyone else living there?'

'I have no idea.' And I hadn't. Guy could have a whole houseful of pregnant ex-girlfriends up there for all I knew.

'But someone must have called,' Shawn persisted. 'Someone with a mobile who was on high ground.'

'I'm sorry, I just can't help you.'

'You look exhausted,' he said gently. 'My advice is to go home and take it easy this evening.'

'That's exactly what I intend to do.'

As I headed back, I reflected on what had to be the most disappointing date ever. I liked Guy, but as I'd told him, I didn't want to have to deal with any of his baggage – or that stupid scarf. Now I had to go and tell my mother that the present wasn't for Lenny, but rather for Guy, something I didn't exactly relish doing.

I pulled into the cobbled courtyard at the Carriage House and tried her writing house, giving three short taps followed by two fast ones – our secret code – and waiting for her to open the door.

Ushering me inside, she raised a hand. 'Don't speak!'

She darted back to Dad's Olivetti typewriter – she flatly refused to use a computer – pounded the keys in a flurry of high activity and finished the sentence with a loud ping as the carriage hit the return.

'You don't get that kind of satisfaction from a laptop,' she said, and leant back in her chair.

'It sounds like *Betrayed* is coming along nicely,' I commented. 'Is this the third in the Star-Crossed Lovers series?'

'Fourth,' said Mum. 'Quite frankly, living in this village is going to give me enough material to last me for decades.'

'Until your true identity is discovered,' I reminded her. 'Then everyone in the village is going to be very upset with you.'

'I already told you . . . Wait, why are you here? I thought you had a date with the handsome Guy?'

'The scarf was for him,' I said bluntly.

Mum's jaw dropped. 'You told him? Why would you tell him we opened it?'

'I had to. I had to tell him that his mother was upset – and she was, Mum. I saw her earlier at the Hall and she wasn't speaking to Lenny at all.'

I waited for my mother to make the inevitable comment about Guy having an ex-girlfriend who was still very much in the picture, but instead she grabbed one of her Post-its.

'Never mind,' she said airily. 'I can still make that work. It will add a nice twist. The reconciliation of Colonel de Lacy Evans—'

'I'm glad my heartache is coming in useful,' I said drily. 'He wants the scarf back.'

'With pleasure.' Mum went over to the metal filing cabinet in the corner and retrieved the parcel from the bottom drawer, all neatly put back together. 'You're lucky I didn't throw it out. I was going to. Did he explain the note?'

'I didn't ask him,' I said.

'Are you going to tell me what happened?' said Mum. So I did.

Her jaw dropped again. 'You think he and Lala the pregnant limbo dancer are . . . well, I just don't know what to say.'

'It shouldn't matter,' I said. 'It was before me, but I don't like the secrecy.'

'You know the saying, the apple doesn't fall far from the tree,' she said with a knowing look. 'But of course, perhaps we're being too hasty to judge. She's got a husband. It must be his. It takes a rare man to accept another man's child. Maybe Lala wants him to be the godfather.'

'But why lie?'

'Anyway, Delia would have told me,' Mum went on. 'She said Guy had been divorced for a year and that his wife had cheated on him when he was risking his life in Afghanistan.'

'Oh. He didn't tell me that.'

Mum rolled her eyes. 'I think you're just nervous, darling – and tired. You always overthink things when you're tired.'

'There is something else,' I said. 'I saw David.'

'Good grief! *Where?*'

'At Dartmouth Antique Emporium,' I said. 'He's divorced.'

'Yes, I know.' Mum nodded. 'I read about it in *Star Stalkers*.'

'Was *that* why you tried to hide that awful magazine from me?' I said. 'It would have been nice to have some kind of warning.'

'I thought it would upset you. I can give you the copy, though. It's quite a good read.'

'No thank you,' I said primly.

'Trudy cheated on him with her cameraman,' Mum said.

'Yes. He told me.'

'Well be careful,' she went on. 'You don't want to be his sloppy seconds.'

'There is no danger of that,' I said. 'That's the least of my problems. I'm convinced that David is here because of the pocket watches.'

'Ah. Don't say I didn't warn you.' Mum thought for a moment. 'Well? How did he look?'

'Different,' I said. 'He was wearing a Barbour and some kind of work boots. I've never seen him dressed like that before.

'Mark my words, he's come to woo you,' Mum declared. 'You are in demand! Three gorgeous men all clamouring for your attention.'

'Don't you dare write about it, and anyway, that's not the point.'

She gave a heavy sigh. 'Why should any of this be our problem? Whatever the Honeychurch clan got up to in the past is nothing to do with us. You're getting too involved with everything, Katherine. You need to stay in your own lane.'

'Stay in my own *lane*? Where on earth did you hear that expression?'

'Some self-help radio programme, but it's true. We both should. I've decided to stop interfering in Delia's marriage. Good luck to her.'

'There's something else,' I said, 'and this isn't very nice.'

As I told her about poor Nick, Mum clutched at her throat in horror. 'Oh good grief. That is awful.'

'He obviously lost control of his motorbike and hit the wall.'

'And you say the police don't know who dialled 999?'

'Apparently not.'

'Don't you think it strange that someone called for an ambulance and didn't wait for it?' Mum said slowly.

'As you said, we should stay in our own lane.' I headed for the door. 'I'm going to take a long bath. Don't work too late.'

It was nearly ten when my window was lit up by the sweep of headlamps and the sound of a car stopping outside.

I jumped up in a panic. Guy hadn't texted me to say he was coming, and I was already in my pyjamas. I had also left the kitchen in a mess.

I heard the crunch of feet on the gravel outside and then a rap at the door.

'Be right there!' I yelled.

I raced to the bathroom and grabbed a white towelling robe off the hook behind the door. A quick check in the mirror confirmed that I did not have chocolate on my chin. I had been quite miserable when I'd got home, having expected to have enjoyed a wonderful evening with Guy. Instead I had devoured an entire tub of Salcombe Dairy Rich Belgian Chocolate ice cream.

When I opened the door, I was surprised to find that it was Shawn, not Guy, who was standing there.

'Can I come in?' he said.

Chapter Twenty

Shawn's eyes widened with embarrassment. 'I'm so sorry. Did I get you out of bed?'

'No, I was watching TV,' I said.

'I know I should have called, but . . .'

I stepped back to let him pass, then darted to the TV to turn down the sound. I'd been watching *The Thomas Crown Affair* on Netflix.

'Oh, good film,' said Shawn. 'I like Pierce Brosnan better than Steve McQueen. Mind if I take my coat off?'

He hung it over the banisters and took in the living room.

'Nice Christmas tree,' he said. 'Mine was too tall. The boys wanted a large one but it didn't fit in the house and I had to lop the top off.'

'My mother bought me mine from Marks and Spencer,' I said. 'Tea?'

He followed me into the kitchen and perched on a bar stool while we waited for the kettle to boil.

'Camomile, lavender, PG Tips, Earl Grey,' I said. 'What would you like?'

'If it's not too much trouble, I'd like coffee,' he said. 'I'm not finished for the night yet.'

I switched on my Keurig coffee machine – a guilty luxury and one that I had not regretted buying for a minute. Besides, the pods were biodegradable.

'Is Peggy taking care of Ned and Jasper tonight?' I said.

'No.' Shawn shook his head. 'Lizzie, that's Helen's mother—'

'Yes, I know who she is.'

'Oops, sorry,' said Shawn sheepishly. 'I'm not supposed to keep talking about my wife.'

'Don't be silly,' I said. 'You loved her deeply and must miss her every minute of the day.'

'She's been gone for years now and I suppose I've been in limbo,' he said. 'Not the Lala type of limbo, I might add.' He took a deep breath. 'I've handled us all wrong, Kat. I'm sorry.'

I felt my face redden. This was not what I was expecting. 'Don't worry, I—'

'No!' He threw his hand up as though he was directing traffic, and then quickly brought it down again. 'Sorry, force of habit. Please hear me out. All I wanted to say was if you ever get tired of your sailor, let me know.'

'He's actually a helicopter pilot.'

'Ah. Bit more glamorous than a policeman.'

'It's still early days,' I said.

Shawn hesitated, then plunged on. 'I'm glad you're letting

someone into your heart. You are far too lovely to be alone. I only wish . . . Never mind.'

I was touched by his sincerity. 'Thank you. That's a nice thing to say.'

'But we're friends, yes?'

'Of course we are.' I smiled, and he smiled back, holding my gaze for just a moment longer than I could handle.

Shawn was a good man. He was a good father and he had obviously adored his wife. I couldn't imagine how hard it was to raise the boys alone and hold down a demanding job at the same time.

The kettle pinged and I was able to busy myself with making my tea and his coffee.

'How's Peggy doing?' I said to break the moment.

'Not good, I'm afraid,' he replied. 'Lady Lavinia called today to tell her that Delia wants to switch cottages.'

'Ah. I heard that too.'

'Gran is very upset about it and told her that they'd have to take her out feet first,' he continued. 'She was born in that cottage and she plans on dying there.'

'I'm sure she's still in shock.' I handed him a cup of steaming coffee. 'Sugar? Milk?'

'Black. It's going to be a long night.'

We took our drinks into the sitting room and sat down on the sofa.

I stifled a yawn.

'I'm sorry, I'm keeping you awake, but this is important.' Putting his mug down on the coffee table, he pulled out his notebook. 'Can we go back to the churchyard last night?'

'Yes. Why? Surely you can't think there's a connection between Nick's accident today and yesterday's attack?'

'We're keeping an open mind,' said Shawn carefully.

'But . . . didn't Nick just come down the hill too fast and hit the triangle?'

'As I said, we're keeping an open mind . . . Oh, I sound just like a policeman.'

'That's because you *are* a policeman, which leads me to ask: why are you here so late?'

'Nick still lives at home,' said Shawn. 'Yesterday he told his mother that he was on the trail of some big story but wouldn't say what it was.'

'Didn't a branch of Nick's family used to live here on the estate?'

'Decades ago,' said Shawn dismissively. 'His mother confirmed that he had purchased a listening device. We found that on his person last night, but since it was connected to his stolen iPhone, we don't know what was on it and Nick refused to tell us.'

'OK . . .' I said.

Shawn looked uncomfortable. 'We were able to trace today's 999 call back to a mobile phone.'

I gasped. 'Whose was it?'

'It was a burner.'

'A *burner*? Here? In Little Dipperton?' I was stunned.

'We were able to triangulate the cellular towers and know that the call was made extremely close to the accident.'

'You mean . . .' I tried to grasp the implication of what he was saying.

'Yes. Someone was with Nick when he came off that motorbike,' he said grimly. 'And that someone didn't hang around to see if he lived or died.'

When I didn't comment, he added, 'There were traces of black paint on the Suzuki's rear mudguard, suggesting—'

'A collision with another vehicle,' I whispered.

'Or a deliberate attempt to finish the job that was started last night,' agreed Shawn. 'Yes – we believe that Nick Bond was murdered.'

Chapter Twenty-One

'You think Nick was deliberately forced off the road?'
I said. 'But Larcombe Quarry and Guy's barn are the only
places there.'

'I have to ask you this,' said Shawn. 'Did Nick know your
boyfriend?'

'You're asking me because Guy drives a black Freelander,'
I said. 'I told you, I was with Guy. I was *following* Guy. He
was just as shocked as I was.'

'Can you account for your boyfriend's movements this
morning after you left the police station?'

'Please stop calling him my boyfriend, and no, I can't, but
he did say he was going to meet his father at Violet's tea room
because Nick wanted to take Lenny's photograph for the
newspaper.'

Shawn wrote that down.

I didn't add that when I saw Lenny at the Hall afterwards,
he had said that the interview had taken place, but that when

I saw Guy, he said that it hadn't. Given that Lala was staying at Violet's B and B, I didn't know what to think.

'All I can tell you is that I met Guy in Dartmouth for lunch,' I said wearily. 'We spent the afternoon together and then we found Nick. Together.'

'So is it possible that Guy returned to Larcombe Barn after he left the police station this morning?' asked Shawn.

'I suppose so,' I admitted miserably. 'But . . . when do you think Nick had the accident?'

'We're still establishing a time frame . . . I'm sorry,' said Shawn. 'I can see you're tired and upset. But you know I wouldn't be asking if it wasn't important.'

He went to get his coat and gestured to the TV. 'Maybe I prefer Steve McQueen after all.'

When Guy texted me goodnight a little later, I didn't reply. Everything was so confusing. I'd been so looking forward to spending time with him, but now I just didn't know.

I woke early the following morning with a deep sense of foreboding.

The gloomy day matched my mood. A heavy mist had settled over the countryside and the air was so cold it hurt to breathe. I donned my thermal undies, two pairs of socks and three sweaters, and somehow managed to put my riding coat over the top.

Mum's Mini was parked outside Delia's cottage, but Lenny's car wasn't there. There were a number of removals boxes piled in the lane, and the door to Peggy's cottage stood wide open.

Delia emerged from Peggy's front door wrapped up in a woollen scarf and one of her hand-knitted bobble hats. She was carrying a standard lamp and waved a greeting.

'Guy told you, didn't he?' she exclaimed.

'Told me what?'

She beamed happily. 'The scarf was a present for him! Not for Lenny at all!'

'Yes, he told me,' I said.

'I feel so silly!'

'Kat!' Mum beckoned from the doorway. 'I thought I heard your voice. You have to come and see right this minute.'

'Mum,' I protested.

'No, Katherine. Really. You have to come right *now*!'

Reluctantly I parked my car and followed them both inside.

'Have you put on weight?' Mum demanded.

'I'm wearing about five thousand layers,' I said.

'And speaking of layers . . .' Delia looked cautiously over her shoulder as if making sure she wasn't overheard. 'Before we go into the cellar, I want to ask you to promise not to mention the scarf situation in front of Lenny.'

'Why not?' Mum demanded.

'I just don't want you to.' Delia thrust her jaw out. 'Do I have to have a reason?'

'It's your life,' said Mum.

Delia smiled. 'Guy always was popular with the ladies.'

'So it would seem,' I said drily.

'Not that he's like that any more,' she added quickly. 'Now he's met you.'

'So what is it you want to show me?' I said, anxious to change the subject.

'Wait! Don't go down there without me,' Delia squealed. 'I need to ring Lenny to tell him to stop on his way home for some more packing tape. I'll be right back.' She headed for the front door.

'Where is Lenny?' I asked Mum.

'Gone to Homebase to get more paint for Guy, apparently,' said Mum. 'They're determined to finish the entire barn by Friday.'

We trooped into Peggy's living room and dutifully waited for Delia to return. It looked like half the place had been packed up. Open cardboard boxes sat on the dining room table full of china plates and serving dishes. Books had been taken off the shelves and stacked neatly, while other boxes held knick-knacks that looked like they could easily break during the short journey next door. One contained Scrabble, Monopoly, Cluedo and mah-jong.

'I think this is all wrong, Mum,' I said. 'And you really shouldn't be getting involved.'

She pointed to the sideboard, where wedding anniversary cards marked sixty years of married bliss.

'Oh no!' I exclaimed. 'When was their anniversary?'

'On Saturday, the day before Seth died,' said Mum. 'Don't you think it looks like a shrine?'

She was right, it did. Framed photographs of the Croppers' lives together over the years were arranged along the top of the sideboard. Many of them showed the couple seated on a wooden bench in front of a large expanse of water. In the background was a ruined brick building with a tall chimney – the same set-up as the one I'd seen next to Seth's collection bucket at the pub.

'Larcombe Quarry,' said Mum. 'All in ruins now, but in my day we used to go there for a bit of skinny-dipping.'

I felt sad. 'They were so young.'

'The quarry mined slate back then,' she went on. 'Many a romantic rendezvous was planned in the foreman's hut.' She smiled at a memory. 'And then his lordship's father closed it down and allowed the quarry to fill with water. That pit was at least two hundred feet deep. We still swam in it, though even at the height of summer it was freezing cold.'

'Which is very dangerous,' I reminded her.

'Yes, but no one bothered about that kind of thing. We didn't wear seat belts, we played outside until dark and there weren't such things as mobile phones.'

'Or in your case, any phone,' I said.

Mum fell quiet. 'Seth proposed to Peggy on that wooden bench – I know what she's going through.' She had tears in her eyes. 'To lose your soulmate . . . Sometimes you don't think you can go on.'

'Oh Mum.' I gave her a hug.

'You'd think I'd be over losing your father now, wouldn't you? I mean, it's going to be two years in April.'

'You'll never get over it,' I said. 'You'll just adjust to the new normal.'

Delia burst into the cottage. 'Lenny's not answering his phone. Let's go – this way!' She opened the door to the cellar and flipped the light switch. 'I'll go down first.'

When we got to the bottom of the wooden steps, I stopped in stunned silence.

The cellar was filled with dozens and dozens of empty bottles, piled at least three feet high. It resembled a sea of glass.

'Gin and vodka,' Mum said gleefully. 'You name it, they're all hidden down here.'

I looked to Delia in amazement. 'But . . .'

Delia thrust an empty vodka bottle in my face. 'Look at the price. I know my prices when it comes to this sort of thing, and I can tell you, this was on sale only last week.'

'Seth had been drinking all the time!' Mum was triumphant. 'He never fell off the wagon, because he was never on it!'

I thought of the collection bucket on the bar at the Hare and Hounds. 'Peggy didn't know, did she?'

'Nope.' Delia was virtually expiring with excitement. 'The door to the cellar was locked. Lenny had to kick it open.'

'Yes,' Mum declared. 'Seth was a total drunk.'

'So you see, Kat,' Delia went on, 'your mother is not to blame for his fall and subsequent death.'

Mum bristled. 'I was never to blame for Seth's fall,' she snapped. 'As I've said a gazillion times, I believed I was giving him water, not gin.'

'Why keep all the bottles hidden down here?' I wondered.

'Because his lordship is a stickler for recycling,' Mum said. 'Or have you forgotten?'

'And obviously Seth didn't want Peggy to know,' added Delia.

I was appalled. 'How can she *not* have known?'

'Perhaps she didn't want to,' said Delia. 'Sometimes people don't.'

'Well, there is that,' said Mum pointedly.

There was an uncomfortable silence.

'Do you want to see the box room?' Delia pointed to a small door underneath the open-tread staircase. 'It's through there.'

'What's in it?' Mum said.

'Just bits of old junk. There's even a car door in there from a Morris Minor. Lenny thought we should leave it, but I said no, a fresh start is a fresh start. Everything must go!'

'But . . . there might be things in there that are important to Peggy,' I protested. 'You're like vultures swarming around a carcass! Frankly, I am disgusted at the pair of you.'

Mum had the grace to look embarrassed, but Delia remained defiant. 'Her ladyship said I should do as I see fit, so I am.'

'I'm leaving,' I said, and showed my displeasure by stomping childishly up the stairs, only to come face to face with Shawn at the top.

'What on earth are you doing down there?' he demanded. 'Where is my grandmother?'

Chapter Twenty-Two

I didn't know what to say, but then I didn't have to.

'Yes, Lenny's going to call a house clearance company and get rid of all this rubbish,' I heard Delia say.

Confusion flooded Shawn's face. 'Who is in the cellar?'

'Delia and my mother.'

'With my grandmother?'

'Um, no.' I wished the floor would open and swallow me up. 'She's not here.'

'I'm sorry, I don't understand.' Shawn scanned the room, and I suddenly saw what he must have seen. A house in complete disarray, with cardboard boxes filled haphazardly with personal effects. 'What are all these boxes doing here?'

I stood there tongue-tied.

Shawn drew himself up to his full height. Colour flooded his face. He was livid. 'What the hell is going on?'

At that moment, Mum and Delia returned from the cellar to be confronted with a very angry policeman.

'Hello,' said Delia gaily. 'Tell Peggy that Iris and I are

going to make sure that her new home is even nicer than her old one. In fact Lenny is going to paint our cottage so that it's fresh for when she returns.'

'Put everything back,' Shawn said coldly.

'But . . . why? Lady Lavinia said we could switch,' Delia whined.

'Did you speak to the dowager countess?' he demanded.

'Not yet,' said Delia. 'But I will.'

'If my grandmother isn't here,' said Shawn, 'then where is she?'

And then I realised that this was not a social call. He looked very worried. 'What's happened?' I asked.

'It seems that Gran has vanished. I was under the impression that she was resting in her bedroom and did not want to be disturbed, but it turns out that she caught the bus back to Little Dipperton yesterday afternoon.'

'*Yesterday?*' I exclaimed.

'She hasn't been seen since,' he added.

'She wasn't here this morning,' said Delia. 'The door wasn't locked and her bed hasn't been slept in.'

'I haven't seen her either,' Mum put in. 'And to be honest, the bus is hardly reliable in this weather. Are you sure she's not at the Hall?'

'Of course I'm sure!' Shawn exclaimed.

'So . . . does that mean that she would have walked from the bus stop all the way home?' Mum said. 'It has to be at least two miles.'

'There's a shortcut through Larcombe Woods,' he said. 'What if she fell? It was below freezing last night. She would never survive a night out in the open, especially if she was hurt.'

No wonder he was frantic.

'Perhaps she stopped off to see a friend?' Mum suggested.

'A friend?' Shawn looked at my mother as though she had suggested that Peggy had stopped off to meet an elephant. 'No. She would have come straight home.'

'Should we all go out looking for her?' I said.

'I can't,' said Delia. 'I've got the lunch to prepare.'

'Clive is Christmas shopping,' said Shawn. 'He won't be free until later this afternoon. I'll ask him to bring Fluffy the bloodhound and we'll see if we can track Gran through Larcombe Woods. I can't think of anywhere else to look.'

'How do you know she actually got the bus to the village?' I said. 'Doesn't she have a cousin in Dartmouth? Maybe she went there.'

'Violet saw her get off the bus just after three yesterday afternoon,' Shawn said. He pointed to the anniversary cards that lined the sideboard. 'It was their wedding anniversary on Saturday. Larcombe was a special place for her. It's where my grandfather proposed, and every year they would return to the quarry to have their photograph taken.'

'I'm riding with Harry this morning,' I said. 'We'll go that way.'

'Honey, I'm home!' came a shout, and Lenny strolled through the front door carrying a roll of packing tape. 'You'll never guess what I just heard. That newspaper reporter is dead – motorbike accident—'

The moment he saw Shawn, his face fell. 'Oh. What's wrong?'

'Peggy Cropper has gone AWOL,' said Delia. 'You didn't see her wandering around the lanes on your way back from Homebase, did you?'

'I thought she was supposed to staying with you?' Lenny said to Shawn.

'Wait,' said Delia. 'Which reporter? That young lad Nick?'

'I'm afraid so,' said Shawn.

'Well he was alive yesterday morning, because Lenny met him at Violet's tea room. He took Lenny's photograph for this Saturday's edition of the *Dipperton Deal*.'

'What time was that?' said Shawn sharply.

'It never happened,' Lenny said quickly. 'He never showed up – maybe because he'd already had his accident.'

Delia's expression darkened. 'You told me that you saw him yesterday morning. I distinctly remember that, because you were late meeting her ladyship.'

I had heard him say it too, but I kept quiet.

'I said no such thing.' Lenny laughed. 'Have you been at the gin already?'

'Guy said that he was going to Violet's tea room so you could meet Nick together,' Delia persisted.

'Guy and I got our wires crossed,' said Lenny. 'What does it matter?'

'What car do you drive, sir?' said Shawn.

'I've got a BMW convertible, but I'm driving Guy's Freelander today,' said Lenny. 'I had to pick up some paint from Homebase. Why?'

'There was some damage to Nick's rear mudguard,' said Shawn. 'Traces of black paint that suggest there had been a collision.'

'That puts me in the clear,' said Mum cheerfully. 'My Mini is chilli red and Kat's Golf is silver.'

'Lord Rupert has a black Range Rover,' Delia put in.

'The problem is that someone called the police to report the accident,' said Shawn, regarding us all keenly. 'But whoever it was didn't wait for help to arrive.'

'A hit and run, eh?' said Lenny.

'Can't you trace the mobile number?' Mum said. 'Isn't that what they do on the telly?'

'It was from a disposable phone,' said Shawn.

'I have a disposable phone,' Mum said. 'It's in my handbag. Feel free to check my call log, but I rarely keep it on. Anyone can buy this kind of thing. It's just a top-up.'

'If you ask me, this has got something to do with that hawk,' Delia said slowly. 'Peggy told me it was cursed. First Seth is crushed to death under a suit of armour, then Peggy vanishes, and now that poor lad has been killed in a motor-bike accident. What have they all got in common? The hawk!'

'Well that's as may be,' said Shawn gravely. 'But for the time being, I would ask you all to be vigilant.'

'No . . . wait!' Delia snapped her fingers. 'Forget the hawk. Perhaps it has something to do with the stolen watches?'

'Watches?' said Lenny sharply.

'That's right. Don't you remember, in the pub? His lordship was offering a reward for any information.'

'I don't remember anything about that.'

'Where have you been?' Delia scoffed. 'It's all over the village!'

'I don't see the connection at all,' said Mum.

Shawn was scribbling in his notebook. 'Thank you,' he said. 'You've all been very helpful.'

'Don't worry,' said Delia. 'I'm sure Peggy will turn up.'

Mum nodded. 'If she's in Larcombe Woods, Kat will find her.'

'I feel like I missed the party,' complained Lenny.

'Don't worry, I'll fill you in,' said Delia.

I couldn't wait to get to the stables. Unlike the Hall, no expense had been spared. The entrance was marked by a grand archway topped with a dovecote and a clock, with another archway directly opposite that led to the service road beyond.

As I gazed at the horses peering over the green-painted half-doors, the bizarre events of the last twenty-four hours thankfully faded away.

I loved being around such noble creatures and felt lucky that the dowager countess encouraged me to ride as much as I liked.

I watched as Alfred led Jupiter out of her loose box, all tacked up and ready for me to mount.

'She's a bit skittish today, Kat,' he said, giving the grey mare an affectionate pat. 'Doesn't like the cold too much.'

With his thatch of white hair, steel-rimmed glasses and jaw like a French bulldog, Alfred seemed more suited to the boxing ring than the stable yard, but the dowager countess relied on him implicitly. He had a magical way with horses as well as possessing psychic powers.

I couldn't help it. I had to ask. 'As you've probably heard, Peggy Cropper has gone missing. Are you getting any signs from the universe?'

He paused for a moment to think. 'She'll be all right,' he said gruffly.

'But where is she?' I asked.

'I only see pictures, and all I can say is that it's dark. Very dark,' he added. 'Here comes Master Harry. Reckon you'll be getting a scolding.'

Harry emerged from a loose box with Thunder, his little black pony. Dressed for the cold in a sheepskin flying jacket, he also wore his trademark aviator gear.

'You're late, Stanford!' he cried as he deftly mounted Thunder. 'We were supposed to meet at o-eleven-hundred sharp!'

'Sorry, sir,' I said. 'Last-minute orders from above. We'll be riding to Larcombe Woods this morning.'

'Larcombe Woods! Oh *wicked*!' Harry exclaimed, dropping his alter ego for a moment before adding, 'Are we going to look for the OBs?' Seeing my confusion, he added, 'Operational bases.'

I remembered that Doreen had said something about those.

'There are more than thirty-two OBs in Devon,' continued Harry. 'They're *everywhere*.'

'Kat!' came a cry. 'Wait!'

Lavinia hurried over looking harassed and worried. The slumber net she wore over her unkempt blonde hair was askew and her navy puffa jacket had a rip in the sleeve.

'Frightful business,' she declared as she joined us. 'Shawn called Rupert and told him that Mrs Cropper is missing.'

Harry's eyes widened. 'Golly! Is that our mission?'

'We *ab-so-lutely* must have her back for the annual Honeychurch gift-giving event,' Lavinia went on. 'It's frightfully selfish of her to go off like that. Do you think she's sulking?'

'I don't think sulking is the right word,' I said carefully. 'Peggy has just lost her husband, and now it would seem she is likely to lose her home too.'

'Home? You mean . . . that little cottage?' Lavinia looked stunned. 'Why on earth would that upset her? What difference does it make? She's only moving next door. Delia needs the cellar for storage purposes, and number one doesn't have a cellar. It's not like I'm banishing her to live in the village.'

'Quite right, m'lady,' said Alfred. 'I can't think of a worse place to live.'

'Thank you, Alfred.' Lavinia was oblivious to his sarcasm. 'We *must* get her back before Edith comes home. What time is her train, Alfred?'

'She gets in at one, m'lady.'

'Oh dear.' Lavinia bit her lip. 'And still no sign of those wretched pocket watches. Kat – you're in the antique trade. Have you heard anything?'

'I'm afraid not,' I said.

'Edith is going to hit the roof. Rupert has offered a *massive* reward, but the only person who came forward was that beastly newspaper reporter. Dreadful chap. Told Rupert a pack of lies.'

Clearly Lavinia had not heard that Nick was dead.

'He had the nerve . . . the *nerve* to come to the Hall!' she exclaimed.

'I'm afraid that was my fault,' I said. 'I didn't know he was banned. I just thought that getting some media coverage for the museum open house would be a good idea.'

'Well . . . he has caused a *huge* stink,' Lavinia said. 'He told Rupert that the watches had been reported stolen years ago, which of course is *ab-so-lutely* untrue! He even threatened to go to the police. He said he had enough information to bring the family down! Even said we could lose the Hall! Rupert is *livid.*'

For once, Lavinia was on the right track.

'Yes,' she ran on. 'He cornered Rupert in the churchyard on Sunday, and then again at the post office yesterday afternoon! Made a *frightful* scene. It's all because of that *dreadful* scandal years ago—'

'What scandal, Mummy?' said Harry.

Lavinia looked startled. 'Oh, take no notice of Mummy. She's just being silly.' She gestured to the clock, which had stood at 9.35 since I had arrived over a year ago. 'Golly! Is that the time?' And with a brief 'Have a good ride, darlings,' she scurried away.

Lavinia's comments were worrying. I knew how much Rupert disliked Nick – he'd made that obvious – and now she had confirmed that the two men had argued. She had also confirmed the fact that Rupert was still in the dark about the insurance scam that had been masterminded by his father all those years ago – or if he wasn't, he certainly hadn't told his wife about it. And I still wasn't sure where the money the children had found in the stumpery fitted in. Perhaps it had something to do with Nick, but I just couldn't be sure. The whole thing was a total mess.

Putting Rupert in the village also put him near Larcombe Cross yesterday, coincidentally at the same time that Peggy had got off the bus. Rupert drove a black car. If anyone had a lot to lose, it was the 15th Earl of Grenville.

Chapter Twenty-Three

Soon Harry and I were on our way. Riding out together had become a regular event that I always looked forward to. I still wanted kids and hoped that at forty it wasn't too late. My thoughts turned to Guy. I wondered what kind of father he would make, but then I reminded myself of his job. Could I handle the long separations? What if he was posted somewhere else and I had to move?

When I first left *Fakes & Treasures*, Mum and I were going to open an antique shop in Brick Lane. It was all I had been thinking about. When she'd upped sticks and vanished to the countryside, I never dreamed in a million years that I would actually move to the West Country, let alone be happy here.

It was one of the more sobering things about getting older. In my twenties I would have just plunged in with Guy and hoped for the best, believing that love would conquer all. There wasn't the baggage that came with past relationships, failed or otherwise. But now I didn't have the time for that kind of indulgence.

I liked to think I was a realistic optimist, and frankly, although I liked Guy a lot, I wasn't sure I liked Lenny and Delia. How could someone so lovely have such awful parents?

There was also my own mother. Shortly before Dad had died, he'd made me promise to look after her. At the time I had thought it was because she might be unable to deal with practical things like servicing her car, or just facing the usual deterioration that went with ageing. As things turned out, his request seemed to have a deeper meaning, because Mum was forever getting herself into trouble – and somehow that always seemed to involve me.

'We should check Larcombe Quarry too, and not just the footpath,' said Harry, breaking into my thoughts.

'Isn't it fenced off?' I asked.

'I know a secret way in. It's at the end of Hopton's Crest. I'll show you.'

'Lead the way, Squadron Leader Bigglesworth,' I said.

Hopton's Crest was one of my favourite bridleways. Named after Sir Ralph Hopton, a Royalist commander in the Civil War who secured the south-west of England for Charles I, the rough track had run along the top of this ridge for over four hundred years.

On one side nestled the small village of Little Dipperton, and on the other, tucked between trees and centuries-old dry-stone walls, lay the Honeychurch Hall estate. Views of Haytor Rocks on distant Dartmoor could be seen on the skyline.

We rode side by side, Harry chattering non-stop about operational bases, his latest discovery.

'They were buried ten feet underground and packed with explosives, ammunition and provisions,' he told me. 'They're very difficult to see because the openings are camouflaged. And when you do find them, you have to climb down a narrow shaft to get into the bunker.'

'Ugh, that sounds claustrophobic.' I had a fear of enclosed spaces – hardly surprising given the fact that not so long ago I had been trapped in one of the secret hides at the Hall with the only escape being via a chimney flue.

'What if Mrs Cropper has fallen into one of them?' said Harry.

'Let's cross that bridge if and when we come to it.'

He went on to tell me how highly trained men from the surrounding villages formed covert auxiliary units that were ready to resist the Germans when they invaded. Following the surrender of France to Germany in 1940, that threat was very real.

Harry was obsessed with both world wars and was a mine of information. I encouraged it. I liked the fact that he was interested in history when so many kids were glued to their tablets and iPhones. It was refreshing. When I asked him where he got his information, he told me it was all in the Honeychurch library.

'The chaps were recruited for their local knowledge,' he went on. 'They had to sign the Official Secrets Act and everything. Then they'd be assigned to the Home Guard. Granny said that she suspected two of the gardeners were part of it, but of course it was a secret, so they wouldn't tell.'

'They must have been very brave men.'

'I would have *definitely* volunteered,' he said enthusiastically. 'Recruits were formed into cells or operational patrols of seven or eight men, all trained in stealth and sabotage. Their orders were to emerge at night to destroy supply dumps, block roads, derail trains and assassinate Germans! But the major said they would only have lasted two weeks before being discovered.'

'You told Major Evans all this?'

'Yes,' said Harry.

'And why did he say two weeks?'

'Sniffer dogs.' Harry's voice was solemn. 'And of course if the railways were blown up, the local people would have been tortured for helping the resistance.'

Hopton's Crest came to an end and opened into a sunken lane. If we turned right, it would take us up to the main road to Dartmouth, which Guy and I had driven down yesterday. If we turned left, we descended to Larcombe Cross and the scene of Nick's accident. There, we could either turn right again to Larcombe Quarry, passing the entrance to Guy's barn, or go straight over to the green lane that eventually wound downhill and came out behind the church in the village below.

Of course I couldn't stop thinking about Nick. It was hard not to. We were riding past the exact place where he had come off his motorbike. The deep groove was still visible in the snow-covered mound.

Harry pointed to the boundary wall, which was no more than six feet tall and part stone, part hedgerow.

'The quarry is behind there,' he said.

Just a few yards further down there was a large gap, and beyond that, the wall had collapsed completely. I was worried. The place was clearly dangerous.

'I don't like that fact that you've been down here, Harry,' I said.

'I'm always careful,' he told me. 'I promise. And I never go to the edge. I'll show you.'

With great trepidation, I followed him to the gap in the wall. Harry reined in and I pulled up behind him.

'See,' he said. 'Over there.'

I was horrified. The quarry pit was enormous, and it seemed to come out of nowhere. The sheer cliff face disappeared into blackness below. There wasn't even a barbed-wire fence between where we stood and the edge, which couldn't have been more than two yards away.

'It's over two hundred feet deep!' Harry said.

'Come back from there,' I said sharply. 'I'm not sure this is a good idea. I've changed my mind.'

'But this isn't the secret way in,' he said. 'The secret way in is down that lane. There's a ruined mining village and everything. You said we had to look for Mrs Cropper. I bet she's down there.'

I hesitated for a moment. 'OK, but on one condition.'

'Anything!'

'You must tell me the truth about finding the blood speckles on the hawk.'

'Oh.' Harry's face fell.

'Harry? That's the deal.'

He straightened his little shoulders. 'I'm afraid I can only give you my name, rank and serial number,' he said, reverting to his alter ego.

'OK, then home we go.' I turned Jupiter around to head back the way we had come.

'Oh no! Please don't,' begged Harry. 'But really, I can't tell you.'

I regarded his earnest face.

'It wasn't me,' he said. 'I swear.'

'That hawk is priceless,' I told him. 'Your father has sent for a specialist in Egyptian artefacts to look at it, at great expense.' This was not yet true, but could be. 'He will take it away for testing and they will be able to find out exactly who tampered with it.'

'No! You have to stop him!' Harry cried. 'He'll be so angry. I swear I didn't touch it.'

'It was Fleur, wasn't it?' I said.

Harry didn't answer.

'Harry, it's all very honourable being loyal to your friend,' I said. 'But when someone does something wrong like that, you need to think very carefully about your friendship.'

'I told her not to do it,' he whispered. 'But she wouldn't listen. And now the bird is angry and that's why so many bad things are happening.'

'That's just superstition,' I said briskly.

'But it's true, isn't it? And if Mrs Cropper is dead . . . She touched the hawk. She told us she did. Mr Cropper did too.'

'Pure coincidence,' I said. 'What exactly did Fleur use on the bird?'

'Red food colouring from the kitchen,' he said miserably. 'You can make fake blood with it.'

I nodded. 'Cochineal. It's a food dye.'

'A dye! Does that mean it won't come off?' Harry wailed. 'I'm sorry, Kat.'

'Don't apologise to me. It's your father you need to say it to.'

'I can't,' he said. 'He'll send Fleur away.'

Personally I thought it would be better for Harry if he did. 'Don't you think she would be happier spending Christmas with her family anyway?'

Harry nodded. 'She told me she misses her mummy.'

'Of course she does,' I exclaimed. 'So will you talk to your father?'

Harry thought for a moment, then nodded. 'OK. I promise.'

'Lead the way, Biggles.'

Ten minutes later, we stopped at a broken gate that was barely visible in the undergrowth. 'That's the way in,' Harry said.

The gate was too rotten to move, but there was an opening beside it that indicated we weren't the first to go this way. It was a squeeze on horseback, but somehow we managed it, even though I practically lost my kneecap on the gatepost. Beyond it was an animal track, and we set off along it in single file.

'Who showed you this secret way in?' I asked.

'William,' Harry replied.

I hadn't heard that name in a long time. In fact I had

forgotten all about the handsome stable manager who had been working at the Hall when Mum and I first arrived. His tenure there had ended in a prison sentence. As far as I knew, Harry still believed that he had gone off on an expedition to the Himalayas.

'He told me that a travelling fair and boxing emporium used to camp in the park in the summer months. Everyone would come down and swim in the quarry.'

'It must have been lovely before it got so overgrown,' I said. 'But it's still dangerous, and somewhere that you should never come on your own.'

The animal track joined a sunken path made up of broken slate and granite. It was flanked by steep banks carpeted in green moss and strewn with exposed tree roots. A canopy of unruly laurel arched overhead. The horses slipped on the path, which was slick with water that ran off from the hillside above. With every step our way grew darker and more sinister.

I tried to get my bearings. It was difficult because the laurel was thick and impenetrable. It seemed to have grown into every available space, choking whatever trees and shrubs had been there before. The effect was creepy.

At last we emerged onto the main track, where an extra-ordinary row of rusting Victorian lamp posts, still covered in snow, disappeared into the undergrowth, creating a Narnia-like landscape.

It was getting decidedly colder. I knew we had to be close to the water, but I still couldn't see it.

Harry told me that at the turn of the last century, when

the quarry was at its most productive, the slate had to be taken out by wheeled wooden carts pulled by donkeys.

'We're riding along the old cart tracks now,' he said. Peering left and right into the dense undergrowth, he added, 'I wonder where the OBs are hidden.'

I refrained from saying it would be like looking for a needle in the proverbial haystack.

At last we reached the ruined mining village – a wheel-house with a tall chimney reaching up to the sky and half a dozen one-storey brick houses with no roofs and gaping windows. Rusting machinery rubbed shoulders with piles of rubble and abandoned mounds of slate. It was incredibly depressing.

I thought of the photographs I'd seen on Peggy's sideboard.

'When did you say the quarry closed?'

'I'm not sure,' said Harry. 'At least seventy years ago.'

I marvelled at how quickly nature reclaimed her territory once man had left.

He pointed to a muddle of wooden planks criss-crossed against the hillside. Someone had spray-painted: *Danger Keep Out*.

'That's the way into the underground workings,' he said. 'There's also a tunnel that they used to transport dynamite, but William and I couldn't find it.'

So far I hadn't seen the water at all. 'Where is the quarry?'

Harry grinned. 'This way.'

We rounded a ruined building, and suddenly there it was. Sheer cliffs embraced all four sides. As I looked up, I could just make out where Harry and I had been standing earlier. He was right. It had to be a couple of hundred feet.

'The bottom of the quarry is under the water and at least another hundred feet down,' he said as if reading my mind.

Ice floes sat on a surface that did not move. It was so still that the silence hurt my ears. To my right was an old wooden jetty. Framed against the wheelhouse chimney, I recognised the bench where Seth and Peggy had sat together.

'There are giant eels in there the size of twelve-foot pythons,' said Harry.

'Who told you that?' I scoffed.

'William,' he exclaimed. 'He said he only swam in there once and he would never do it again. One touched his leg. It had teeth the size of a great white shark.'

'You won't get *me* swimming in there,' I said with a shudder of revulsion. 'It sounds disgusting.'

'And the water is so cold that you would die within seconds,' Harry said with glee.

It was hard to imagine this derelict and deserted place being full of life and laughter all those years ago.

And then I saw it. My stomach gave a lurch, and I quickly dismounted.

'What's wrong?' said Harry anxiously.

Under the bench in the snow was an empty packet of Fisherman's Friend cherry-flavoured lozenges – Mrs Cropper's favourite cough sweet. So she had been here, and presumably not that long ago given the fact that the wrapping had not turned into pulp. I shoved it into my pocket.

'Peggy!' I called out, and Harry joined in. We shouted

until we were hoarse, but all we heard was the echo of our own voices.

'Where is the footpath back to Little Dipperton?' I said finally. 'We need to tell Shawn that we think she was here.'

But Harry didn't answer. He was staring out over the water and had gone very quiet.

'What's the matter?' I said.

He pointed a tremulous finger. 'What's that? Is it . . . is it . . .'

My heart turned over as I saw what he was looking at.

Out in the water across from the jetty, a figure was lying on an ice floe.

'Is it a body?' he whispered.

For a brief moment I had thought so too, but then my rational mind kicked in. The figure was far too small, and the wrong shape.

'No,' I said. 'Thank God.'

'What is it, Stanford?' In his relief, Harry had reverted to his alter ego. 'An ammunition drop?' He began to dismount. 'Let's go and inspect it.'

'No, Harry. Stay right here.'

I handed him Jupiter's reins. I was about to step onto the jetty, but had second thoughts. It just didn't look safe. I decided to walk around to the other side and have a look.

It wasn't far, but the path was just a ledge that followed the waterline and was only two feet wide. I started to think about the eels.

As I drew closer, I sighed with relief. 'It's only a black

dustbin bag,' I called back to Harry. Had someone come all
this way to fly-tip?

And then my eye caught a splash of pink caught in the
reeds. And another. Then a third – a dark yellow this time.

I reached down to scoop one up, only to stare in astonishment.

It was Monopoly money.

Chapter Twenty-Four

'**What is this doing here?**' **I asked Harry as I hurried back.**

'Money! So we were right, Stanford,' he said. 'The Germans have been dealing in ammo—'

'This is not the time for games!' I said sharply. 'Take off your goggles, please.'

Harry gasped. 'I'm not playing games.'

'Take them off now!'

He hesitated for a moment and then did as he was told. I showed him the money. 'Is this yours?'

To my dismay, I realised that I was looking at a little boy who seemed just as confused as I was.

'No,' he exclaimed. 'I don't even like the game. It's boring.'

'But you *have* been down here.'

'No,' he said again. 'I promise.'

'Or Fleur has.' I was furious, but in truth I was also frightened. These kids seemed to roam wherever they wanted at will. 'Please don't lie to me.'

'But I'm not!' Harry wailed.

I thrust the notes into my pocket and mounted Jupiter. 'Let's go home.'

We retraced our steps and didn't speak again until we reached Little Dipperton. The footpath back to the village wasn't far at all.

As we clattered past Violet's tea room, Lala came rushing out and waved us down. She seemed upset. Dark circles sat under her eyes and her face was devoid of make-up, making her look deathly pale. She wore her hair pulled back into a ponytail.

'Where were you riding today?' she asked.

'We've just come through Larcombe Woods. What's the matter? Is everything all right?'

'You didn't see Angus anywhere?'

'No. Why?'

'He went for a walk yesterday and didn't come back . . . Well, he must have come back at some point, because our car has vanished.' She stepped closer to Jupiter and went on in an urgent low voice, 'I think something awful has happened to him.'

Harry was watching us, white-faced. 'He touched the hawk, didn't he? I told him not to! Bad things happen to people who touch the hawk.'

'Oh shut up!' Lala said hysterically.

'Don't speak to him like that,' I snapped.

Lala's face crumpled as though she was about to cry. 'Oh God, I'm sorry. It's just . . . something is wrong. I don't understand why he would just disappear and not tell me where he was going.'

'Has he done anything like that before?' I asked.

'No!' she said. 'Never. If the car hadn't been missing, I would have thought he'd got lost in Larcombe Woods.'

'Why would he have gone there in the first place?' I asked.

'I don't know.' She shrugged. 'He just wanted to explore a little.'

'Obviously you've tried to call him.'

'I've left messages, but it goes straight to voicemail.' She looked so worried that my heart went out to her.

'Then you need to call the police,' I said.

'No! No police,' she declared. 'Don't worry. I shouldn't have told you. I'll wait and see if he comes back today.'

Harry didn't say another word on the way home. I felt terrible for speaking to him the way I had, but the thought of what could happen down in the quarry should they go there unsupervised just filled me with horror.

Back at the stables, I was surprised to see Mum's Mini parked just outside the archway.

I found her in the courtyard talking to Alfred. She waved, and pointed to where the formidable dowager countess, Lady Edith Honeychurch, was hammering on the tack-room door. Dressed in a neat navy coat and hat, Edith looked as though she had come straight from the railway station.

'Lavinia! Stop all this nonsense!' she was shouting. 'Come out now!'

Harry and I dismounted, and Alfred led Thunder away, followed by a very subdued little boy.

'What are you doing here?' I said to Mum, taking in her smart appearance. It was unusual for her to visit the stables

– especially in kitten heels – even though I knew that she loved horses.

'The dowager countess is *furious*,' Mum said in a low voice as she walked alongside me to Jupiter's loose box. I led the mare inside and shut the half-door. Mum leant over it.

'Why is Edith furious?' I asked as I removed Jupiter's saddle.

'Can't you guess? Lavinia has locked herself in the tack room and is refusing to come out.'

'Tell me what happened,' I said.

'*Well* . . . it all started when I offered to pick her ladyship up from the station,' Mum began, hardly able to keep the note of glee out of her voice. 'Wait . . . any news of Peggy?'

'No,' I said. 'Go on. You didn't tell Edith about the cottage switch, did you?'

'Of course not,' Mum said. 'I just told her that Lavinia had something important to discuss with her and that she should ask her what it was.'

'Oh Mum,' I said. 'I told you to keep out of it.'

'But I did!'

Jupiter thrust her nose into my mother's hand, searching for treats. She was in luck. Mum produced a handful of pony nuts from her coat pocket and fed them to her.

'Quiet! Her ladyship is coming!' Mum whispered.

Edith was bristling with anger. I saw Lavinia dart from the tack room and run off in the direction of the house.

'I leave for exactly four days and this is what happens,' the dowager countess fumed. 'First of all Rupert tells me that two *priceless* pocket watches have been stolen, then I learn that we've lost our butler – frightful, I know – and now the cook has vanished too.' She shook her head with dismay. 'And to top it all, he's talking gibberish about it having something to do with disturbing that dried-up old bird.'

'And what if it has?' Mum said tentatively.

'Of course it hasn't,' Edith declared. 'The curse ended with my marriage to Rupert's father. The whole thing is nonsense.'

'But what if there is some truth in it and the curse has returned?' said Mum. 'Let's not forget the newspaper reporter. He's dead too. We think he must have touched the bird.'

'What newspaper reporter?' Edith demanded.

Mum looked to me for support, but I was focusing on putting Jupiter's winter rugs back on.

'Nick Bond had a motorbike accident,' she said. 'He came to the open house to write about the legend of—'

'Nick *Bond*?' Edith's expression darkened. 'Oh good *God*, not that family again!'

'I believe he was related to the former gatekeeper here,' Mum said. 'As you know, I am in charge of the Honeychurch archives, and apparently—'

'Yes, yes, I know all about that *incident*,' said Edith with disgust. 'Was he actually here at the Hall? How on earth could that possibly have happened?'

'It was my idea.' I realised I was actually nervous. 'I didn't know there—'

'Of course you wouldn't know,' Edith cut in.

'I did wonder why his lordship looked so angry when he saw Nick,' Mum said, which only seemed to fuel Edith's fury.

'This is exactly why I was against the open day in the first place!'

'Do we know why the family is banned from the Hall?' Mum asked gingerly. 'I'd like to make a note of it for my files.'

'I *beg* your pardon?' Edith said.

'It's just that his lordship . . . Oh, nothing,' Mum mumbled.

'I will not tolerate this disobedience,' Edith said.

'With all due respect, your ladyship,' I said, struggling to keep my temper. 'No one told me about this so-called family feud with Nick's relatives. Secondly, I . . . I don't believe the pocket watches have been stolen. They will probably turn up somewhere.' There. I'd said it.

'I'm sure they *will* turn up somewhere,' Edith snapped. 'Given the outrageous reward that Rupert is offering. He may say no questions asked, but as far as I'm concerned, if it's one of our people, they will be out on their ear, and if it's some blow-in from up country, they shall be prosecuted to the full extent of the law.'

'And I'm positive that Peggy will come back once she's got over her wobbly,' Mum added.

Edith gave another snort of disgust. 'Both of you!' she said. 'Come with me. Now.'

'Where are we going?' Mum asked. 'Only these shoes . . .'

But Edith was already halfway across the courtyard and heading for the archway that led to Honeychurch Cottages.

I looked at Mum. 'You are in deep trouble,' I said.

Sure enough, the dowager countess stopped outside

number 1, where Delia, bundled up in her winter coat, stood in the road.

'Good grief!' Edith exclaimed.

Behind her we saw Peggy Cropper's pink sofa wedged in the doorway, half in and half out.

It began to sleet.

Delia sniffled into her handkerchief. 'Oh, your ladyship,' she said. 'What a terrible misunderstanding. Lady Lavinia told me that you had agreed to the cottage switch. You must think me so heartless! So *heartless*!'

'What a fibber!' Mum muttered.

'Where is your husband?' Edith demanded. 'Where is the major?'

'Um. Out,' said Delia. 'He's gone with our son Guy to buy more paint.'

'How did you move this sofa?'

'Um. I did it myself. I'm quite strong,' she added. 'It just got jammed in the doorway. Do you think if we turn it sideways—'

'Put it back,' Edith commanded. 'Iris and Katherine will take one end and you and I the other.'

I was appalled. 'Your ladyship, you can't—'

'I am perfectly capable of moving a sofa,' she said. 'I'm not in the grave yet.'

Mum and I clambered over the sofa into Peggy's sitting room to pick up our end, while Edith and Delia took the other.

'On the count of three, we will lift it,' said Edith. 'Mrs Evans and I will push and you and Katherine will pull.'

'Yes, m'lady,' Mum said meekly.

'Poor Peggy,' Delia said between sobs and puffs. 'What kind of friend must she think I am? What with her losing her husband and now this muddle.'

Suddenly the sofa shot into Peggy's sitting room, sending Mum and me flying onto the carpet. Mum started to giggle.

Edith ignored us. 'Mrs Evans, you will be cooking luncheon today.'

A transformation came over Delia's face. Her tears were gone.

'You won't be disappointed,' she beamed. 'Would you like a choice of menus? I can give you three. I always keep a selection of gourmet ingredients in my kitchen. I like to follow Nigella Lawson – although she does seem to inject the suggestion of sex into her recipes—'

Edith's eyebrows disappeared under her hairline. 'Good Lord.'

'Yes, I agree,' Mum put in. 'I much prefer the Barefoot Contessa. I always feel I could invite her to dine at my table, but with Nigella you'd never know if your husband would be safe – not that you should have to worry about Lenny any more.'

Delia shot her a look of pure venom. 'He said it only happened once, Iris.'

'Mrs Cropper swears by Mrs Beeton,' Edith put in. 'And her recipes are good enough for me.'

'Mrs Beeton died of syphilis, you know,' Mum said. 'According to Wikipedia, she caught it from her husband on their honeymoon.'

'I did not know that, Iris,' said Edith. 'Still, it didn't seem to affect her ability to concoct the most delicious recipes. Her mutton pie is excellent.'

'If Nigella's too fancy, I can always fall back on my namesake Delia Smith,' said Delia desperately. 'But what do I know? I'm just the housekeeper.'

'Yes, that is exactly what you are, Mrs Evans,' Edith said sternly. 'My daughter-in-law is not the sharpest tool in the shed and is easily manipulated. Peggy Cropper is family, and I always promised that she could stay in her cottage and keep her position for as long as she desired. So I suggest that if you aren't happy with that arrangement, you look for employment elsewhere.'

Mum caught my eye and winked.

Delia went white. 'You mean . . . Lenny and I . . . But we wouldn't have anywhere to go.'

'Surely Major Evans has an army pension?' Edith declared. 'And with all the fame he's garnering from his derring-do, perhaps he won't need to work. Next thing we know, he'll be writing his war memoirs.'

Delia nodded. 'He has talked about—'

'Our people don't like flash, Mrs Evans. It's common.' Edith surveyed the living room with its half-filled boxes. 'And put all these things back where they belong. Immediately.'

Delia hesitated. 'I thought you wanted lunch. Can't Iris sort this place out? She's a lady of leisure. She doesn't work.'

Mum opened her mouth to protest, but shrank under the dowager countess's flinty glare.

'I don't care who does it,' said Edith. 'Just get it done.' And with that, she turned on her heel and left the cottage, with Delia scurrying after her.

My mother stood there in shock.

'Gosh,' I said eventually. 'That was brutal.'

'I told you so,' said Mum. 'Delia made a big mistake.'

'Let's get all this put away,' I said. 'Before Edith comes back to check on us.'

Mum picked up an old black-and-white photograph of a group of teenagers posing on the bench by the quarry. She pointed to a small, skinny girl with unruly dark hair and wild eyes.

'That's me,' she said. 'I was younger than the rest of them, of course. Back then you could get into the underground workings. The tunnels went on for miles, but I suppose the roof has all caved in now.'

I told her about my adventure with Harry that morning, and about finding the Monopoly money on the edge of the water. 'Two five-hundred-pound notes and one one-hundred,' I said. 'I also found this.' I pulled out the Fisherman's Friend packet with its distinctive diagonal red-and-white stripes.

'Those are Peggy's ghastly lozenges,' said Mum. 'She must have gone to the quarry after all.'

'That's what I thought,' I said. 'Can we find the Monopoly game that was in one of the boxes here? I just want to see if the money—'

'Where did you find that?' said a sharp voice.

We turned to see Shawn standing in the doorway.

Chapter Twenty-Five

'**You really do have a habit of turning up at the right time Shawn,**' said Mum. 'Is there any news of Peggy?'

'No,' said Shawn. 'We've got Fluffy the bloodhound coming to lend his assistance later today. I've come to get an item of Gran's clothing – presuming her clothes are still here.'

'Delia didn't get as far as packing up the bedroom,' said Mum. 'I had nothing to do with it. Nor did Kat. We're only here because we were told to put it all back by the dowager countess.'

'But I found this.' I handed Shawn the empty Fisherman's Friend packet.

Shawn's eyes widened. 'Gran's favourites.'

'Surely other people eat those horrible things,' Mum pointed out.

'Unlikely,' said Shawn. 'The cherry ones are hard to find. I have to order them for her online. Where did you find it?'

'Larcombe Quarry,' I said. 'By the bench next to the water.'

'It was their wedding anniversary on Saturday,' said Mum helpfully. 'Perhaps she just wanted to go back there and remember. Kat's father and I eloped to Gretna Green, and after he died, I often took his ashes up there. I'd strap the urn in the front seat of my car and we'd take a tour of Scotland. I found it comforting.'

'I didn't know that,' I said. 'Oh Mum, I wish you'd told me. I could have come with you.'

'At least it gives us a place to start looking,' said Shawn. 'Would you have time to come with me, Kat, and show me exactly where you found this?'

'Of course,' I agreed, although it was not something I really wanted to do.

'I'll just grab something of Gran's. Excuse me.' He headed for the latch door in the corner of the room, and we heard his heavy footsteps go up the stairs.

'I see how it is,' Mum teased.

'How what is?'

'Shawn's looking for an excuse to have you all to himself.'

Moments later, he rejoined us with an oversized black T-shirt emblazoned with the Rolling Stones' iconic lip and tongue logo. 'I think this will do.'

'Good heavens,' Mum said. 'Surely that can't be Peggy's?'

Shawn grinned. 'She's a diehard Stones fan.'

Mum seemed impressed. 'Just goes to show you never really know someone, do you?'

'We'll have to go separately, Shawn,' I said. 'I've got to view a sale this afternoon. It's my last chance before the auction tomorrow. I'll go straight on from the quarry.'

Mum gestured to my riding attire. 'Smelling of horse?'

'Oh. Right. Damn. I'll pop back and change and meet you at Larcombe Cross in twenty minutes.'

Shawn and I left our cars at Larcombe Cross. It felt strange being so close to Guy's barn – as if I was doing something behind his back. Having relented, I had replied to his text this morning, but he hadn't answered mine.

Shawn opened the boot of his car and began to take out some equipment – an ice pick, a telescopic boathook and a coil of rope. Then, to my surprise, he retrieved a drysuit and proceeded to pull it on over his clothing.

'You're not thinking of going into the water, are you?'

'I might have to.'

'But surely . . .' The thought was horrifying, 'You don't think Peggy might have done something drastic, do you?'

'No. I don't. But I was a boy scout. Our motto was "Be Prepared".'

I thought back to the Monopoly money and told him about finding the notes.

'Why would she take them down there?' he asked. 'It makes no sense. And you say they were near the jetty?'

'I'll show you exactly where.'

I took him the same way that Harry had taken me earlier. The path was treacherous, and both of us had to concentrate on keeping our footing. As we picked our way down, Shawn began to talk about the science of ice.

'It's all about calculating snow coverage, external temperature, water depth and the size of the body of water,' he said behind me.

'Sounds complicated.'

'Thick and blue, tried and true,' he quoted. 'Thin and crispy, way too risky.'

He proceeded to explain the significance of the various colours of ice.

'Light grey to dark black is dangerous,' he warned. 'Ice melts even if the air temperature is below zero degrees Celsius. It's just not safe. Did you know that water-saturated snow freezes on top of the ice and forms another thin layer? Most of the time it's weak, because air pockets tend to make it porous. It can look deceptively firm.'

'I didn't know that,' I said.

'We want it blue to clear, because that's high-density, very strong and the safest ice to be on if it's thick enough. You don't want it any less than four inches thick.'

'Oh,' I said. 'I'll make sure to remember.'

'Of course mottled and slush ice can often be deceptive,' he continued. 'It looks thick on the top but it's rotting away at the centre and base. Give that a wide berth. The shoreline is the weakest . . . Sorry, am I boring you?'

'Actually, no,' I said, and to my surprise, he wasn't. It was strange. I used to think his lectures were tedious, but now I found his nerdy side rather sweet.

And then I felt my feet go from under me on the slippery slate surface, and I crashed down heavily on my back, severely winded.

'Kat!' Shawn cried out. 'Are you OK?'

I just lay there for a moment, unable to catch my breath. Why was I so clumsy? My elbow was so painful I was sure I'd broken it. I thought I was going to throw up. Slowly, though, the nausea subsided.

Shawn stood over me, looking concerned. 'Let me help you up.'

'Honestly, this is the second time in two days that I've fallen,' I said. 'I hit my elbow in the exact same place as I did in the churchyard.'

Transferring his tools into one hand, he offered me the other, pulling me up with such force that I toppled against him. I smelt his musky scent and felt the hardness of his body through the ridiculous drysuit.

I had never been so close to him before. I could feel the atmosphere between us shifting dramatically. Instead of letting go, he kept hold of my hand. When our eyes met, he suddenly threw the equipment to the ground and in one quick movement caught me by the waist and pushed me against the mossy bank.

Before I knew what was happening, his lips sought mine. Electricity surged through my body, leaving me dizzy, and instinctively I started to kiss him back. I couldn't help it.

Just as quickly, he broke away. His eyes were ablaze with a passion I felt certain was reflected in my own.

He carried on staring at me. I was flustered. How could this have happened? What about Guy? I felt awful and yet oddly happy. I had just been kissed by Shawn the policeman and I had liked it.

'Shawn, I . . .'

But he had already turned away. Picking up the tools from the ground, he strode on ahead, slipping and almost falling twice in his haste to get away from me.

'You don't know the way!' I cried, but he pretended not to hear. 'Turn left when you get to the bottom!'

I stumbled after him, my emotions churning. He didn't look back once.

I caught up with him at the ruins. Shawn seemed to have composed himself whereas I was still a bundle of nerves.

'Interesting place,' he said. 'I came here as a teenager but I haven't been back since. Where did you find the empty packet?'

'I'll show you.' I led him through the brick buildings to the water and pointed out the bench.

'And obviously you called out?'

'Yes, of course,' I said. 'But we should try again.' So we did, but there was still no answering cry.

'Fluffy will find her,' he said. 'I'm sure of it.'

I just hoped that she would be found alive.

'Where was the Monopoly money?' he asked.

'Over there.' I pointed. 'In the reeds.'

He looked across the water towards the black dustbin bag on the ice floe. There seemed to be another bag beyond it now that I hadn't noticed earlier. He stiffened, and I knew that he was thinking the exact same thing I had when I saw it earlier in the day.

'It's just rubbish, I think,' I said. 'Someone has been fly-tipping.'

'Perhaps we should take a look.' He headed for the jetty, putting one foot on the boards to test if they would hold his weight.

'You can't walk along there,' I said, aghast. 'It doesn't look safe. If you fall in, you may well have the drysuit, but Harry told me there are eels in there the size of twelve-foot pythons.'

'Don't worry, I'm a policeman.' He gave me a wolfish grin, and suddenly, right at that moment, I knew that something between us had changed forever.

He dropped slowly to his hands and knees. The jetty jolted violently and sank a few inches but then seemed to steady itself.

'Please be careful,' I said.

'The key is to distribute your weight evenly,' he said. 'If you fall through the ice, the first thing to do is to get your breathing under control. Once you've done that, you can kick your way out. Try to get onto the ice like a seal, then roll away from the hole.'

He set off at a cautious crawl, dragging his telescopic boathook along with him. As he reached the end of the jetty, he extended the hook to its full length and, after several attempts, managed to snag the black dustbin bag and drag it towards him.

It must have been incredibly heavy, because he didn't seem to be able to haul it onto the jetty. In fact, it suddenly disappeared beneath the water.

Shawn gave a yelp of alarm and sat bolt upright on his haunches.

I swear my heart stopped beating. 'What's wrong? Is it an eel?'

'Over there.' He pointed to what I had thought was a second bag. It was floating on the surface, and my mind struggled to make sense of what it could be.

Before I realised what was happening, Shawn had thrown himself into the water and struck out for what I guessed had to be a body.

Panic rose in my chest. *Please don't let it be Peggy*, I said to myself over and over again. *Not Peggy. Not Peggy.*

I grabbed the rope that he had left at the end of the jetty and looked around for anything that might work as a weight. I picked up a large stick and quickly tied it to one end.

'Shawn! Here!' I screamed, and hurled the stick out over the water. It struck him on the head, but he caught it. His other arm was clamped around the upper torso of the unknown person.

It was hard to pull them in, but with Shawn swimming with one arm and kicking out, I managed it. As he came closer, I saw to my relief that the body was not Peggy Cropper.

It was Angus Fenwick.

Chapter Twenty-Six

The next hour went by in a blur. We were back at Larcombe Cross. The ambulance had arrived, Clive turned up with Fluffy in the police K9 Vauxhall van, and then suddenly Guy was standing beside me, his face creased with worry. He was wearing a coat over a pair of olive-green overalls splattered with cream paint.

'I saw the flashing lights from the barn,' he said. 'But I never imagined that you would be here. What's going on?'

The Cruickshank twins appeared carrying a stretcher and loaded it into the ambulance. Angus's body was covered in a sheet.

'Who is it?'

'Angus Fenwick,' said Shawn grimly. 'He was staying at Violet Green's B and B with his wife.'

Guy turned ashen. 'What happened?'

'It looks like he drowned,' said Shawn. 'The quarry is very dangerous. Mrs Fenwick told Kat that he went for a walk yesterday and never returned.'

'You think he got lost and fell into the water?' asked Guy anxiously.

'We don't know,' Shawn said. 'But we do have to find his wife.'

'Poor Lala.' My heart went out to the young woman.

I realised I was shivering violently. Guy put his arm around me. 'Come up to the house,' he said. 'You're freezing.'

'Yes, please take her.' Shawn's expression was hard to read. 'I don't think she should drive home quite yet.'

I didn't dare meet his eye, and felt an unexpected pang of guilt.

'What did you find in the black dustbin liner?' I asked. 'It sank like a stone.'

'Newspapers,' said Shawn. 'And more Monopoly money.'

'*Monopoly* money?' Guy said sharply.

Shawn regarded him with curiosity. 'Do you play the game?'

'Well . . . yes. Doesn't everybody? But I haven't done for years. It must be some childish prank.'

'What do you mean by that?' Shawn cocked his head.

'I mean . . .' Guy laughed uneasily. 'I don't know. I mean . . . don't kids play in quarries all the time?'

'I may need to ask you some questions a little later, sir,' said Shawn. 'What with Nick Bond's accident here yesterday and then today's drowning. Yours is the only house in the area and you may have seen something and didn't realise it was important.' He thought for a moment. 'What colour is your car?'

'I drive a black Freelander,' said Guy. 'Why?'

'Just double-checking.' Shawn scribbled something in his notebook.

Guy turned to me. 'I'll drive your car up to the barn, Kat. Get you inside and warmed up.' He gave Shawn a look of triumph, but as Guy turned away, Shawn caught my eye and winked.

'Right then,' said Shawn. 'I'll just fetch my gran's Stones T-shirt and Fluffy will show us what she's made of.' He gestured for Clive to get Fluffy out of the van.

'Is that a bloodhound?' asked Guy.

'They're going back down to the quarry,' I said. 'I'm sure your mother told you that Peggy Cropper is missing.'

'The old butler's wife?' Guy seemed surprised. 'But why would she have gone to the quarry?'

'That was why I took Shawn down there in the first place,' I said. 'I think she's still there somewhere.'

'I had wondered what you were doing, especially as you didn't come up to say hello – or offer to paint a wall.'

It was an attempt at humour, but I wasn't in the mood.

'Shawn's worried sick about his grandmother,' I said. 'I found something that I thought belonged to her.'

'Oh.' Guy looked startled. 'Where?'

'Down by the water's edge.'

'The water's edge,' he repeated.

'Harry and I were riding there this morning.'

'I thought nobody went to the quarry,' said Guy. 'It's too dangerous.'

'Well clearly Peggy did.' I was getting irritated and I didn't know why.

'But . . . why would she have gone down to the quarry?' he persisted.

'It was a special place for her and her husband,' I said. 'Apparently it was where he proposed to her, and every year they had this tradition of having a photograph taken in a particular spot.'

'At the *quarry*?' Guy laughed. 'I can't think of anywhere more unromantic.'

'It wasn't like that years ago,' I said defensively. 'Apparently it was *very* romantic.' As I said it, the memory of Shawn's kiss hit me afresh and I felt my face grow hot.

'I seem to always be saying the wrong thing,' said Guy. 'I know you're upset. Give me your car keys and we'll drive up to the barn.'

'Smart move to put snow tyres on these wheels,' said Guy. The narrow lane rose fairly steeply. Just fifty yards up on the left, a granite sign said: *Larcombe Barn*. Guy pulled into a hardcore-covered apron and parked next to a black BMW convertible. My heart sank.

'Is your father here?'

'He borrowed my Freelander to pick up materials,' said Guy. 'He's gone back to Homebase. Come on. Let's get inside. This wasn't how I planned on you seeing my home for the first time.'

The converted stone barn was perched on the top of a bluff. A cement mixer stood next to a stone garage that was nearing completion. Slabs of slate were neatly stacked along a post-and-rail fence that marked the boundary line.

'We won't get the tarmac down on the drive until the spring,' said Guy. 'I hope you can imagine what this will look like once the hedge and plants have all grown in.'

The views were spectacular.

Inside, the barn smelled of new paint and wood polish.

'Gosh, it's warm in here.' In fact it was sweltering.

'I'm having problems regulating the temperature at the moment,' said Guy apologetically. 'I've got the woodburner specialist coming out tomorrow. Can I take your coat?'

I was happy to relinquish it.

He hung it over the custom-made newel post at the base of an exquisite bespoke oak staircase that led to the living area upstairs.

'Do you like it?' He sounded nervous, and I was touched. I tried to push Shawn's mad moment to the back of my mind.

He gestured to the flagstone floors. 'Under-floor heating – but there's no need to take off your shoes. As you can see, everything is in disarray.'

'Hardly,' I said, looking at a neat row of empty paint cans that sat on sheets of newspaper in the vestibule. 'You're so tidy.'

'That's my naval training. I would show you my hospital corners, only the bed hasn't arrived yet and I'm having to sleep on an air mattress.' He smiled, but when I didn't respond, he added, 'What's wrong? I've been looking forward to this Christmas for so long, and—'

'I'm sorry. It's not you. It's me – or rather, it's everything.'

'You've had yet another terrible shock today.'

I nodded. 'First Seth Cropper dies a horrible death right

in front of me, then there was Nick's accident yesterday – and now, seeing Angus Fenwick in the quarry . . .'

'All accidents, Kat,' said Guy earnestly. 'Every one of them.' He smiled. 'Maybe there is some truth in the curse of the Honeychurch Hawk.'

'It's not funny,' I snapped. 'And now Peggy Cropper's missing. Don't you feel *anything*?'

He recoiled, stung. 'Of course I do. But you forget that I've seen far worse. I've been in war zones, Kat . . .'

'Oh, yes. Of course you have. I'm sorry.' I felt awful.

'Some of the images that haunt my dreams are so horrific that I suppose I've learnt how to disconnect a part of my brain,' said Guy. 'Sometimes it makes me come across as callous, but I can assure you I'm not.' He reached for my hand. 'Let's go upstairs and have a cup of tea – or something stronger. I've got a bottle of that lethal Honeychurch Gin if you'd prefer.'

'Tea would be lovely,' I said.

As with most barn conversions, the living area and kitchen were combined in one enormous open-plan area. Larcombe Barn had gabled ceilings inset with a series of skylights. On one side there were floor-to-ceiling windows, with a French door that led out onto a raised deck overlooking the valley. Empty stone troughs stood ready for spring planting.

In the living area, half of the floor was covered in paint-splattered dust sheets. A pair of A-frame stepladders supported a plank so that the ceiling could be painted.

'It's really lovely, Guy.' And it was.

'I'm glad you like it,' he said. 'I apologise for the lack of furniture.'

Against the rear wall was a long leather sofa in a dark shade of plum. A coffee table sat on a vast Aubusson rug of cream, plum and navy. There was nothing else in the living area.

'Dad and I should have finished painting by tomorrow. I'm hoping the rest of the furniture will arrive in time for Christmas.'

Next to the windows stood a SkyWatcher 120-mm mounted telescope and stool.

Even though it was the middle of winter, the trees surrounding the quarry were dense. I couldn't see the water below. For a crazy moment I wondered if Guy had spotted Shawn and me kissing, but then I reminded myself that even a high-powered telescope did not have X-ray vision.

Guy came up behind me and slid his arms around my waist. He nuzzled my neck and I let him. *Get a grip, Kat!*

'The sky is spectacular out here at night,' he said. 'It's so clear. There is no end in space – that concept fascinates me. No end! Can you imagine? Oh – look down there.'

Far below we could see the beams of two torches moving through the undergrowth. 'Your policeman and his faithful sidekick, I presume.'

'Shawn is not my policeman,' I said.

'We all know he wants to be.'

When I didn't answer, Guy stepped away. 'I'll make some tea.'

The kitchen contained top-quality Viking appliances along

with a dark-green double Aga. The units were all made of oak. Four bar stools ranged along the granite central counter, in the middle of which sat a Charlie Brown Christmas tree.

'Nice tree,' I said.

'You've got to love Charlie Brown,' said Guy. 'What's your favourite Christmas movie?'

'*Elf*, I suppose,' and I couldn't help but smile. It was such a stupid movie, but it always made me laugh.

'Mine too!' Guy grinned.

As we waited for the kettle to boil, I peeped through an archway that opened off the kitchen. A spiral staircase led to a gallery above. 'Utility room and steps down to the garden through there,' said Guy. 'And upstairs is my studio.'

'Studio?'

'I told you. I wanted to be an artist. It's a hobby of mine. I'll show you my paintings later.'

Suddenly, out of nowhere, a mobile phone began to ring. I had left mine in my Golf. Guy retrieved his from his pocket, but the sound was coming from somewhere else. We looked at each other in confusion.

It rang three more times and then stopped. A moment later, it started again. It was bizarre.

'It's coming from . . . I think it's coming from the direction of the *sofa*!' I said in amazement.

The ringing stopped for a moment, then began yet again. Guy strode to the sofa. He felt down the sides of the cushions before moving the sofa out from the wall and picking up a plain brown envelope. Tearing it open, he upended the contents.

A pay-as-you-go mobile phone clattered onto the floor.

Swiftly he turned off the ringer and put the phone back into the envelope.

I waited for him to say something, but he didn't. His expression was one I could only describe as furious.

But before I had a chance to question him, there was the sound of someone hammering at the front door, and a woman's voice screaming to be let inside. 'I know you're there, you bastard! Open the door!'

'What's going on?' I asked.

'Stay right here,' Guy said in a tone that frightened me. 'I will deal with this.'

There was no question of me staying *right here*. I followed him to the top of the stairs and watched him open the front door.

There on the doorstep stood Lala, holding a mobile phone. She was hysterical. 'What the hell have you done to my husband?'

Chapter Twenty-Seven

I didn't have time to react, because Lala launched herself at Guy right there in the doorway, pounding his chest with her fists. 'Where is he? Where is he? Is he here? He must be here!'

Guy, though, was far stronger and grabbed her wrists, clamping them by her sides. His face was mottled with rage.

'I told you to keep away from my family,' he hissed. 'And you can cut out the husband crap. We all know that's not true.'

I was speechless.

'Bastard!' Lala screamed again, and kneed Guy viciously in the groin. He went down with a crash, groaning in agony. She stepped over him and hurried up the stairs, only stopping momentarily when she saw me waiting at the top.

She pushed me roughly aside and looked around the vast room, bewildered. 'Where's Angus?'

And then I realised: *she doesn't know that Angus is dead. She doesn't know!*

She began circling the room like a dervish, even opening the kitchen cupboards as if he might be inside them. Then she disappeared under the archway, and I could hear her thundering up the spiral staircase. But I did nothing. Just stood there in shock.

Guy staggered up the stairs and managed to speak. 'Let me deal with this, Kat. You should go home.'

'I'm not going anywhere,' I snapped. 'You lied to my face. I asked you if you knew that woman and you said you didn't. Is she pregnant with your child?'

He shook his head vehemently. 'This is not what you think it is.'

'And what *do* I think?' I demanded.

Lala returned through the arch, her eyes wild and frightened. 'Angus came up here yesterday. He told me he did! He told me where he was going in case something happened.'

'Why don't you tell her?' I said to Guy.

Guy's expression was stony. 'I wasn't there. Why don't you?'

I stood in an agony of indecision, then had a sudden thought. 'How did you get here this afternoon, Lala?'

'I walked,' she said. 'Why?'

'You didn't see the police at Larcombe Cross?'

'I saw two police cars, yes,' she said. The colour drained from her face. 'Why? What's happened?'

'Angus is dead,' I said. 'He drowned in the quarry.'

For a split second, she didn't react. Then she swayed, before pitching forward and hitting the flagstone floor with a sickening thud.

'She's fainted!' I exclaimed, and dropped to her side. 'God, I hope she doesn't go into labour.'

'Undo her coat,' Guy said, kneeling beside me. 'Give her some air. She's overheating.'

Together we undid the snappers and the zip, then we both stopped in shock. Lala's baby bump had shifted dramatically to one side.

It would appear that she wasn't pregnant at all.

Guy thrust his hands angrily up her jumper. 'What a sly, cunning—'

'Guy!' I was outraged. 'At least let me . . .'

'Go on then. Do it!' He got to his feet, muttering a string of expletives.

'Get her some water,' I told him. My hands touched a silicon fake belly. 'I don't believe this.'

Guy returned with a glass and threw the water into Lala's face.

'Guy!' I shrieked. 'For heaven's sake!'

Spluttering, Lala shot bolt upright, her shock turning to indignation, and then scooted away from me in terror.

'Get out,' hissed Guy. 'Go!'

She rolled to one side and got to her feet, her expression mutinous. 'I know what you've done.'

'And I know what *you* have done, Lala,' Guy spat. 'Get out, before I call the police. I don't want to ever hear your name again, do you understand?'

Lala stormed away, pausing briefly at the top of the stairs. She swung around and pointed an accusatory finger at Guy.

'This isn't over,' she said. 'Not by any means. You tell Daddy that. Tell him from me.'

And with that, she was gone. The door slammed, leaving us in silence.

I stayed sitting on the floor, trying to take in what had just happened. 'You need to call the police.'

'I can't. Not yet,' said Guy. 'I can explain, but . . . not yet. Please trust me.'

'Trust you? You lied to me.'

'I swear there is nothing going on with that woman.'

'Her husband is dead—'

'He wasn't her husband.'

'What? Then who the hell was he? What is going on?' I demanded.

Guy just shook his head.

'This isn't working. I'm sorry.' I stood up and headed for the stairs, desperate to get away.

He leapt forward to bar my way.

'Let me go, please,' I said.

'This has nothing to do with me,' he said quickly. 'It's . . . Dad.'

I looked into his eyes and saw such despair that I knew he was telling the truth.

'Please just hear me out,' he begged. 'Come and sit down. Please, Kat.'

I allowed him to lead me back to the sofa and noticed the envelope containing the burner phone. A wave of anger hit me. 'You can start by explaining that.'

'Angus and Lala gave the phone to Dad a few days ago

because he wasn't answering his own,' said Guy. 'They left it on the front steps of the Hall.'

'Oh, you mean just like the scarf from Harrods? The gift that you claimed was meant for you?'

'I had to say that. I didn't want my mother to find out – or the Queen.'

'The *Queen*?'

'Dad's award for gallantry. He's had an impeccable military career. He served his country. He saved those kids in the caves ... Why should this one indiscretion ruin everything he's worked for?' Guy raked his fingers through his closely cropped hair. 'They've been blackmailing him for months.'

'Before he even moved to Honeychurch?' I was amazed. 'But what about the other woman? The woman your father ran away with.'

He seemed taken aback. 'You know about Jennifer?'

'You think I was born yesterday?' I said, exasperated. 'Your mother was distraught when she started working at the Hall – and, I may add, she told everyone that she was a widow and that your father was dead.'

'Dad told me. He was very upset,' Guy said.

'Oh I am sorry to hear that,' I said sarcastically.

'OK, yes, Dad lied, but it was just to protect my mother. You have to understand that. He loves her.'

I gave a snort of disgust. 'Nice way to show it.'

'Look, I only found out about this whole blackmail thing at the pub on Sunday night, and that was by accident.'

'Am I supposed to feel sympathy?'

'Dad wasn't to know that Lala would pretend she was carrying his baby. They were demanding child support and everything!'

'And he was stupid enough to believe the child was his?' I was stunned. 'Didn't he ever question it? I mean . . . his age, for starters!'

Guy shrugged. 'Yeah, well . . . Dad's ego has always been a problem.'

'I assume he never paid them any money, which was why they hunted him down.'

'Oh, he paid them all right,' said Guy bitterly. 'He naïvely thought they would stop once he had parted with thousands of pounds. But of course people like that never do. When Dad moved hundreds of miles away, he thought they would never find him—'

'But his name appeared in all the newspapers,' I said. 'How could he have been so stupid?'

'Jesus, Kat,' Guy exclaimed. 'No one is perfect. This all happened before my mother agreed to give him a second chance.'

'And I suppose that makes it OK? And what about Angus? How did he happen to end up in the quarry with a bin bag full of newspaper?'

At this, Guy faltered. 'Dad would never deliberately hurt anyone. I . . . I don't know how that happened.'

'That reporter, Nick? His accident happened just down the road.' A terrible thought hit me. 'Lenny has been helping you to paint the barn, hasn't he?'

'Yes. So?'

'Was he painting here yesterday while we were in Dartmouth together?'

Guy looked uncomfortable. 'Why?'

I gestured to the burner. 'He was the one who made the phone call, wasn't he?'

At first I didn't think Guy was going to answer my question, but then he took a deep breath. 'Dad told me that he found Nick and that he was already dead.'

'But why didn't he stop and wait?' I demanded.

Guy gave a heavy sigh. 'He told me there was no phone signal there, so he came up here to make the call. I . . . I don't know what to say. I don't know why he didn't wait for the ambulance.'

Nick had originally been on the trail of the pocket watches, but now I wondered if he had found out about the major being blackmailed. It would have made national headlines for sure.

'Did your father attack Nick in the churchyard on Sunday evening?' I asked.

'My father is not a murderer, Kat,' was all Guy said.

'So why hide the burner phone?' I persisted.

'He could hardly leave it at the cottage. My mother goes through everything. She searches his pockets all the time. She would have suspected that he was having another affair.'

'Because she doesn't trust him, and with good reason! You have to go to the police,' I said again. 'Didn't you hear Lala's threats? This is not going to go away.'

'I . . . I can't. I just can't.' Guy seemed so small and lost that for a moment I felt a pang of sympathy.

'What would you have done if it was your mother in this situation?' he said suddenly.

I was about to retort that I couldn't imagine my mother ever being in this kind of situation, but then I realised that she lied all the time. Apart from hiding her Krystalle Storm identity, she had an attic full of cash that, should it be discovered, would almost certainly lead to a prison sentence. And that was just the beginning.

I kept my mother's secrets because I loved her, and even though I didn't agree with what she was hiding, I would never betray her.

Wasn't Guy just doing the same?

'Don't let my father's indiscretions come between us,' he said. 'I've done nothing wrong here. I told him not to give in to the blackmail. I begged him to go to the police, but he refused.' Guy seemed close to despair. 'What else could I have done?'

There was the sound of a car pulling up outside.

'It's Dad,' he said.

My stomach turned over. Lenny was the last person I wanted to see.

'Don't say a word,' said Guy. 'You don't know anything at all. Just let me figure something out. Please, Kat. Let me do it my way.'

'All right,' I said grudgingly.

'And don't tell anyone else either,' he begged. 'Let's not spoil everyone's Christmas.'

'Honey, I'm home!' came a cheerful voice below, followed by the slam of the front door.

I felt bile rise in my throat. I had never particularly liked Lenny, but now I detested him. Mum had been right to have her suspicions, but I was certain that not in a million years would she ever have guessed what he had really been up to.

Guy quickly picked up the envelope with the burner phone and pushed it under the sofa, out of sight. As he did so, a heavy rubber-clad torch rolled out. He swiftly kicked it back under just as his father appeared at the top of the stairs carrying two tins of paint and a long-handled roller. He too was dressed in overalls.

'Sorry,' Lenny said with a grin. 'Did I interrupt the lovebirds?'

'I was just leaving,' I muttered.

'Not on my account,' he said with a laugh.

'I'll walk you back to your car,' offered Guy.

He followed me outside and opened my car door. I hesitated, wondering if I was becoming paranoid.

'Why was there a torch under the sofa, Guy?'

He looked blank.

'When you hid the envelope again, a torch rolled out and you kicked it back underneath.'

'Did I?' he said. 'I don't remember.'

'I saw you.'

He gave an exasperated sigh. 'Jesus, Kat. Here we go again! What is wrong with you? Why all these stupid questions?'

'I'm tired,' I said. 'I've got to go.' I slammed the car door and drove away.

I was bitterly disappointed. I could understand Guy's loyalty to his father – of course I could – but even though I knew he was covering for him, I suspected he was a lot more involved than he let on.

Lenny had known all about the quarry because Harry had told him about the World War II OBs down there. It was a short walk from Little Dipperton to the ruined mining village and would be a perfect location to hand over cash. I now wondered if the stumpery had been used for such a drop too, but of course the kids had found the money first, which had soon put a stop to that.

It would explain why Angus was at the quarry, but why his car had gone missing and the significance of the Monopoly money and the bag of newspaper was a mystery.

Lala had said that Angus had not returned from his walk, and that their rental car had vanished.

And then it hit me with a blinding flash.

Angus's body was not supposed to have been found.

If Peggy Cropper hadn't gone missing, Harry and I wouldn't have ridden to Larcombe Quarry and I wouldn't have spotted the empty packet of Fisherman's Friend or the Monopoly money.

Lenny had a lot to lose, and the Queen of England and his award for bravery was only the tip of the iceberg. Blackmail? A man of his stature fooled by a young girl pretending to carry his child? The ensuing scandal would end his marriage, destroy his military reputation and put paid to his pension.

I was convinced that he had deliberately lured Angus to

the quarry. Maybe Nick had found out what was going on and followed them. I just didn't know.

One thing I did know was that Guy was wrong.

Lenny was a murderer.

Chapter Twenty-Eight

Pleading a headache, I refused Mum's offer of a Marks & Spencer ready meal and a game of Scrabble and went straight home to Jane's Cottage. I had not made it to the saleroom to view tomorrow's auction, but I decided to go early in the morning, before it started.

I ignored texts from Shawn to call him and from Guy claiming that everything was going to be OK.

My thoughts turned to Peggy. What if she had seen Lenny in the quarry with Angus? We knew she had walked that way. Had Lenny got rid of her too? The water was a hundred feet deep, to say nothing of the carnivorous eels. She would never be found.

The problem was that I had no proof whatsoever.

If I voiced my concerns, it would almost certainly destroy what was left of my tenuous relationship with Guy. It would also ruin my mother's friendship with Delia, to say nothing of the possibility of Delia losing her home and Lenny going to prison.

And I could be wrong.

I took a long bath and half a sleeping pill – something I rarely did – and fell into a dreamless sleep.

For the first time in years, I actually overslept, and woke up in a panic. The auction!

I dressed in record time, but got stuck in traffic. A lorry had jackknifed on the main road.

When I got to Luxtons, all the spaces had been taken in the car park, and by the time I had managed to find a spot in a nearby residential street, I knew I had missed the white Dicky Bear and the entire reason why I had wanted to go to the sale in the first place. Still, there were a few more lots I was interested in that would come up later in the afternoon, so I decided to stay.

As I reached the entrance to the saleroom on the High Street, I bumped into David.

'I've been waiting for you,' he said. 'It's not like you to miss the bears. You could have got them for a steal.'

'A lorry jackknifed and I got stuck – excuse me . . .'

'I'll come in with you,' said David. 'One bear didn't even make the reserve. In fact, I nearly bought it for you – the white Dicky Bear.'

'What?!' For a moment I forgot about everything else. I was seriously disappointed. I had expected the bear to go for a lot more than the reserve of £3,000. An irrational wave of misery welled up inside me.

'I didn't know you wanted it *that* badly,' teased David, but his smile soon changed to concern. 'What's wrong, Piglet? Are you OK?'

The stupid nickname tugged at my heart. Suddenly I yearned to be back in the familiarity of my old life, secure with the man I had spent over a decade with – a man who had always supported me, loved me, even though ultimately he could not commit to me.

'You haven't called me that for a long time,' I whispered.

'Come on,' he said gently. 'Let me buy you a cup of tea and you can tell me everything – or tell me nothing at all.'

'Not a good idea,' I said, but even as the words came out, I knew that I wanted to talk to him. At the same time, I wasn't stupid. It was as I had suspected when he had turned up at the Emporium. David had driven two hundred miles from London for a reason, and that reason wasn't me.

'On one condition,' I said.

'Name it.'

'That you tell me about the case you're working on.'

He laughed. 'It's a deal.'

We found a glass-fronted café called Eileen's among the selection of charity shops, betting shops, a pawnbroker and a newsagent's that lined the street.

'In here,' David said.

I regarded him with surprise. He would never have set foot in a place like this a year ago. 'Seriously? You want to eat here?'

'They do the best all-day breakfasts,' he said. 'Trust me.'

Steps down led to a handful of red Formica-topped tables and metal chairs with plastic padded seats. The place was packed with customers – mostly labourers – and smelt of bacon.

'Morning, Eileen,' David called out to an elderly woman wearing an old-fashioned floral housecoat. She greeted him with a smile.

'Go and sit down,' he told me. 'We have to order at the counter. What would you like?'

'Just a cup of tea.'

'You need to eat something.'

'Just tea,' I said again, and took the only free table, next to a steamed-up window.

David headed over to place our order. I watched him chatting to Eileen and sharing a joke. A couple of people turned to stare at me and then back at him, no doubt wondering if we were together again. A few nudged and whispered. David stopped to talk to them too – something he would never have done before. His sense of superiority had always been a source of irritation to me, but as I looked at him in his brand-new Barbour jacket, I wondered if he really had changed.

Delia believed that Lenny had changed. Guy did too, and yet his father's old life had caught up with him, as old lives always do.

David returned carrying two cups of tea and sat down opposite me. 'I've been in every one of those charity shops since I got here on Monday . . . Kat, what is it?' He reached across as if to take my hand, but I put it quickly into my lap.

'Nothing,' I said. 'Really. Why don't you tell me what you're doing down here. We made a deal, after all.'

'You know I can't do that,' he said.

'You promised!'

'And you knew I wouldn't tell you, so let's cut the crap, shall we?' He looked into my eyes. 'Tell me all about Lieutenant Commander Guy Evans of 825 Naval Air Squadron.'

I was taken aback. 'I don't remember telling you any of that.'

'Your helicopter pilot just bought Larcombe Barn near Little Dipperton for four hundred and twenty-five thousand pounds,' David went on. 'He was married to a German artist but they were divorced a year ago. No children.'

I was aghast. 'You're checking up on him?' Of course, I knew that David had all kinds of access to people's private files – that was his job, after all – but I was still annoyed. 'That's private information.'

'Maybe it is,' said David. 'But my intentions are sincere. I just want to make sure that my successor is a good man.'

'I don't want to talk about my personal life,' I said primly. 'And I don't want to hear about yours either. That's not why I agreed to have breakfast with you.'

'Fair enough. So tell me, how is Kat's Collectibles & Mobile Valuation Services going?'

I was happy to talk about the business, and soon we were discussing our shared passion for art and antiques as if we were still living together.

Slowly I steered the conversation to Honeychurch Hall and the museum room open day to see if he would mention the insurance scam. But he didn't, which made me all the more certain that this was the exact reason why he was here. He knew something about the pocket watches, and it was my guess that it had to be connected to the auction at Luxtons today.

When I told him about the mummified hawk, he didn't dismiss the rumours at all. 'Four people who touched the bird have either died or vanished,' he mused. 'Interesting.'

'It's just superstitious nonsense, isn't it?' I said.

'I'm open-minded.' He polished off the last mouthful of his fried eggs and bacon. 'But think of the curse of the pharaohs. The bird has been stuck for decades in a sarcophagus in the attic; it might have been oozing blood all the time it's been up there.'

'Harry admitted that his friend had put tiny drops of cochineal along the bindings, which I'm sure Rupert is going to be furious about.'

'Can I come and see the hawk?' said David. 'I'm not going back to London until tomorrow afternoon – all being well.'

'I don't think that's a good idea,' I told him. The risk of him recognising another object on the stolen goods list was too great.

'You mean your mother wouldn't approve? Krystalle Storm, the international romance writer.'

'You promised to take that secret to the grave,' I reminded him.

He put his hand on his heart. 'It's a promise I swore to keep, and I will.'

We fell into an easy silence. After a moment, I looked out of the window and gave a start of surprise.

Lenny Evans was emerging from Prestige Pawnbrokers directly across the street. He wore a heavy coat, a black woollen beanie and a face like thunder. I wondered if Guy was with him.

'What's the matter?' David said. 'You look as if you've just seen a ghost.'

'I'm not sure. I just saw . . . a client of mine leaving the pawnbroker's opposite.'

'A client?'

'Well . . . not a client. It's Guy's father, actually.'

'And you think he's up to no good?' said David.

'I don't trust him, nor do I like him.'

'Do you want to find out?' said David. 'You always had good instincts, and you may as well make use of me whilst I'm here.'

Chapter Twenty-Nine

David took my arm and we weaved through the traffic to cross the busy street. He seemed almost too eager to help. Suddenly I was struck by the most terrible thought. What an idiot I was! Was it possible that Lenny had found the wretched watches somewhere, and that was what he was pawning? But it was too late to turn back now. David was already opening the door to Prestige Pawnbrokers, *in business since 1912*.

I took in the double-fronted windows full of a variety of oddments: shelves of old lamps and rotary-dial telephones, a saxophone, a fur coat, a stuffed swan and a glass display case of jewellery. A man who looked as if he had walked straight out of *The Sopranos* stood up from behind the counter as we stepped inside. A radio played low in the background, broadcasting horse racing 'live from Doncaster'.

'Hi, Bill,' said David. 'I bet you didn't expect to see me back again so soon.' He turned to introduce me. 'This is my friend Kat Stanford; Kat, this is Bill Sykes, not to be confused with his namesake from *Oliver Twist*.'

Bill's expression was guarded. 'I already told you to look around. I'm hiding nothing. I play strictly by the rules. Been here for fifty years, and my dad before that—'

'Yes. So you said,' David put in. 'Just a quick question. The man who left a couple of minutes ago? Black beanie?'

'Yeah. Major Leonard Evans. Read about him in the papers,' said Bill. 'Saved a lot of kids caving. Why? What about him?'

David stiffened. I could sense his excitement and realised I had been holding my breath too. 'I told you not to lie to me, Bill,' he said. 'Show me the watches.'

'Watches?' Bill shook his head. 'I don't know anything about watches.'

'This is my final warning.' David's voice was icy.

'Don't you threaten me,' Bill retorted in a tone designed to put David's hackles up. 'He came in to pick up a crystal necklace and earrings that he brought in six weeks ago—'

'A *necklace*?' said David sharply.

Of course! It had to be Delia's. Lenny was despicable. He must have pawned it to raise some cash, and now, with Angus dead, he was buying it back.

Bill retrieved an old leather-bound ledger from under the counter and opened it. Turning the book around to face us, he jabbed a manicured finger at the description – an antique art deco Pools of Light rock-crystal orb necklace with matching earrings.

'Unfortunately, they'd gone,' he went on. 'I sold them last week. He wasn't happy, but that's the risk you take and I told him so.'

'Thanks,' said David. 'Anything else?'

'He said he was going to the auction.'

Once we were out on the street again, David checked his iPhone. 'Damn. I've missed a call. I've got to get to the saleroom.'

'Me too,' I said.

He grabbed my hand to cross the road, just as Lenny drove by in Guy's Freelander. He was alone. Our eyes met and my stomach gave a jolt of anxiety. Not only had he spotted me exiting the pawnbroker's, he'd seen me with David, and we were holding hands.

By the time we arrived at Luxtons, I was a nervous wreck. David's disappointment at the pawnbroker's had morphed into a state of euphoria. I knew that mood. It meant that he was closing in on a case.

Johnny, a short, stocky man in his sixties, greeted us at the door. I knew him well. He oversaw the cataloguing of all the items that passed through the warehouse and into the saleroom. But this morning his face was grave.

'I'm sorry, Mr Wynne . . .' Noticing me standing there, he stopped.

David's face fell. 'Kat can hear what you have to say,' he said curtly. 'Out with it, man!'

'Both pocket watches have been withdrawn.'

'*What?*' David was furious. 'When?'

'About an hour ago.'

'I told you to call me immediately!' David exclaimed.

'I left you a message,' Johnny said defensively.

David pulled his iPhone out of his pocket again and muttered something under his breath.

'What was the seller's reason for withdrawing them?' he demanded.

'When he first brought them in, late Monday afternoon, I wasn't here. George told him to wait until the spring, when we would be holding a sale of fine watches, but he was most insistent that he wanted them in Wednesday's sale.' Johnny shrugged. 'I suppose he changed his mind.'

'And George is off today?' said David.

'He's gone skiing. Won't be back until January. I thought I told you all this.'

'Talk me through what happened today.'

'The chap turned up about an hour ago and said he planned on taking my colleague's advice. I have a signed receipt . . . here.' He pulled a piece of paper out of his pocket.

David flipped the receipt, clearly annoyed. 'It's just a name and a phone number. Where's the address?'

'He brought the items in fair and square – he produced a certificate of authenticity,' said Johnny. 'I gave them back to him. What can I say? Now if you'll excuse me, I have work to do.' He turned away grumbling.

David handed me the receipt. 'Does this name seem familiar to you?'

I stared at it in astonishment. The receipt read: *Angus Fenwick.*

'You know him,' David said. 'I can tell by your face. Is it someone who lives on the estate?'

'I don't know anything,' I said quickly. I couldn't believe that Lenny had used Angus's name.

I braced myself for David's anger, but instead he said, 'Look, let's cut to the chase here. You know that I know about the insurance scam in 1990. And yes, that is why I'm here – although seeing you was an added incentive.'

I didn't answer.

'I know you have a copy of the police report and a list of the items that were allegedly stolen on that night. You *know* those watches were on there, Kat – shall I describe them to you?'

Still I didn't answer.

'Pleading the Fifth, are we?' David was exasperated. 'You don't owe these people anything! A crime was committed. I need you to help me here.'

'I don't know what you're talking about,' I whispered, and looked down at the floor.

I felt fingers lift up my chin and turn my face to his. 'Kat, are you in some kind of trouble?' he said gently.

'No, of course not.'

'Is this anything to do with your mother?'

'My mother?' I exclaimed. 'No! Not at all.'

'Then it must be your boyfriend. You're protecting him.' He dropped his hand and his expression changed to one of disappointment. 'If you won't tell me, then I can't help you. I will solve this case. You know I will. What has happened to you? You used to have integrity.'

And without another word, he snatched the receipt from me, shoved it into his pocket and strode away.

His insult stung, especially since there was a ring of truth to it, but I would never betray the Honeychurch family. The irony was that Mum and I were convinced that those above stairs didn't even know about any of this. But David had a point. Why did I feel I had to keep it a secret?

My heart wasn't in the sale any more. I just wanted to get home as quickly as possible.

It was only as I turned into the tradesman's entrance at the Hall that I remembered something Johnny had said.

Lenny had brought the watches in late Monday afternoon. Angus's body wasn't found until Tuesday. This had to mean that Lenny already knew that he was dead. Somehow he had to have been involved. The thought made me sick to my stomach.

Lenny couldn't have known about the insurance scam. He wouldn't have known that the pocket watches had been flagged on the Art Loss Register and become the subject of an investigation. The precaution of putting them in Angus's name had completely backfired.

But where on earth had he found them in the first place?

As I passed the entrance to the Carriage House, I saw Shawn's panda parked in the courtyard. I slowed down, wondering whether to go inside. My mother would notice straight away that something was different between us. But then it hit me that he might have news about Peggy.

He was sitting at Mum's kitchen table when I walked in, sipping something from a tiny liqueur glass. He jumped up smiling, his pleasure at seeing me so obvious that I blushed.

'I was just about to leave,' he said. 'I've been looking for you.'

'Peggy's been found,' Mum declared.

'Thank heavens!' Relief washed over me. Peggy was safe. Now was the time to tell Shawn everything, but even as I thought it, I just couldn't. Not yet.

'Where was she?' I asked.

'She'd fallen into some kind of disused bunker,' said Mum.

'It was an operational base built during the war,' added Shawn. 'They're dotted all over Devon.'

'Harry's going to be excited to hear about that,' I said. 'Where exactly was it?'

'That's the strange thing,' he said. 'It was in the woods, nowhere near a path at all.'

'But she's OK?'

'A sprained ankle and a touch of hypothermia, but yes, she'll be fine. She's staying under observation at Totnes Cottage Hospital for a few days.' Shawn raised his tiny glass. 'So we're celebrating with Honeychurch Gin.'

Mum handed me a gin and tonic – a full-sized one – and we toasted Peggy's safe return to civilisation.

'Aren't you on duty?' I asked Shawn.

'It's just a thimbleful.' He grinned. 'And I must say, it's excellent. You'll be glad to know that I have inspected Iris's still, and I think the less said about it the better.'

He drained his glass and headed for the door, only to stop and say, 'Oh . . . there is something else. Lala Fenwick has gone. Violet said a taxi came to pick her up and take her to Totnes station. She didn't pay her bill. When Clive went to Totnes to find out which train she'd taken, he found the Enterprise rental car.'

'Isn't that astonishing?' Mum exclaimed.

'We'll be looking at the CCTV footage at the railway station,' Shawn said. 'I believe that whoever moved that car hoped it would trick us into thinking that Angus had gone back to London alone.'

'Good heavens,' said Mum.

'The interesting thing is that we found the car keys on Angus, along with his phone.'

'So how did the car end up at the railway station?' Mum asked.

'It was either hot-wired or towed,' said Shawn. 'Hopefully the answer will be on CCTV.'

My heart sank. Guy's Freelander had a tow ball hitch.

'We were able to open the glove box in the rental car,' he went on. 'Inside was an Ordnance Survey map of Little Dipperton with the Honeychurch estate circled in red ink. There was also a receipt for a burner phone and a series of newspaper clippings about Major Evans.'

I found I couldn't speak.

'Is there anything you're not telling me, Kat?' he asked.

What was I supposed to say? Repeat the conversation I'd had with Guy about his father? I stood there paralysed, but I knew I had to say something.

'Lala wasn't pregnant,' I blurted.

'Ah,' said Shawn, not looking remotely surprised.

'Not pregnant?' Mum shrieked. 'Why on earth would she pretend to be?'

'You *knew* she wasn't pregnant,' I said to Shawn.

'We've been working with the North Yorkshire Constabulary,' he admitted. 'Nor was she Angus's wife.'

'Not his *wife*?' Mum repeated.

'You're beginning to sound like a parrot,' I said.

Shawn smiled. 'But I can happily confirm that she does hold the world record for limbo dancing.'

'Well thank God for small mercies,' said Mum drily.

'As I have told you before,' Shawn continued, 'just because we're a tiny unit doesn't mean we are buffoons.'

'And what about Nick Bond's accident?' I said.

'We're taking paint samples from his lordship's Range Rover and your boyfriend's Freelander.'

I desperately wanted to tell Shawn that Guy had loaned the Freelander to his father, but that would only create more questions that I just couldn't answer yet.

'Nick had made a lot of enemies,' Shawn went on. 'We are in the process of recovering information from his iPhone.'

'But . . . I thought it was stolen?' I said. 'That night in the churchyard when he was mugged – he said it was stolen!'

'He lied,' said Shawn. 'He told his parents that he threw it into the undergrowth.'

'But he'd been hit over the head. How could he have done that?'

'There were two blows,' said Shawn. 'According to his mother, the assailant struck him once on the shoulder and tried to grab his phone. Nick lobbed it into the undergrowth before being struck a second time and getting knocked out. When he went to pick up his motorbike on Monday, he picked up his phone too.'

'Was that what you were looking for in the undergrowth on Sunday evening?' I said.

'No.' Shawn shook his head. 'I believed him when he said his phone had been stolen. I was looking for whatever had been used to hit him.'

I recalled Nick's refusal to admit to Guy that he had been struck, confirming my suspicion that it had to have been Lenny. 'Nick didn't have any idea who had attacked him?'

Shawn shook his head. 'Of course everyone knows that there was bad blood between his family and the Honeychurch clan. Lady Lavinia told me that Nick said he had vital information that could easily bring them down.'

'Surely you don't think it was his lordship?' Mum said with dismay. 'I've never seen him as a violent man.'

'Well, witnesses said that they saw his lordship talking to Nick in the churchyard on Sunday evening,' said Shawn. 'I'm confident we'll get to the bottom of this. But I won't if I stay here.'

And with that, he left.

Chapter Thirty

I told Mum everything I knew including the things that Shawn did not. She listened with her mouth open, shocked by the blackmail, angered by Lenny's deceit and surprisingly protective of her friend.

'But the pregnancy,' she said in astonishment. 'Who on earth does Lenny think he is? Mick Jagger?'

'Guy said he really believed it.'

'I told you people don't change,' said Mum. 'Although having said that, I believe Shawn has.'

I remembered Shawn's kiss again and didn't dare look my mother in the eye.

'Do you think I'm blind?' she teased. 'Something has changed between you. I saw it the minute you walked into the kitchen. Remember *Pride and Prejudice*? There's that scene when Georgiana Darcy is playing the piano at Rosings Park and someone mentions Wickham. Elizabeth saves Georgiana from humiliation, and after that, Darcy looks like he could eat her alive. Those smouldering I-want-to-rip-your-clothes-off—'

'I don't want to talk about it,' I said quickly.

'Well I do,' Mum said. 'Shawn and I had a lovely conversation before you walked in. Delia was right when she said he'd been going to counselling. He said he realised he was ready to give you his heart; that he couldn't live without you, and if he had to fight for you, he would.'

'Very funny,' I said. 'You probably wrote that this morning in *Betrayed*.'

'Me?' Mum put her hand on her heart. 'I swear it's what he said – well, maybe not word for word, but that's what he meant.'

We laughed, and I felt a little bit better. 'You are impossible.'

'And you are in demand,' Mum said. 'Enjoy it, darling. When you get old, you'll look back on the time when you had three men vying for your attention.'

'Don't be silly,' I said, and reached for the gin bottle.

'So is Guy on the way out?' Mum said.

'I told you, I don't want to talk about it.'

'Well at least tell me how you feel about Dylan.'

This time I didn't bother to correct her deliberate misuse of David's name. 'A bit confused,' I said. 'He's so much a part of my life – my old life – and seeing him again brought up a lot of feelings for me. He seemed different somehow, though. I almost felt sorry for him.'

'I'm sure he's not happy about you outwitting him yet again,' she said.

'I didn't outwit him. We just got lucky.'

'I like the way you said that – *we* got lucky.' Mum smiled.

'We're part of the Honeychurch family here, aren't we, and that's why we want to protect them.'

I realised she was right. 'Yes. I suppose we do.'

'Everyone is covering for everyone else,' she went on. 'But trust me, Lenny will get his comeuppance. Life has a way of making sure of that.'

'Who will get their comeuppance?' Neither of us had heard Delia walk in the front door. She looked furious.

'We were just talking about Kat's old boyfriend David,' Mum said hastily. 'Whatever's wrong?'

'I've just about had enough!' Delia blinked.

Mum nodded to the gin bottle on the kitchen table. 'Shawn just gave me the all-clear. We're still in business. Let's pour you a drink and you can tell me all about it.'

Delia took off her coat and threw it on the floor. 'It's Lenny.'

'Of course it is. I'd be angry too,' said Mum. 'She wasn't pregnant. It was just a trick.'

'Pregnant? Who wasn't pregnant?' Delia frowned as she helped herself to a glass from the oak dresser and filled it to the top with neat gin.

'That young girl,' said Mum. 'Lala the limbo dancer from the Peppermint Panda nightclub.'

'What's *she* got to do with anything?' Delia said impatiently. 'No. I've had enough. I'm going to divorce Lenny and to hell with the Queen and her medals!'

'I could have told you that a leopard never changes its spots,' said Mum.

'If you're going to go on about that little indiscretion, I'm leaving,' Delia fumed. 'I'm talking about Lenny's money problems.'

'No one should give in to blackmail,' Mum agreed. 'But he did bring it on himself.'

'Blackmail? What are you talking about?' Delia demanded again. 'He was tricked by some Nigerian investment company in Lagos . . . What? Why are you looking at me like that?'

'Um . . . we're surprised that Lenny was taken in by such a scam,' I said quickly.

'All our savings!' said Delia. 'The bank statement arrived and I got to it first. Cash withdrawals totalling thousands of pounds!'

'A Nigerian investment company,' Mum repeated. 'Well, that's new and original.'

'And now Peggy is coming back,' Delia raged on. 'She's too old! She should retire! I can't live like this.' She drained her glass and slammed it on the table, letting fly a torrent of language that would make a sailor blush.

'Go on . . . let it all out,' Mum said.

'I was fine living on my own,' Delia declared. 'I liked being married to someone who was a hero, but I didn't need him living in my house.'

'Oh,' said Mum, surprised.

'You can't possibly understand,' Delia continued. 'We rarely saw each other, and it suited me fine.'

'Well you soon changed your tune,' said Mum. 'Just weeks ago, you would have died without him.'

Delia ignored the jibe. 'When we had our little holidays, they were always so wonderful and romantic.'

'Ah.' Mum nodded knowingly. 'It's hard to keep the romance alive when reality steps in. I suspected as much.'

'But seeing him day in, day out . . . I feel trapped! Claustrophobic! And now he wants us to leave Honeychurch because of all that business with Peggy's cottage and the dowager countess being so cross. He's asked Guy for a loan to buy a boat so we can sail around the world! I don't want to sail around the world. Guy is furious. He just bought Larcombe Barn so he could be near us. It's such a mess!' She burst into noisy tears.

I was lost for words. It seemed that Lenny's life was falling apart from every angle.

Fortunately the phone rang. Mum jumped up to answer it.

'It's the little French girl. She sounds upset.'

'Fleur?' I said.

'She's not really French,' said Delia. 'She's been looking for you everywhere, by the way.'

I took the receiver but didn't have a chance to speak. Fleur was chattering away at top speed, and the tone of her voice was beginning to scare me.

Finally I understood exactly what she was saying. 'What do you mean, Harry has gone to the quarry?'

'He's gone looking for the cook,' said Fleur.

'But . . . Peggy Cropper was found last night,' I said. 'When did he go?'

'About two hours ago,' she said. 'He took the quad bike as far as the estate boundary and told me he was going the rest of the way on foot.'

'Did he take his two-way radio?' I said.

'I . . . I don't know,' said Fleur miserably.

'You know very well that he's only allowed to go off on his own if he takes the radio.'

'Then he must have done. Yes,' Fleur stammered.

'Who told him Peggy was at the quarry?' I demanded.

Fleur hesitated. 'All he said was that it was on a need-to-know basis, but he's . . .'

'What, Fleur. He's *what*?'

'He said he thought she might be in the underground workings and that he knew he could get in.'

I turned cold. 'I'll go and find him,' I said. 'You'd better tell Harry's father straight away.'

'No!' Fleur exclaimed. 'Monsieur is so angry already. Harry told him about the hawk.'

'That's just too bad,' I said, but I was pleased that Harry had kept his promise. 'Stay where you are. Keep your handset switched on. I'll be in touch.'

I disconnected the call and relayed Fleur's message to Mum and Delia, who seemed to have recovered from her own outburst thanks to this latest drama.

'That girl is trouble,' she said. 'His lordship hit the roof when Master Harry told him about the food-colouring trick on that moth-eaten bird, and the little minx said it was all Harry's idea. He was so upset, poor lad. His lordship banished him to his room.'

'When was this?' I said.

'Last night. He's been grounded for the rest of the week.'

'Clearly not,' said Mum. 'He must have escaped.'

'Mum, please call Shawn and tell him I am going back to the quarry,' I said.

'And I'll call Guy,' said Delia pointedly. 'After all, he is your boyfriend.'

'But we don't need Lenny,' Mum added.

'You won't get Lenny,' Delia replied. 'He drove into Newton Abbot to meet our bank manager, to see if there's any way we can get his money back from that crook in Lagos.'

'Good luck with that,' said Mum drily.

She followed me to the front door, looking worried.

'I really think you should let Shawn handle this. Get him to take that dog.' She thought for a moment. 'Should I come with you?'

'I'll be fine,' I said. 'Just remember to let him know where I am.'

I left my car behind the church and went on foot up the green lane. Harry would have left the quad bike at the gate where Honeychurch land ended and the footpath through Larcombe Woods began.

I broke into a jog. If my gut feeling was right, he should have left a spare radio handset in the dry box, as he was always told to do. Once I got hold of that, I would be able to contact him.

Sure enough, when I reached the bike, it was there – a bright yellow Motorola T402. Even better, it was fully charged – and taped to the back was the configuration code so I could tune into the correct frequency.

I was ecstatic.

Quickly I switched the radio on, and was treated to an earful of static.

I hit the button. 'Calling Squadron Leader James Bigglesworth, do you read me? Over.' I had no idea what the exact terminology was, but thought that sounded about right.

There was no reply.

I tried twice more, but there was still no answer.

I jogged back to the place where Harry and I had got into the quarry yesterday morning. Dusk was beginning to fall and the temperature had plummeted. I hurried along the track, growing increasingly jittery as I made my descent to the ruined mining village.

I soon came to the clearing in front of the water. It was eerily silent, deathly still. A thin mist drifted across the surface.

Even thought it wasn't yet dark, I used the flashlight feature on the radio handset and scanned the area calling out for Harry. There was no reply.

The powerful beam lit up the entrance to the underground workings. To my relief, the wooden planks were in place. But if he hadn't gone in there, where could he be?

I clicked the button of the handset and tried to contact him again, but there was still no answer.

Shawn had said that Peggy Cropper had fallen into an operational base bunker. Was it possible that Harry had managed to find it too?

The moment I had that thought, I realised it made no sense. Harry had come here looking for Peggy. He wouldn't have known that she'd been found in the OB. He had to be here somewhere.

I was exasperated. I tried the radio again, but this time dropped the role-play. I was getting cold.

'Harry,' I said wearily. 'I know you can hear me. This is not funny. Come out right this minute.'

Still no response.

My exasperation shifted to a gnawing sense of unease. Something felt off. Something was wrong.

I hit the button one last time. 'OK, Harry,' I said. 'Have it your way. I'm going home.' I'd let Shawn deal with it – no, Rupert should. After all, he was Harry's father.

That was when I heard the crunch of boots behind me.

I spun around. A figure was standing in the shadows of the ruined wheelhouse.

'Harry?' I said nervously. 'Is that you?'

'No, it's not Harry,' came a friendly voice. 'Thought you'd need an extra pair of hands to look for the little fella.'

It was Lenny.

Chapter Thirty-One

Quickly I shoved the radio handset into my pocket. 'What are you doing here?' I said.

'What kind of greeting is that?' Lenny teased. 'Fleur told me that Harry had come down here. She was worried, and rightly so. Biggles needs our help.'

I stood there, unsure what to do. Delia had said that Lenny had driven into Newton Abbot. He must have changed his mind.

'She called us at the barn,' he went on. 'She was in a terrible state.'

'Why would she call you there?' I said.

'She was looking for you because Harry had gone off to hunt for Peggy Cropper. He obviously hadn't heard that she'd been found.'

'Yes, that's right,' I said, and scanned the area. 'Is Guy here?'

'He's gone back to the house to get some rope,' said Lenny.

'Rope? What do we need rope for?'

'To rescue Biggles.'

So Harry *was* here. I felt a rush of anxiety. 'Where is he? Is he hurt?'

Lenny moved towards me, smiling. Automatically I stepped back.

'Our illustrious leader has only gone and got himself stuck in the access tunnel.' He pointed to the other side of the quarry. 'It's over there. It was drilled at the end of the nineteenth century to carry dynamite from the top road down here to the blast site.'

I didn't need to wonder why Harry would have gone in there. It was exactly the sort of thing he loved to do, but even so, I was growing suspicious.

'How did you find him?' I asked.

'Instinct,' said Lenny. 'Keep calm, luv. You know this is my area of expertise. As I said, we just need some rope. Guy will be back in a minute. Come on, I'll show you where Harry is.'

I had learnt to listen to my instincts years ago, after being stalked by a fan. The night I'd come home late and found the young man in my bed was a night I would never forget. Back then I had ignored the warning prickles that had raced up and down my spine whenever I saw him buying his coffee at the same time as me at the little coffee shop on the way to work. He was a stockbroker and wore a smart suit. He was polite and friendly. I never suspected for a minute. It was then that I realised that bad people came in all shapes and sizes.

Regardless of whether Lenny was dangerous or not, my priority had to be making sure that Harry was safe. I just needed to be careful. Help was on its way.

'Follow me,' said Lenny. 'Ladies before gentlemen.'

'Age before beauty,' I retorted, and ushered him ahead. There was no way I was going to step in front of Lenny Evans. Every nerve ending in my body was urging me to run, but I couldn't – not until I had found Harry.

I followed him past the last of the ruined buildings towards a mossy dell full of branches, root wads and trees. It reminded me of the stumpery, except that this place was cradled by high embankments lined with overhanging laurel.

'Just a little further,' he called back over his shoulder.

Even though I was following him, I was poised for flight and keeping my eyes open for an escape route. I was quite sure I could outrun him if it came to that.

A fresh-water spring tumbled down the embankment from above and flowed on towards the quarry. Chunks and sheets of slate and granite covered with moss and lichen climbed up the sides. The place smelt dank.

I stopped walking. It was bitterly cold. I could see my breath coming out in uneven puffs. My heart was pounding. 'I think we should wait for Guy.'

Lenny turned to me and pointed ahead. I could make out a long crescent-shaped hole that was just visible above a mound of debris and leaf mulch. 'He's in there,' he said. 'The access tunnel would have come out in a sunken lane close to Little Dipperton, but the roof must have collapsed. Looks like he squeezed in not realising there was a steep drop.'

I hesitated.

Suddenly my two-way radio crackled into life, breaking the nerve-racking silence. I pulled it out of my pocket.

'Stanford, Stanford,' came a voice. 'Do you read me, over?'

I couldn't believe it. It was Harry! I was so relieved. 'Thank God. Are you OK?'

'Escape successful,' he said. 'Give us your position, please. Over.'

'The major and I are here. Rescue imminent. Over.'

There was a rush of static electricity and I couldn't hear what Harry was saying. 'Repeat question,' I said. 'Over.'

I still couldn't hear, but I could make out a smattering of words: German spy, trap – and *run*.

And it hit me in a blinding flash.

Harry wasn't at the quarry.

Guy wasn't coming.

Fleur had lied.

It had all been an elaborate ruse to get me here.

Lenny spun around and knocked the two-way radio out of my hand, then ducked down, snatched it up and hurled it into the undergrowth.

I threw myself at the embankment and began to scale the slate-covered slope. There had to be a way out at the top. But it was like walking on marbles. I kept slipping, and every tree I reached for came away in my hand. I'd managed to climb halfway up before my foot skidded out and I found myself sliding all the way back to the bottom, where Lenny was waiting.

'Now that was silly, wasn't it?' He stood over me. When I looked up, I thought my heart would stop beating.

He was holding a Glock pistol, and it was pointed right at me.

'I'm sorry, Kat.' He looked sad. 'But I can't let you ruin everything. Up you get.'

For a moment I was so shocked that my mind just didn't register the possibility that he would use the gun. I fought to stem the rising tide of panic.

'You're scaring me,' I said. 'Whatever you've done, it's not worth this. If this is about you being blackmailed—'

'Guy told you that?' He seemed shocked.

'Go to the police,' I urged.

'Too late, luv. That ship has sailed.'

'Guy's worried about you,' I went on.

'Guy knows everything,' Lenny said with a bitter laugh. 'In fact, if he hadn't interfered, no one would have got hurt.'

'*Guy?*' I was horrified. 'Guy is involved in all this?'

'Never give in to blackmail, Dad,' Lenny said, mimicking his son's voice. 'That's what he said, and I listened to him.'

'You told him,' I said.

'Sunday night.' Lenny shook his head as if hardly able to believe it himself. 'Astute, that's my son. He knew something was up.'

'Don't do anything stupid,' I said. 'Guy idolises you.'

'Fenwick had been blackmailing me for months.' Lenny went on as if I hadn't spoken. 'I had two more payments and then we were finished. It was agreed. But then he changed his mind. Claimed they never got the last instalment.'

'The stumpery,' I said suddenly. 'Was that where you left the money?'

Lenny seemed startled. 'How do you know about that?'

'Because Harry and Fleur found it in there,' I said. 'They gave it to Rupert.'

He let fly a string of curses. I knew I had to keep him talking. Shawn would be here any minute.

'And for whatever reason, Rupert kept it – presumably to offer as a reward for information about the pocket watches that you attempted to sell at the saleroom,' I said.

'You know about that?' He was surprised. 'I needed the cash.'

'Where did you find the watches, by the way?'

'The box room in the cellar next door,' he said. 'I've put them back now. How was I to know they'd been reported as stolen property? Looks like the butler did it.' He gave a short laugh at his own joke.

'You see?' I exclaimed. 'No one need know about that. And the other things were just accidents.'

Lenny shook his head. 'Guy said that people like that never stop. Fenwick followed me to Devon. He gave me the burner phone to make sure I took their calls.'

'And why send a scarf with the note? "With you for always, forever"?'

'He was turning up the heat,' said Lenny. 'They came to my home! My pub! They threatened to go to the newspapers.'

'The newspapers? You mean the *Dipperton Deal*?'

'That reporter . . .'

'Was it *you* who attacked Nick in the churchyard on Sunday evening?'

'He was spying on me,' said Lenny. 'Recording my conversation with Lala.'

'He was following a lead on something else . . . another story,' I said. 'You just happened to be there at the same time.'

For the first time, Lenny seemed off balance. 'No. That's not true.'

'Didn't you see Rupert in the churchyard on Sunday night?' I said incredulously. 'You must have done. He was talking to Nick.'

Lenny hesitated. 'Why did Nick want to meet me at Violet's tea room?'

'He wanted your photograph for the newspaper.'

'No. He picked it because that's where Angus and Lala were staying. He wanted to see my reaction. It was a trap.'

'Lenny,' I said. 'Nick had left his motorbike at the Hare and Hounds on Sunday night. Violet's tea room was the most logical place to meet you.'

'But then he must have followed me,' Lenny persisted. 'Explain that! When I got to Larcombe Cross on my way to see Guy, that kid just came out of nowhere on his motorbike.'

'Nick was an off-road motorbike enthusiast,' I said. 'He was taking a shortcut home.'

Lenny's face crumpled. 'Jesus. That was an accident, I swear. All I wanted to do was talk to him. I tried to get him to stop. It was just a tap. The next thing I know, he's lying against the wall with a broken neck.'

'And you called for an ambulance,' I said. 'That's why I'm telling you to go to the police. It was just a terrible accident.

The same as Angus drowning in the quarry was an accident – wasn't it?'

Lenny hesitated. 'Yeah. It was. I told him it was the last payment he'd ever get from me and just threw the bag of newspapers onto the ice. I suppose he went to get it and fell in . . . But I'd told him not to worry, that I'd always take care of my child.'

'Lala told you that you were the father of her child.' I couldn't believe he'd been taken in so easily.

'I've got used to the idea now,' he said with a hint of pride. 'I think I'll enjoy being a father again now that I'm retired.'

'Lenny,' I said. 'Lala wasn't pregnant.'

He smiled. 'Nice try.'

'You can ask Guy. He was there when we found out.'

Lenny went very still. He just didn't seem to comprehend what I had said. 'Baby's due in June. It's a boy. That's what she told me.'

'Lenny—'

'She worked out all the dates,' he added. 'I remember the night it happened.'

'She fooled you,' I said. 'She was wearing a fake pregnancy belly. Guy saw it. She came to the barn. He threw her out and told her to leave you alone.'

Lenny stood there, bewildered. As he lowered the gun, I saw my chance, leaping to my feet and ploughing my shoulder into his stomach with all the force I could muster. He fell over and dropped the pistol. I pounced and managed to kick it out of his reach. He rolled to his feet, elbowing me out of the way and catching me on the chin. I cried out in pain, but

I was desperate and flung myself at his back, throwing my arms around his neck and trying to pull him over backwards.

He threw me off, but I hurled myself at him again as he reached down for the pistol. Our hands collided and we staggered towards the water's edge. There was a deafening pop as the gun went off, frightening scores of birds that exploded from the trees in a cacophony of indignant cries.

I fell back, but got to my feet again, throwing myself at him once more and grappling for the pistol. I bit his hand hard, and this time he let go. The gun flew in an arc and landed in the water. Furious, Lenny lashed out and caught my cheek, sending me stumbling backwards onto the ground.

I sat there trying to catch my breath as he crouched at the edge of the lake, tentatively poking at the water with a stick.

I saw my chance and staggered to my feet, reaching him in three quick strides, shoving him hard. He toppled into the water and went under. When he surfaced, he was screaming in terror. 'Help! Help! Get me out! Get me out!'

I scoured the edge for the pistol, surprised to see it lying on a ledge in the shallows.

A very small eel floated by, and then another . . . and another.

I looked at the hero in the water begging for his life. He was thrashing about, fighting off some unseen monster and, like a fool, moving further away from the bank.

That was when I remembered his fear of snakes – and presumably that included eels. I knew he wouldn't be able to survive for long in the cold water. I couldn't let him drown. I'd have to go in.

As I pulled off my coat, I heard the sound of barking, and voices shouting my name.

'Big one just swam by, Lenny,' I taunted now I knew that help was near. 'The size of a python.'

'Oh God have mercy!' he wept. 'Please, please . . . get me out!'

Shawn, Guy and Mr Chips burst into view. Shawn was wearing his drysuit and didn't even hesitate. He plunged into the water and struck out for Lenny, who was babbling with terror.

'Shawn!' I cried. 'Be careful . . . please be careful!'

Lenny grabbed onto him, and to my horror, the pair went under the water, resurfacing only to go under again. Lenny had Shawn in a stranglehold from behind and took him down with him yet again. They emerged coughing and spluttering.

Guy threw a rope, but it fell short.

'Do something!' I screamed. 'Guy! He's drowning him! Oh God!'

At that moment, Shawn slammed his head viciously back into Lenny's face. Lenny loosened his grip and began to sink, but Shawn grabbed him under the arms and held on fast.

Guy threw the rope a second time and Shawn caught it, and somehow we managed to pull them both to the bank. Once they were on dry land, Mr Chips darted forward and sank his teeth into Lenny's sopping wet trouser leg. Lenny didn't cry out. He just lay there, a broken man. Mr Chips lost interest and sat down.

'Shawn . . .' I realised I was close to tears and could hardly speak. 'I thought you . . .'

'Everything is going to be all right.'

As I stepped into his arms, it seemed the most natural thing in the world. I didn't even mind that he was drenched.

It was only when I pulled away that my eyes met Guy's, and in them I saw sadness.

'Dad won't give you any trouble now,' he said, and turned away, leaving the three of us and one little dog at the water's edge.

Chapter Thirty-Two

After a short and impersonal text asking for some time to think, Guy vanished. I asked after him twice, but all Delia would say was that he felt responsible for Angus's death because it had been his idea to stuff the black dustbin bag with newspapers and throw it into the water. Lenny had added the Monopoly money because, according to Delia, it was a 'nice touch'.

David too seemed to have disappeared off the face of the earth, until, on the morning of Mum's drinks party, the postman arrived with a Christmas card from him. It was a formal family portrait of himself, Sam and Chloe with Ella, their adorable Labrador puppy, in front of a perfectly decorated Christmas tree.

After our last communication, I was relieved to hear from him – especially given the cryptic postscript, which read: *Don't worry – all your secrets are safe with me.*

'You haven't heard the last of him, Kat,' Mum said darkly. 'Just you see. He'll be back.'

'But not for the pocket watches,' I pointed out. 'They're back in Peggy Cropper's cellar – that's what Seth must have been talking about before he died. Maybe he was trying to tell Rupert.'

'Well his lordship hasn't a clue,' Mum said. 'He's still offering a reward for their safe return.'

'Presumably Lenny's thousand pounds that the children found in the stumpery,' I said. 'Ironic, isn't it?'

There was a tap at the kitchen door and Shawn poked his head in.

I hadn't seen him for a few days, and I felt a rush of butterflies. He sported a hideous tie covered with brown Christmas puddings that bore a startling resemblance to cowpats. Seeing my expression, he said, 'I know. Sorry.'

'You haven't come to arrest me, have you?' Mum joked.

He smiled. 'Not this time.'

'We're having a little party,' said Mum. 'I hope you'll stay.'

'I'd love to, thank you. I thought you'd both like to know that we apprehended Lala at the Peppermint Panda club in Leeds a few days ago – that's why I haven't been around. She admitted to everything. In exchange for a lighter sentence, she's agreed to help with the ongoing investigation into a sextortion ring involving high-ranking officers in the armed forces—'

'Good heavens! I read about that in *Star Stalkers*!' Mum exclaimed. 'What will happen to Lenny now?'

'Put it this way,' said Shawn. 'He won't be having tea with the Queen any time soon.'

'Good,' Mum said.

'There's something else.' Shawn brought out his iPhone. 'I forwarded a video recording from Nick's mobile to my own. I think you'll find it interesting.'

Mum and I stood behind him as he tapped the play arrow. The footage was of the museum room open house. Over the sound of animated conversation and laughter, we heard Frank Sinatra singing 'White Christmas'.

Nick had videoed Mum giving Seth the glass of gin – 'I was told it was water,' she said for the umpteenth time – and then Seth draining half of it before placing the glass on the windowsill behind the jousting suit. He had then zoomed in on Angus and Lala as they headed over to look at the hawk. We saw Lala pretend to touch it, heard Harry's protests, watched Mr Chips dart in to attack Angus, and winced as the couple toppled onto the flagstone floor.

'This is the bit I want you to see,' said Shawn. 'Watch carefully.'

Off camera we heard a voice cry, 'I'm here! Stay where you are! Everything is under control!'

Nick swung the iPhone around to show Lenny framed in the doorway brandishing an umbrella. As he pulled in for a close-up, Lenny's face registered shock, then fear.

Nick zoomed back to Lala, who could be seen blowing Lenny a kiss and patting her round stomach. Off camera Mum could be heard shouting, 'Seth! Move! Move!' followed by the sickening sound of falling metal as the jousting suit collapsed.

Mum and I looked at each other, stunned.

'I knew it,' I exclaimed. 'I knew it was him!'

'So it *was* Lenny's fault!' Mum said. 'He pushed the armour over.'

'Not deliberately, but even so . . .' Shawn tucked the iPhone back inside his trench-coat pocket. 'There's more. Nick had recorded a conversation in the churchyard between his lordship and Douglas Jones, who just happens to be Nick's great-uncle – Nick's mother Anne is Douglas's niece.'

'Ah, one of the Jones clan. I must write that down for my below-stairs family tree.' Mum whipped out a Post-it note and did just that.

'Douglas Jones demanded a thousand pounds in exchange for keeping quiet about a break-in at the Hall that took place three decades ago,' Shawn's expression was grim. 'He implied that it was an inside job.'

'An inside job?' Mum said, deliberately not catching my eye. 'How ridiculous! The man must be mad.'

'My father was the investigating officer at the time, and I can assure you there was no question of him ever covering up something like that,' said Shawn.

'Presumably Lala must have arranged to meet Lenny in the churchyard around the same time,' said Mum. 'Lala and Lenny. They sound like a singing duo from the seventies.'

'Lenny thought that Nick had been recording his conversation,' I said. 'What about the black paint you found on the Suzuki mudguard?'

'It was a match for the major's BMW convertible,' said Shawn. 'We also managed to get the CCTV footage from Totnes railway station. It clearly showed your boyfriend's

Freelander towing the Enterprise rental car on Monday night and leaving it in the station car park.'

My heart sank. 'Did you manage to see who was driving the Freelander?' *Please don't let it be Guy.*

'It was Major Evans,' said Shawn. 'There is no reason for us to suspect your boyfriend of any involvement other than withholding vital information from the police.'

'Actually,' said Mum, 'Guy's not her boyfriend – well, not any more.'

'Mother!' I was mortified, especially as I had yet to tell Guy that.

Shawn turned red and mumbled, 'Good to know.'

'Did you find out whether Lenny had a licence to keep a gun?' Mum asked suddenly. 'He deliberately lured Katherine to the quarry with that terrible story about poor Master Harry.'

'I don't think he would have used it, though,' I said. 'He just wanted to force me into that access tunnel and . . .' I couldn't finish the sentence. If Lenny had had his way, I knew I would have died in there.

'Many retired military officers keep their guns,' said Shawn. 'So yes, in his case he had a permit. As for luring Kat to the quarry – Fleur was given five pounds to tell that story. But then if it hadn't been for Fleur, Harry would still be locked in the meat larder.'

'Ah, the meat larder,' said Mum. 'I know it well.'

'What enticed Harry to go in there in the first place?' I asked.

'Apparently the major suggested that it would be a good

place for a secret briefing,' said Shawn. 'Fleur suffered a crisis of conscience and came clean. She should be on her way to China now. His lordship thought it best if she returned to her family. She won't be coming back to Little Dipperton.'

'There you are!' Delia entered the kitchen all smiles. 'Merry Christmas!' She and Mum were dressed in identical Marks & Spencer little black dresses.

Mum gestured to the countertop, where there was an array of gin, wine and beer. 'Help yourself. Mulled wine is in the saucepan on the hob. Ice in the bucket, sliced lemons somewhere around there.'

'Don't you just love Christmas?' Delia trilled. 'Oh . . . nibbly things too. Yum.'

I was taken aback by her cheerful demeanour. Her husband was under arrest on two counts of manslaughter and one of attempted murder, and here she was acting as if she had just won the lottery. It was then that I noticed she was wearing the most stunning crystal necklace and matching earrings.

'Where did you find your grandmother's crystals?' I exclaimed. 'They are beautiful.'

'Tucked behind a cushion on the sofa. I have no idea how they got there,' she said. 'It's funny how I was more upset about losing those than I was about losing my husband!' She laughed. 'I'll go and get Peggy. I parked her wheelchair in the carriageway.'

'Gran's *outside*?' Shawn exclaimed. 'She must be freezing!'

'It's a lovely day,' said Delia. 'We walked – or rather I walked and she let me push her.'

'I'll go and fetch her,' said Shawn and left the kitchen.

I raised a quizzical eyebrow and mouthed to Mum, 'Necklace? Earrings?'

As Delia helped herself to a gin and tonic, Mum whispered, 'Alfred knew someone who knew someone . . . He can be very useful when it comes to missing items.'

Moments later, Shawn returned with Peggy in her wheelchair. Mum thrust a drink into her hand.

'I owe you an apology, Iris,' said Peggy. 'I didn't know that Seth had been drinking on the sly for years.'

'I didn't tell her, I promise,' Delia said.

'She didn't,' Peggy echoed. 'When I heard that I might lose my home—'

'But you're not going to now,' Delia protested.

Peggy raised a hand to silence her. 'Let me tell the story! On Monday afternoon I caught the bus to Little Dipperton and walked home. I was so upset when her ladyship told me that Delia was in the process of switching cottages without me even being there. Touching my things! *Moving* my things!'

'But they're all back in their place now, Peggy,' said Delia.

Peggy scowled. 'That's when I discovered that the door to the cellar had been forced open. Seth always kept it locked because he told me the stairs weren't safe. When I saw what was down there, I couldn't believe it.'

'And that's when you realised that Seth had been drinking all the time,' Mum declared.

Peggy's face filled with sadness. 'I feel like my marriage was a lie.'

'Tell me about it,' said Delia darkly. 'Mine too.

'But you had a *good* marriage,' Mum insisted. 'Seth was a good man.'

'Are you saying that Lenny wasn't?' Delia put in.

'I think you should both remember the happy years you spent with your husbands,' Mum said diplomatically. 'To be loved is a wonderful gift, no matter how it turns out in the end – and let's face it, both Seth and Lenny just wanted to protect you.'

I regarded her with surprise, but I knew that in essence she was talking about herself, and perhaps explaining just a little bit why she never told my father all her secrets.

'But I will say that your Lenny was no hero,' Peggy added. 'I saw everything! That poor man Angus fell into the water and he did nothing to save him. Nothing at all! Just watched him drown!'

Delia bristled. 'He doesn't like snakes,' she said. 'And you didn't do anything to help either.'

'I was frightened,' said Peggy. 'I'd gone to the quarry to reflect on my marriage, and suddenly there's a *lunatic*—'

'Ah, this is where the party is,' said Rupert at the door. 'Room for two more?'

He squeezed in with Harry, who was carrying a box trailing scraps of wrapping paper. To my surprise, Harry was not wearing his Biggles attire, but jeans and a dark green Christmas sweatshirt with a robin on the front.

'You won't believe what's just been delivered!' he enthused. 'Look!'

Inside the box was a complete set of Biggles first editions.

Mum and I exchanged horrified glances. She mouthed, 'Dylan?'

'When did this arrive?' I asked nervously.

'A courier brought it all the way from London,' said Rupert. 'I'm sure you know more about it than we do. Very kind.'

'And there's a note.' Harry beamed happily and passed it to me.

It read, *To Squadron Leader James Bigglesworth, with thanks from the British government for keeping the Germans off our beaches.*

'I let him have an early Christmas present,' said Rupert almost apologetically. 'To make up for having to send Fleur home.'

'To be honest, she was really high-maintenance,' said Harry ruefully. 'I hope all girls aren't like that.'

Everyone laughed.

'Harry has something to tell you all,' said Rupert.

Harry took a deep breath. 'I'm announcing my retirement from the RAF. Effective immediately.'

'Oh, Master Harry!' Peggy wailed. 'No more Biggles?'

Rupert gestured to the box of books. 'A fitting end to a distinguished career,' he said. 'Tell them what you're doing instead.'

'Father has enlisted me in the 3rd Totnes Sea Scout Group,' Harry said excitedly. 'We have to wear a uniform and everything, and there are lots of activities, like learning to surf and abseiling and paragliding and kayaking and *camping*! It's going to be wicked!'

'Congratulations,' I said. Harry was growing up. 'They're very lucky to have you.'

'You'll have so much fun, Harry,' said Shawn. 'I went up through the ranks in the scouts.'

'And I wished I could have joined.' Rupert ruffled Harry's hair. 'My father wouldn't let me.'

'This definitely calls for a celebration,' Mum said. 'A glass of Honeychurch Gin, milord?'

'We might need it for the task in hand,' said Rupert. 'I'm looking for a volunteer to put the lid back on the sarcophagus and return the hawk to the attic.'

'I'll do it,' said Shawn.

'No, I'll do it,' said Guy, suddenly appearing in the doorway.

'What a lovely surprise!' Delia exclaimed.

'No, really, *I'll* do it,' said Shawn with an edge to his voice.

'I don't believe in all that superstitious nonsense,' said Guy.

'Well I *do*,' said Shawn. 'And I'm prepared to take the risk.'

'Oh for heaven's sake,' Mum said. 'Why don't you take one end each?'

There was a tap on the door, and this time it was Alfred who peered inside.

'It's like Piccadilly Circus in here today,' Mum muttered. 'Come on in, Alfred.'

'Just to say I put the hawk back in the attic, milord,' he said.

Everyone breathed a sigh of relief. Guy stepped forward and whispered into my ear. 'Kat, can I have a quick word in private? It's important.'

My stomach dropped. Regardless of what did or didn't happen with Shawn, I knew I had to tell Guy that it would be better for us to stay as friends.

We stepped out into the hallway, and he shut the kitchen door to make sure we wouldn't be overheard.

'I wanted to get you alone so I can apologise for how I handled everything,' he said quietly. 'With my dad . . . all of it.'

'You don't have to apologise, Guy—'

'The torch you saw under the sofa,' he said quickly. 'Yes . . . it was my father's. When I walked you back to the car on Sunday night, Dad had already told me about being blackmailed. He'd said he was certain that Nick had overheard his conversation with Lala in the churchyard, and that she was pregnant. When you and I found Nick unconscious . . . I just had a hunch that Dad might have had something to do with it.'

'So when I went to call for an ambulance, you found Lenny's torch and hid it.' I was annoyed. 'You lied to me again.'

He shrugged. 'I'm sorry. What do you want me to say?'

'Well . . . I appreciate you telling me now.' I took a deep breath. 'Guy, I need to be honest too—'

'I already know what you're going to say,' he said. 'Shawn's a lucky man, even if his taste in ties is appalling.'

'This has got nothing to do with Shawn.'

'Really?' said Guy. 'When he dived into the water to save my dad, I saw your face. At that moment, I knew that your heart belonged to another.' He gave a sheepish smile. 'Ugh.

Sorry. That sounded as if it came right out of a Krystalle Storm novel.'

Despite everything, I had to laugh.

'Full disclosure,' he grinned. 'My mother's a big fan, and I borrow her books. You should read them.' He offered his hand, and I took it. 'Friends?'

'Yes,' I said. 'Friends.'

As Guy left, Shawn joined me in the hall holding two frosted crystal tumblers with fir tree stirrers. 'Fancy a Honeychurch Gin and tonic?'

I nodded. 'I thought you'd never ask.'

As we gently touched glasses in a Christmas toast, he looked into my eyes and said, 'Here's to the future.'

I smiled. 'I'll drink to that.'